Light

Shadows – Book Two

by

Amber Lacie

85,400 words

2016 Gray Publishing Paperback Edition
Copyright © 2016 by Amber Lacie

All Rights Reserved. In accordance with the U.S. Copyright Act of 1976, the scanning, uploading, and electronic sharing of any part of this book without the permission of the publisher or author constitute unlawful piracy and theft of the author's intellectual property. If you would like to use All Rights Reserved. In accordance with the U.S. Copyright Act of 1976, the scanning, uploading, and electronic sharing of any part of this book without the permission of the publisher or author constitute unlawful piracy and theft of the author's intellectual property. If you would like to use material from this book (other than review purposes), prior written permission must be obtained by contacting the publisher at amberlacieauthor@gmail.com.

Thank you for your support of the author's rights.

FBI Anti-Piracy Warning: The unauthorized reproduction of distribution of a copyrighted work is illegal. Criminal copyright infringement, including infringement without monetary gain, in investigated by the FBI and is punishable by up to five years in federal prison and a fine of $250,000.

Cover Art by Willsin Rowe
Copy and Line editing by Kris Matury-Turner
ISBN 978-1523424412

CONTENTS

Acknowledgements 7
Prologue 9
Chapter 1 18
Chapter 2 30
Chapter 3 44
Chapter 4 55
Chapter 5 69
Chapter 6 85
Chapter 7 99
Chapter 8 115
Chapter 9 128
Chapter 10 144
Chapter 11 156
Chapter 12 171
Chapter 13 178
Chapter 14 186
Chapter 15 203
Chapter 16 213
Chapter 17 219
Chapter 18 229
Chapter 19 240
Chapter 20 255
Chapter 21 268
Chapter 22 282
Chapter 23 293
Chapter 24 303
Chapter 25 311
Chapter 26 320

Epilogue	331
Other Books by Amber Lacie	336
About the Author	337

Visit Amber Lacie's website for the latest news and updates.

Website: http://www.amberlacieauthor.wix.com/author-blog

Twitter: @amber_lacie

Facebook: www.facebook.com/amberlacieauthor

Warning: This book contains scenes of adult sexual nature and may contain graphic violence. This is for mature audiences only, especially those wanting a roller coaster ride and wet panties.

eBooks are not transferrable. No part of this book may be used or reproduced without written permission, except in the case of brief quotations in articles and reviews. This book is a work of fiction and any resemblance to persons, living or dead, or places, events or locales is purely coincidental. The characters are productions of the author's imagination and used fictitiously

ACKNOWLEDGMENTS

To my readers and betas, thank you so much for your support. Knowing someone else is enjoying reading my books as much I as I enjoy writing them is absolutely an amazing feeling.

To my husband who I've driven extremely crazy during the process, I love you to the moon and back again.

To my children, thank you for letting me have just a few minutes and sometimes hour to myself so that I could write, even if it was only when you were sleeping or bribed with movies and Legos. I love you both.

To anyone else who thinks they deserve to be acknowledged, but for some reason, or another you've been skipped, you obviously didn't bribe me with enough wine or coffee. Do better next time.

I hope you enjoy the conclusion and final installment of Eve and Theron's story. I fell in love with them, and I hope you do too.

PROLOGUE

THERON

Then

I'm walking along the beach, looking for rocks to skip across the water. I hate being here. I'm so bored, but at least I'm not with him. He had to take my mom in for more testing today. I am not sure what they are looking for, but I'm not stupid. I am fourteen and I'm not a child anymore. I push my sunglasses up on my nose, and I see a bright glare on the water. It catches my attention. I shade my eyes with my hand to get a better look, and that's when I see her.

A beautiful angel is sitting on the beach with her friends. I can see her laughing. Her smile is bright and full of life. The sun is behind her, giving her hair a golden look to it. I notice one of her friends is a boy. I am suddenly jealous of him, and I'm sure it's just the start of things.

I think about going over to introduce myself, once or twice, but I stay over here where it's safe. She doesn't know me, and I don't know her. It's easier when I keep to myself. No one teases me, or expects things from me. No one knows my name, and I can blend in with everyone else. I watch her and her friends for a while. They are bouncing a beach ball back and forth to each other, while wading through the waves. The wind catches it, taking it away, and landing it at my feet. I stare at it for a second, before I reach out to grab it. My hands clasp around the ball, and I look up into the most beautiful blue eyes I have ever seen.

"You caught it."

I did, but I don't respond. Words chase each other around in my mind, and I'm suddenly confused about which ones to use. She stares at me for what feels like minutes, until I finally hand over the beach ball.

"You could play with us. It's just me and my friends."

I stare blankly at her, wishing she could reach into my head and grab my thoughts. I know if I tell her my name, she'll figure it out. Everyone always does.

"It's cool, if you don't want to talk. Wait, oh my God. Can you talk? I didn't even think about it. I'm sorry if I've upset you." She starts chewing on the inside of her cheek. She looks so nervous. She's actually worried that she has upset me. How could a complete stranger care about me? The thought makes me smile, just a little bit.

"Yes." My voice croaks.

"Good. Wait. Yes, what?"

Once again, I am speechless. I just stare into her blue eyes, while she tucks strands of her long brown hair behind her ears.

"So, you can talk?"

"Yes." My voice is much firmer this time, but it's still hoarse.

"Right. So anyways, my friends and I are trying to play a game. We could use another player." She turns around to walk away. She looks like she might be twelve or thirteen. I know I'm older than her, but it's not by much. I watch and she looks back over her shoulder, flipping her hair. She may be younger than me, but I have never seen anything more beautiful in my life. She yells something, but I can't quite make it out. She stops and turns around, almost losing her footing in the sand. She starts laughing and it is the most beautiful sound. I stand up and start walking over to her to see if she is okay.

She has a huge smile on her face, and she grabs my wrist, as I get closer to her. "Good. I'm glad you're going to play."

I never said that I was, but I don't correct her. My skin is buzzing where she touched me, and it's the first time I have felt alive in a while.

"So these are my friends, Kayla and Matt. We all go to school together." She points her finger back and forth between her friends. I smile a huge grin, when she refers to the boy as just her friend. "Guys, this is…Um…I don't actually know his name."

They all stare at me, and I just shrug my shoulders. They don't need to know my name. I might tell her eventually, but not them. They continue to look at me, and I notice the girl wink at me.

"Well, it's kind of a secret. I'm not supposed to say because his family is so famous. He's going to play with us. Okay?" She winks at me again.

"Eve, is he dumb?" Her name is Eve and it is perfect. Her friend with curly blonde hair seems to have an issue with me.

"No." This time my voice is steady and calm.

"See, Kayla? He's fine. He just doesn't like talking. It's cool." Eve takes my hand, and pulls me into the water with her. We play, bouncing the beach ball back and forth, for a little while. Eventually the other two leave to race up and down the sand dunes. It is just Eve and me sitting on the beach. I like it better this way. I scoot closer to her until our legs are touching. She makes my skin feel hot and alive. My heart is racing. I don't want to scare her away, so we sit for a long time just watching the waves hit the shore. I spend most of my time at the beach with, Eve.

My dad is being a complete ass. He doesn't want me making friends with "locals". According to him, we are better than they are, and should act like it. He took my bike, but I hid my skateboard before he could find it. He started locking me in my room, but I still sneak out. I have to see her. She is the only one that makes me feel even slightly stable with all of this going on. I hate him.

My mom wants me to avoid him. She says he is coming to terms with things, whatever that means. I heard the doctors in her room the other night. She is dying. She won't tell me, but I know. She has stage four cancer. I am not sure how much longer she will be here with me. I'm scared. If she goes, I will be alone with him. He told me he hated me the other day. He said it is my fault that my mom is sick. He said she has been dying since the day she gave birth to me. I know he is lying, but it still hurts.

It is so odd the way your mind works, while you're dreaming. One minute, I am on the beach with Eve, and the next I'm walking into my mom's room. I wonder if I did break her because she looks so small in her large bed. I open my mom's window to let in some fresh air. It's really hot outside, but there is a soft breeze today. She says she likes the smell of the trees. I walk to her bedside and start combing her hair. She can't really do it anymore. Her arms get tired too quickly.

For some reason, I tell her about the friend that I made at the beach. I tell her all about, Eve and how beautiful she is. The words flow out of my mouth like a waterfall and I can't catch them fast enough. I tell her Eve is short for Evelyn, but I like to call her beautiful. My mom smiles at me, as I tell her every detail about my time with Eve. I set her brush down on the table beside her bed. My mom gently grabs my hand and I carefully sit down beside her. She looks so fragile. I am afraid if I breathe too hard by her, she will shatter into a million pieces and scatter into the breeze.

"Theron, I'm so happy you have finally made a friend. She sounds absolutely amazing, sweetie. I love the way your face lights up when you talk about her. When, I go—"

I cut her off with a wave of my hand. I am not doing this. "Mom, no. I don't want to talk about it."

"No, sweetie, you need to hear this. When I go, I want you to keep her as a friend. Your father is a cold, angry man. I do not want him to dilute you with his poison. Hold onto her. Keep her. You'll need her."

"You're not going anywhere. I need you."

"Baby, I know. I am trying to hold on for you, sweetie, I really am, but it's getting harder every day. I love you so much it hurts. You deserve to be loved. Promise me."

"I can't. I'm not doing it. You can't go. I don't want to be alone with him."

My mom's hand softly touches my chin, turning my face towards hers. "I will love you whether I am here in this place with you, or if I'm floating above you with the stars. A mother's love never ends. Now please, promise me you'll let her love you. Keep her. Hold onto her friendship as long as you can. I believe she's going to be your light in a very dark time." Tears fall from her eyes, sliding down her cheeks.

I can't let her down. I don't want to disappoint her, so I do it. "Okay. I promise."

THERON

Now

That was the last conversation that I had with my mom. Her speech went downhill after that. She died about two weeks later. My dad was destroyed. He swore that I did something to kill her. He acted as though just my presence was vile enough to take a human life. I wasn't allowed back at the beach. I couldn't sneak back out, either. He had me sent away, so he wouldn't have to look at my murderous face anymore. Those were his exact words. What kind of parent tells their child they have a murderous face? What kind of parent blames their child for spreading cancer? Mine does.

I kept my promise to my mom, even through college. I never let Eve go. Her beautiful smile is locked away in my memories. She saved me from myself that summer. I was ready to go with my mom. I wasn't sure how exactly, but I looked into different ways that I could kill myself. I was never able to go through with it. Every time I pictured Eve's face, I felt a little bit of hope. I became an adult that summer. Death will do that. Every minute I spent with Eve, I felt my heart get lighter. She made me feel as though I mattered. We could sit by each other for hours and not say a word. I felt needed, wanted, and most importantly, I felt loved. The memory of her is the only thing that kept me from falling into an abyss of despair all of these years.

My eyes are closed tight, refusing to let in any light. I am sitting against a wall. My shoulder feels like it's burning. It is probably from the glass table I broke and pushed in front of the door, but people were still trying to get in. So, I rammed into it with my shoulder. It shattered. Everyone left me alone after that. I feel like I am going to throw up. The only thing keeping me somewhat calm is rocking my body back and forth. I'm gripping onto my legs, trying to stay in this reality. First my mom, and now my gram. I am completely alone. I feel void and empty. I was mad at first, but there are no words to describe how I feel now. I know he did this. I don't know what he said to her, but I know it pushed my gram over the edge. He will pay for everything he fucking did. He will suffer for hurting Eve, and I will make him pay for everything he has ever done to hurt my gram.

My gram is fucking gone. No, no, no, no, this can't be real. I chant "no", over and over again, trying to wish this all away. I hear glass crunch, alerting me to someone else being in the room with me.

I stop rocking to yell at whoever is in the room, "Leave. I said I want to be fucking alone. Fucking leave!" Chanting once again, I start rocking back and forth. This isn't real. I swear that I can smell

Eve's perfume. I must be losing my fucking mind. I feel a soft hand rest on my forearm. My skin feels like lightening is crawling across it. It can't be her. I walked away from her. I let her go.

"Theron."

I stop rocking. Holy fuck. My sweet, beautiful angel is actually here.

"It's Eve. I am here to help you, but I need you to look at me first. You're bleeding and I'm worried about you."

Fuck. I don't want to bring her into this, but he already did. He hurt her to get to me, and now he has taken the only family that I have left. Fuck him. I look up into her beautiful eyes and see pure fear. She's frightened. He has fucking scared her.

"Thomas did this. He did this! He fucking took her from me. He has taken everything from me. He's going to pay for this. I will ruin him. I won't stop until he has felt every ounce of pain he has brought into my life. I will fucking destroy him." My words are dark and laced with venom. I mean everything that I have said. She doesn't say a word. Her bright blue eyes just stare into mine. She is my light, but dark shadows are taking me over. I need to keep her, so that I don't lose my mind. I put my hand over hers, and she gasps. Turning my head, I look away. I must really be a monster.

CHAPTER 1

EVE

He is sitting on the floor, gripping my hand. I finally got him to move, but we've only made it to a section of the floor where there's no broken glass. At first he wouldn't move, but once he saw I was kneeling in glass, he followed me to the other side of the room. He wouldn't sit in a chair, so I slid down the wall, and he sat next to me. He hasn't spoken since I first came in here. I check the time on my phone and notice I've been in here with him for over an hour. The wall I built around my heart starts falling apart as I sit with him. Just the feel of being close to him, seeps into my heart causing it to thump hard in my chest. Seeing him so utterly, destroyed is killing me. I want to save him from all of this.

I need to get him out of here. He needs his shoulder checked, and I need to get him home. I don't want him to get upset or put off by any of my movements, so I plan everything out in my head as far as I can. I even contemplate different problems or scenarios that could come up.

"Theron." I hear him take a sharp breath, but he doesn't say a word. "Babe, I'm sorry. I'm so very sorry, but we can't stay here. I need you to let me help you. Your shoulder is cut up, and I just want to make sure that you are okay. Then, Evan will drive us back to my brother's place, okay. We don't even have to go to your place. Just come home with me. Please, babe."

He looks up at me with dark, void eyes. I'm really hoping the idea of me needing him will work. He stares at me for a few minutes, and I hold his gaze. "Please, baby. Let me take care of you. I need you home with me, I need to feel you." I notice a light flicker in his dark eyes, I know I have his attention. I stand and pull him up with me. He clings to my hand, as we walk over towards the door.

"I'm going to open the door now, it's the only way out. The doctors are going to check your shoulder, and then you are coming home with me. I won't leave you." I bring his hand up to my lips and gently place a kiss on the back of it. I open the door to see a devastated Evan, leaning against the wall across from us. He looks at me, and then over to Theron. "Evan, Theron needs his shoulder looked at. After we have the all clear from the doctors, we will need you to drive us back to my place. Theron will be staying with me."

"As you wish, Miss Evelyn."

Theron squeezes my hand. It's painful, but I'm doing my best to ignore it. Evan follows Theron and me as we walk over to the emergency room registration.

"Excuse me, but he needs to be seen. He cut his left shoulder pretty badly. He was in the waiting room and had an accident."

"Accident? More like a temper tantrum. Have a seat and fill out these forms. Someone should be with you shortly."

I let out a big sigh. I understand that he has had a mental breakdown, but she doesn't have to be such a bitch about it. I hand the forms to Evan, since he would be able to fill in more blanks than I could. Theron, has finally released his death grip on my hand, and is now holding my arm. It seems like we wait forever for someone to call Theron's name, but it has really only been about twenty minutes.

We follow a nurse into a private room and she pulls the curtain around us. She hands me a gown for Theron and I help him pull off his shirt. The nurse's eyes roam his chest, and I give her a deathly stare. If she wants to live while we are here, she had better keep her gaze professional. She takes his blood pressure, and then makes some notes in her chart before walking out of the room. I help Theron slip on his gown. I start to help him with his jeans, but he stops me.

"Don't. They only need my shoulder. I'll let them look at it because you are here. Then we are leaving. We can stay at Robert's tonight, but then I am going home. I'm going to run him into the ground." Theron's eyes are dark and cold. I keep quiet and sit beside him in the sterile room. Thoughts cross my mind of what he may be capable of. He's such a calm person, I can't picture him being violent. Although right now, I wouldn't put it past him.

Theron got eight stitches in his shoulder. The cuts were not as bad as they seemed. Once the doctor cleaned off all the dried blood, there was only a few scratches and one deep laceration. He has to have his sutures removed in ten days. The drive to Robert's was so quiet; all I could hear was Theron breathing. Evan parks the car. Turning my head, I try to give Theron a soft smile. I want to tell him everything will be okay, but I know that is far from the truth. Softly taking my hand in his, I help him out of the car. His grip on my hand tightens, as we walk into the beach house.

I can't imagine the pain he is going through right now. I may have lost a close friend, but now he has lost all of his family. I won't count his dad as family. He's more of a sperm donor. He may have given Theron some of his DNA, but that is all he has given him. A real father wouldn't treat his son like this. I'm tempted to ask Theron if he knows what exactly Thomas said to Isa, but I don't want to push him any farther. He is already broken and falling apart. I don't want to run the risk of completely destroying any shred of my Theron that may still exist, even if he is lost, lurking in dark murky waters.

He follows me downstairs to my bedroom. I open the door, and gesture with a wave of my hand for him to go in. He doesn't let go of me, instead he pulls me along with him. He still hasn't spoken, but his breathing is definitely softer, easier. I start to sit on the bed, but he stops me with his hand. He holds his palm up in front of me, and then raises his index finger on his other hand.

"What? Why am I waiting? I want to help you." My voice pleads with him, but I'm not sure he hears me.

He sits on the bed, propping pillows up behind him and spreads his legs open. Curling his finger, he motions for me to join him. I crawl up on the bed and make myself at home, laying between his legs with my head resting just above his waist. My head rises, as he takes a deep breath. "I know you want to help me." His fingers run through my hair, grazing my scalp, sending goosebumps crawling across my flesh. I shouldn't have waited so long. I should have gone to him. Stubbornness seems to be my flaw with him. I mentally take a deep breath, needing to clear away my stray thoughts. My focus should be on Theron and what he needs. He lets out a sigh and twirls my hair around his fingers. "Eve?" He pulls me from my thoughts, as guilt settles in my stomach. I don't want to make this about me.

My heart slams hard in my chest. I don't know why, but I suddenly feel scared. "Theron." My voice is flat, not knowing what to expect next.

"I know you want to help me, but I'm not sure what's going to happen. This could be a dark path and I don't want to taint you. I don't want to poison you."

I roll over onto my stomach and place my palms flat on his stomach, under my chin. His beautiful eyes are full of concern. "You won't. I'm with you. Whatever path you go down, wherever this leads, I will follow you. I shouldn't have stayed away. I was stubborn, selfish, and blind. You needed me as much as I needed you."

"I did and I do. Are you sure about this?"

"Absolutely."

"Okay. I'm going to tell you what I know. My gram was an amazing woman. She was beautiful, loving, caring, cunning, and vengeful. Thomas hurt her a long time ago. She tried for so long to gain his love. All he did was destroy everything she had. He ran my grandfather's name into the dirt after he passed. Gram never forgave him. Do you remember how I said I sold my shares of Rowe Incorporated?"

"Yes." I wonder where this is going. Wanting to give him my full attention, I move my body so that I am straddling his waist with my palms resting flat on his chest.

He traces the back of my hands with his fingers, slowly moving them up and down my arms. I watch his chest rise as he takes a deep breath. "I sold them to my gram. Not directly, of course, Thomas would have noticed immediately. Instead, I sold them to a company that was being ran by Evan at the time. Gram purchased the company under her maiden name, and that was the beginning of GILF." At the mention of his gram's business, a slight smile plays in the corner of his mouth. Even in death, Isa can make him smile.

"Evan was running a company? I thought he was Isa's driver?"

"Technically, he was. Evan is quiet, but he's a brilliant man. She saw something in him that most people ignored. She knew he could do more for himself than he was. Evan started his business with a little financial help from her. He was a cunning businessman and had already acquired two other businesses under his belt when I sold him my shares. Of course, Gram was aware of my moves before I actually made them. Evan confided everything in her. He loved her so much and he didn't want secrets."

Theron says something else, but I don't hear it. I'm lost in thought. "Evan loved her? Like they were an item?"

Theron stares blankly at me, almost shocked. "It was apparent to anyone who knew them, but they kept it a secret from most."

"How old is Evan?"

"I don't know. I've never asked. He's worked for Gram for about twelve years now. My guess, late forties or early fifties. What does this have to do with anything I'm telling you?"

"It doesn't. I am sorry. I can't believe they had a thing is all. There's a big age gap there."

"Hmm. I've never looked at it like that. He loved her and took care of her. I never questioned an age difference. I don't think love cared about it either." I can hear the irritation in his voice.

"I'm sorry. I side tracked us."

"It's fine. Back to what I was saying…Gram knew what I was doing. Thomas had hurt her and she wanted to prevent him from hurting anyone else, so she bought Evan's company. GILF is mainly ran by Evan. When I moved back here to make sure she was okay, she told me what she was planning on doing. I'm not sure how far she got, or what the outline was. I'll need to talk to Evan about that."

"Don't jog around the plans, Theron. I want to know what we are getting into."

He sighs, running both hands through his hair. "Fine. Gram was smart, probably a little too smart, but she was also very sly. She approached members of the board at Rowe Inc. One by one, she informed them of her intentions and when they were on board with the idea, she bought them out. She had a contract drawn up for each member. It would allow them to hold their positions, salary, benefits, and shares until she acquires all twelve signatures from the current board, besides Thomas. Once she had the contracts from each member, her hold on the company would be at fifty-one percent. Then if you add in the shares she bought from me, her hold would equal out to a little over fifty-seven percent. She would hold majority, and all rights to the company. She would eliminate the need for Thomas and his position, completely taking over."

"How could she have that much hold in the company without him noticing? Wouldn't he have an eye on what percentage he owns?"

"He does know how much he has. The board collectively, without his share, holds in at thirty-seven percent. Isa never sold her shares. My grandfather was smart enough to leave her a percentage in his will. Thomas hasn't accounted for it. I'm sure he thinks of it as his, since she's his mother it would be left to him in her will. However, just before I found you again, Isa had her lawyers change her will. He gets nothing. I let it slip the day you broke your hand, but when I told Gram, she said he hadn't mentioned it yet. He's not worried about my hold, because according to him, I was stupid and sold it to an infantile company."

"But what about the board? Surely he would know if and when they sold."

"No, he has no clue. The contracts go into effect at the timing of the last signature. They have all signed non-disclosure agreements. They are legally bound not to speak of the contract until it has been in effect for more than sixth months. It would provide enough time for Gram to decide what to do with the company."

"This seems so unreal."

"It took me a little while to wrap my head around it as well. The clincher is that technically, the contracts and agreements were made with GILF. Gram never stepped foot in any meetings. She would provide the terms and contracts, but Evan dealt with them all personally. They see him as the front man of the company. Gram was just lurking in the shadows."

"She's brilliant."

"Yeah. She was." His voice drops, along with his eyes. I want to be able to fix this for him, to take away his pain, but I can't. A drop of water hits the back of my hand. I lift his chin with my fingers. Another tear slides down his cheek. I try to make eye contact with him, but he keeps looking away.

"Look at me."

Giving me a soft shake of his head, he whispers, "No."

"Babe, look at me. Let me help you. I know you are hurting."

Beautifully colored eyes look into mine, and one lone tear streams down his face. I wipe it away with my thumb. He shivers under my touch.

"Don't."

"Don't what?"

"I know that look. I don't need your pity or sadness. This isn't the first time that I've lost someone."

"I'm not trying to give you any look. I hurt for you."

"Well, don't. I don't need you to." His eyes glaze over, and any light that was left fades into the darkness.

"I just…"

"You just, what?" His voice booms, sending shards of ice cutting through me and I jump. I don't know how to respond or what to say. Theron's mood has done a complete one-eighty. He brushes my arm with his fingers, and I tense under his touch. "I'm sorry. I've never been good with handling this. Let me handle this my way. Okay?"

Words fail me, so I simply nod my head. I feel like I'm holding my breath. I am so afraid that he's going to snap. I climb off his lap, moving to sit beside him. His hand runs up my back, sending heat scorching across my flesh.

"Beautiful, don't be afraid of me. I would never hurt you."

"You did once, already."

"That's a low blow, Eve, and you know it."

"I'm sorry, but you did. You left me in the middle of the night, and all I got was a note. Who does that?"

"I was trying to give you what I thought you wanted. I never meant to hurt you the way I did."

I take a deep breath, looking up at the ceiling, trying to keep my tears from falling. "It's fine. I'm here now. What do you want to do, babe? It is late. We should get some rest if you still want to go back to your place tomorrow."

"We probably should. I know you want to stay with me, and I am all for it. God knows, I can't handle the thought of being without you, but I don't want to look like I'm hiding. I don't want to give, Thomas the pleasure of thinking he has beat me down. I want to stand my ground and fight him."

"Okay. Tomorrow we will leave for your place. I'm sure Evan could use some company and help with everything."

"Let's not talk about anything else. I'm done for tonight."

I don't say anything else. Theron slips off his jeans, and carefully pulls his shirt over his head. He hisses a bit through his teeth, I'm sure his shoulder stings. I slip off my clothes, pull a t-shirt on, and then replace the old tape on my splint with new tape. I can feel Theron watching me.

"Did you ever see a doctor?"

"Yes. It's fine. I have an appointment on Thursday for my last check up, and then I won't need the tape or splint anymore. My hand will be as good as new." I lay down beside him. He pulls me towards him, curling himself around me with his front to my back. I can feel his breath on my neck.

"Good. So, two more days?"

"Yep." My voice is tight, as I do my best to ignore his touch.

CHAPTER 2

EVE

My eyelids are so heavy, but I know I need to open them. Slowly, light enters my eyes. It must be early morning because the sun is just starting to make its appearance. I roll over and grab my phone off the floor, trying my best not to disturb Theron. Glancing at the screen, I check for the time. It's ten after six. My body is stiff as I stand and stretch my muscles. I quietly ruffle through my belongings and grab some clothes for the shower. I glance over my shoulder to make sure that Theron is still asleep before I head into the bathroom.

The design of this house is so strange. I'm not sure who the floor planner was, but I know putting a bathroom in the living room is beyond odd. Setting my clothes on the sink, I glance up at the mirror to see my reflection. I don't just feel tired, I look it. Bags hang under my eyes, my hair is in a tangled mess, and my complexion is pale. I turn on the shower, letting it warm up. The mirror is completely, fogged with steam, by the time I have the energy to step into the hot shower.

The water beats into my back, as I roll my shoulders under the hot stream. I've just finished rinsing the conditioner out of my hair, when a thought occurs to me. What if Theron doesn't know where I am? I turn off the water and step out of the shower, grabbing a towel to wrap around me. The bathroom is full of steam, so I crack the door just a little bit. I'm ringing the water out of my hair when I hear someone yelling for me. Securing my towel around my body, I open the door to listen for who is calling for me and follow the voice. At first, I think Robert is screaming, but as I get closer, I realize that it's both of them.

I hear a loud thud echo down the hallway and I take off running. Swinging the bedroom door open, I charge into my room to find both of them fighting on the floor. "What the hell is going on?" Neither of them respond. Robert is trying to pin Theron to the floor. His feet are straddled over Theron's waist and he is using his elbow and forearm to hold down Theron's chest.

"Fuck you. Get the hell out of my house!"

"I swear that if you try to take her from me, I'll fucking kill you." Theron's chest is heaving. They are both out of breath.

"I said, what the hell is going on?" My voice booms into the room, causing them to cease their movements.

Robert sits up, taking his arm off Theron's chest. "Eve, I'm sorry. I just…"

Before Robert can finish his thought, Theron grabs his arms and flips Robert underneath him. He hovers over Robert's face. "You should be fucking sorry. Do. Not. Ever. Try. To. Take. Her. From. Me. Again." Each word Theron says is followed by a jab of his finger into Robert's chest.

Gently placing my right hand on Theron's shoulder, I lean down to grab his arm. "No one is taking me anywhere. I was in the shower." The look in his dark eyes is absolutely, frightening. "I was in the shower." My voice is quiet and soft.

The fog over Theron's gaze clears, as he jumps up from the floor, backing away from us. He looks down at Robert, who is now sitting up, rubbing his chest. "I'm sorry. I didn't mean to, I didn't know." He glances down at his shaky hands, looking lost and confused.

"Theron, I was in the shower. I'm okay. I didn't want to wake you." My feet pad softly across the floor, closing the gap between our bodies. His hands grasp my hips and pull me towards him.

"I didn't…I'm sorry."

"Shh. It's okay." I wrap my arms around his waist, placing my head on his chest.

Robert stands and walks around us, avoiding bumping into either of us. "You two are both incredibly fucked up. Seriously fucked in the head. I'm going upstairs. Sort your shit out." He stops just before the door, turning around to face both of us. "I'm assuming you've lost your mind because your grandma passed. I'm sorry for that, but don't ever accuse me of keeping anything from you. The next time you flip shit, you had better reign it in. Get your head straight. I am serious, man. If you pull that shit near or around my sister again, I'll fucking kill you."

"Robert!" Why can't he just walk away? It's obvious this isn't a normal situation.

"You." He raises his index finger, pointing it directly at me. "Don't you, 'Robert' me. You didn't see what I saw. That man is hurt and crazed. He doesn't own you. You're not a piece of property. I do recall having to pick up the pieces after he left in the middle of the night, only leaving a note behind. Where was he then, huh? If he loved you so much, how could he walk away from you like that?" He moves his finger to the side, pointing it directly at Theron. "You better not hurt her again. I'll hunt you down. You think you're in pain now? You have no fucking idea what I will do to you. This is your last warning."

I can feel Theron's muscles tense in my hold. I need to calm him down. "Robert, I'm okay. Theron's okay. Please just go." I nuzzle my face into Theron's chest, breathing in deep. He always smells so incredible. Standing like this, with his arms around me, feels like home despite the craziness still looming in the air. I feel Theron relax in my hold and I know that Robert has left. I start to move my hands up and down his back, but he pushes my arms away.

"Why would you do that?" I'm left standing cold and vulnerable in just a towel, as Theron turns away from me. Hissing through his teeth, he tries to roll his left shoulder. Why is he so hot headed?

"Theron, your shoulder! Did you hurt it? Let me see it, so I can check your stiches."

"It's fine. I'm fine. I don't need to be inspected."

"Do you love me?"

"Are we doing this right now?"

"Yes, we are doing this right now. Do you love me?"

He spins to face me, taking my hand in his. "Of course, I love you. I don't have a choice. I was born to love you. I was made just for you. I have loved you since I was fourteen, and I'm never going to stop loving you. You're the reason I breathe. The reason I live." His thumb brushes over my skin, sending bolts of electricity coursing under it. "Do you love me?"

"Of course, I love you. I don't have a choice. You're my person, Theron. I was born to love you."

"I'm your person?"

"Yes. Now, can I please look at your shoulder?" He doesn't reply, but simply takes a seat on the edge of the bed. I crawl into his lap, straddling his waist. Pulling the collar of his shirt to the side, I inspect his sutures. They look red and angry, but they aren't bleeding. I let out a sigh of relief knowing that he didn't tear any. Carefully fixing his shirt, I place a kiss softly on his shoulder. "You're okay for the most part. It's really red, but you aren't bleeding." He won't look directly at me. I gently slip from Theron's lap and take a step back.

He takes a deep breath, dropping his head to his chest. "I hurt you."

"You did, but it doesn't matter now. Let me get dressed and throw some clothes in a bag. Then, we can leave. Okay?"

"I don't know if that's a good idea. I don't foresee this getting any better. There's a lot that needs to be dealt with. Are you sure you want to come with me?"

"We are both broken. You more so than me, but we are both broken. I'm not leaving you."

"Thank fuck for that. I might be able to say, I can let you go, but I can't do it. I just can't. I need you."

Leaning down, I place a soft kiss on his cheek. "I know you do, and I need you." I throw on a summer dress and slip my arms into a light button up sweater. I toss what clothes I can fit, plus some of my shower stuff into a bag. I'm so stretched between houses. I really need to gather my things, and just decide on a place. At this rate, I am going to end up losing everything. After a quick search of the house, I find my ballet flats in the kitchen by the front door. I slip them on and reach my hand out for, Theron. He holds my hand and carries my bag to the car.

"Can I drive?"

His question catches me off guard, and I stop to face him. "Yeah, sure. No problem." It seems like an odd request, but I already feel like I'm walking on eggshells with him, so I toss him the keys.

"I just need to stop somewhere first. Is that okay?"

"It's fine. You just threw me off for a second. Let's go wherever you need to. I'm yours all day, and most likely for the next couple of days. I should at the least give Olivia a call over at the bookstore to let her know what's going on."

He nods his head and we both slide into the car. We drive for a few minutes, neither one of us talking. The air is thick with questions we both want to ask, but neither of us want to make the first move. We take a turn down a gravel road, marked private. I watch the trees pass by, as we drive slowly down the rocky path.

"Do you like it?"

"What?"

"The bookstore? Do you like working there?"

"I really do. I feel in my element there."

"Good. That's good."

We pull up into what I think is a driveway, but I'm not sure. There's not much of a house left. I can see some bricks left from the foundation, but what catches my eyes is the stone fireplace standing alone. Overgrown grass and tall, weeds surround its base, while vines crawl up it, reaching towards the sun. Theron, steps out of the car and walks closer to where the house once stood. I watch him, as he softly sits on the ground. His expressions change like the wind. Contentment, anger, and sadness all wash over his face. I hesitate for just a moment, before stepping out of the car, quietly shutting my door so I don't disturb him. He watches me, as I approach him, his eyes never leaving me. I sit down on the grass beside him. I am quiet for a moment, as I pick a bright yellow dandelion growing beside me. It's too bad the weed isn't white and full of seeds, I could really use a wish right now. I spin it in my fingers, turning my head slowly to look at Theron. How can such a broken man make me feel so whole?

"Babe, where are we?"

He grabs a twig from the ground and starts drawing in the gravel at our feet. "This used to be my mom's house. She grew up here. My grandparents died in a car accident a few years after my parents were married. They left my mom everything. The house was old, but it wasn't completely run down. A little bit of love and hard work would have made it beautiful again."

"What happened?" Pulling petals off the dandelion, I start chewing on my cheek. Theron, stares at the fireplace and suddenly I see a lost little boy, instead of a man.

"I was probably about seven or eight the last time my mom came here. She got into a fight with Thomas. He wanted to sell it because he felt she spent too much time here. The thing was she very rarely came here. She just wanted to hold onto it since it was all she had left of my grandparents." Theron takes a long breath and scratches out his drawing in the dirt. "There was a beautiful flower garden that wrapped around the house. She would stop by to water it and take care of the weeds. Any time spent here was time spent away from Thomas. He already hated how much time she spent with me and the house proved to be an added distraction. He finally agreed not to sell it, since the house meant so much to her."

"So, he just left it to rot?" I never understood Thomas' jealousy of Theron, but to be jealous of a house seems insane.

"Sort of. A couple weeks later, the police informed my parents that someone burned down the house. They found an empty gasoline container and some rags, but there were no leads on who did it. My dad collected the insurance money, but never fixed the house. He kept the land, but that was it. I heard my mom crying one night, begging him to let her fix it. He told her there was no reason for her to go there ever again. He didn't want her to become upset by the damage the fire had caused. When she argued, he told her it was easier to get rid of a house than a person. I don't think she ever brought it up again."

"That's just awful."

"This is why I brought you here. I wanted to show you what he is capable of. He won't let anything stop him, and he will go to any means to get his way. He wants to destroy me. Right now, you are the only person I have left. You're the only good thing that I have. He's going to try to take you away from me again, and I'm afraid of what lengths he will go to. This is why I have to get to him first. I'm going to finish what Gram started and take everything away from him. I'm going to leave him so broken that he will never be able to get close to you or me again." He breaks the stick in his hand in two. I'm not sure if it was intentional, but he looks at his hands, as if he didn't know he broke it. Shrugging his shoulders, he tosses the sticks in the tall grass.

I am not sure if his words should scare me or not, but all I feel his hatred for Thomas. "I get it." Placing my hand on his knee, I look out at what's left of the burnt remains. "I bet this place was beautiful."

"It was, especially the garden, but you've seen that."

"What?"

"The garden was the only thing untouched by the fire. It was odd how only the house burnt, but the garden continued to thrive. I don't think my mom ever knew the flowers made it through the fire. I used to sneak here when she was sick. My gram followed me here one day. I was sitting in between a bunch of Gladiolas, when I saw her walking up the path. She never asked me anything. She just sat down beside me and held my hand. I remember spending that day laying in the garden with her pointing out different shapes in the clouds. It's one of my favorite memories." A soft smile plays on his lips, as he looks towards the house. "That night after dinner, Gram took me with her into the library. It was our space. Thomas hated books. Anyways, she told me how she always wanted a garden. She asked me if she could move my garden my mom left me, to her house. The way she called it my garden, made me feel like I still had a piece of my mom left. A piece Thomas had no claim to. I agreed and she hired a landscape company. Of course she's added to it over the years, but the flowers and the stones from my mom's garden are still there."

"It's beautiful." I'm sure he knows, but I decide to tell him anyways. "Your gram loved you very much."

"Yeah." Theron stands and brushes the dirt from his jeans. "On that note, we should go. Evan needs us." He pulls me up from the ground and I follow him back to the car.

It turns out that Theron's mom's house is really close to his gram's. When we pull up to the circled drive, I notice Evan sitting outside on the steps. Theron helps me out of the car and keeps my hand clasped in his, as we walk towards the house. We stop at the steps and he drops my hand, taking a seat next to Evan. Running his hand through his hair, he looks over at Evan. "Have you been out here all night?"

"No. A little. I didn't know where to go. I came home and the house was just too empty without her here. I couldn't handle it, Theron. Everywhere I looked I saw her face, her smile, and I swear I heard her laughter." His shoulders heave, as he drops his head back into his hands. "I wasn't there. Thomas, asked me to leave and I refused, but Isa told me to go. She said she would be okay. I stepped out for a minute and checked my email. The next thing I know, machines are alarming, and Thomas is being escorted out of her room. I could hear him screaming at her."

A sob like I have never heard in my life, escapes Evan's throat. It's like I can physically hear his heart being torn apart. It's awful. His body is violently shaking, as he cries. "I rushed back to her, but the nurses wouldn't let me in. I just wanted to hold her hand, to let her know that I was close, and to let her know that I loved her. Eventually, the nurses moved and my sweet, Isa was laying peacefully. I grabbed her hand, and brushed her hair out of her face."

Theron's face pales, as he wipes away the tears escaping his eyes. He gently wraps his arm around Evan's shoulder. "I'm so sorry, Theron. I'm so sorry." Evan cries as if he is begging for forgiveness.

"It's okay. You didn't know. I would have done the same. You only did what she asked." He squeezes Evan shoulder, as an offer of comfort. I stand still with tears streaming down my face, as I watch them both break in front of me. Watching someone break is so surreal. Everything else fades, and I swear that if you look close enough, you can watch fragments from their soul dissipate into the air around them.

"It's not okay! You don't understand. I brushed her hair out of her face, so I could look into her beautiful bright green eyes. I wanted to see them shine back at me. I don't know what I was looking for. Maybe it was hope that she was still here with me or that she would be okay? I don't know, but I know I didn't find it." Evan pushes Theron's hand off his shoulder, while tears stream down his face. "I watched her beautiful emerald eyes dull in front of me. I watched as the life left her eyes. All I could do was whisper, 'I love you,' over and over again. I don't even know if she heard me. What if she didn't hear me? What if she died thinking that she was all alone? I didn't abandon her. Oh God! Why did I leave her?" Evan pushes himself up from the step and walks out towards the trees growing between the houses. Theron doesn't follow him. He stares blankly out into the distance. At first, I thought he was staring at me, but his gaze is empty. He's looking right through me.

I turn my head towards Evan, as I hear a loud bellow rip from his chest. My feet won't move. I'm frozen still as I watch him pummel his fists into a tree. "Theron. Shit, Theron!" My voice snaps Theron back to reality. He follows my gaze and jumps to his feet.

"What the fuck? Evan, stop it!" He takes off towards the trees. I wish I could follow him, but my mind isn't connecting my thoughts to my feet. Theron runs full force into Evan, knocking him away from the tree. "What the hell are you doing?"

Evan tries to throw a punch at Theron, but it's messy and slow. He steps to the side, as Evan's fist cuts through the air beside him, causing Evan to fall to his knees.

Theron lays his hands on Evan's shoulder. "Stop, Evan. Please, stop."

"I want to die."

"I know."

"I want to go with her."

"I know. Eve, can you help?"

I nod my head and will my feet to move. The skin on Evan's knuckles is ripped, bloody, and barely hanging on. His fists are raw. Kneeling down, I take my sweater off and wrap it around both of his hands. "Theron, we need to get him inside."

"I don't want to go in there. It's full of her." Evan's voice breaks and once again he falls apart, but this time in my arms.

I look up at Theron, hoping he will have an answer, but his expression is once again vacant. "What if you stayed in the guest house? There's an extra bedroom. He could stay with us, right?"

Theron looks at me confused for a second before he realizes what I'm saying. "That's a good idea. Come on, man. Let's get you inside and cleaned up."

It takes both of us to get Evan standing on his feet. We walk into the guesthouse and my stomach sinks as the realization hits me that this isn't over. There are now three broken people trying to hold together the pieces they have left. Thomas is responsible for two of them, and I have my own agenda with him after the stunt he pulled with Bridgette. This isn't going to end well for him.

CHAPTER 3

EVE

I've often wondered why the doctor's office can charge you if you are late to an appointment, but if they are running late, we still have to pay them. It seems only the patients are responsible for being on time. I turn the page in the magazine and I'm greeted with a gorgeous blonde. According to the ad, if I use their shampoo, I can look just like her. A snort escapes me, as I roll my eyes. If I had a makeup artist, photo shop, and airbrushing, I am sure I could look just like her. Her perfect figure, with her perfectly, glossy hair is definitely, false advertising.

There's a gentleman sitting two seats down from me. We are the only two people in the waiting area. He's coughing and keeps wiping his nose on the back of his hand. Why did he have to choose a seat so close to me? My face contorts into disgusted horror, as I watch him wipe his nose, cough, and then put back the magazine he was reading onto the table in front of us. I hold back the urge to gag, as I set down the magazine I was reading, and grab my hand sanitizer from my purse. Theron jokingly calls my purse luggage, but its size is definitely suiting when I have to defend myself against plague boy, two seats down.

I hear my name being called, so I collect my things. Plague boy gives me a little wave, as I walk past trying to avoid brushing up against him. The nurse must understand my sense of disgust because there is definitely a sense of sympathy in her expression. I am only in the room for a couple of minutes before the doctor comes in.

"Good morning, Evelyn. How are we today?"

"Fine, but it's more of a good afternoon, now."

Glancing down at his watch, he checks the time. "Oh, I guess a good afternoon is in order. How long have you been waiting?"

"About an hour or so."

"Yes, well that can happen. Some appointments take longer than others."

I'm not sure what appointments he's referring to. I never saw anyone except me and plague boy the entire time I was in the waiting area. I'm curious if his appointments were due to him running late. I let out a sigh of frustration and I mentally kick myself. It's not the doctor's fault my patience is running thin. I tried to argue with Theron and Evan that they would need me today, since the wake is this afternoon at two, but they wouldn't listen. Theron insisted that I keep my appointment, so I could get the all clear from the doctor. I don't know why it's such a big deal, it was only two broken fingers.

The doctor removes the tape and splint from my fingers. I give them a little flex, and I am able to move them with ease. "You healed up rather nicely. I'm not going to give you any restrictions or anything like that, but please be careful. No more punching. Agreed?"

"Agreed." I take the papers he hands me, and head to the front desk to check out. As I hand the receptionist my debit card, I look out the office window and notice a pink note tucked under my windshield wiper blade. There's no way that it's a ticket, I am parked in a parking lot. I'm barely aware of the receptionist handing me back my card and wishing me a good day. I am too distracted to give her a reply, so I just simply give her a nod of my head.

As I push open the glass doors, stepping into the parking lot, I take a deep breath to calm my nerves. My heart is thumping so hard in my chest that I'm sure if anyone was within ten feet of me they would be able to hear it. I carefully pull the note out from under the wiper blade of my car. My stomach sinks as I read the words.

Troubles in paradise? I notice you're driving your own car. No more fancy rides for you? That must be awful. Just because you are there for him now, doesn't mean it's going to last. I am betting on it.

What the hell? I quickly scan the parking lot to see if I can recognize anyone, but of course, I'm alone with a bunch of empty cars. Gripping my keys tightly in my hand, I slide into my seat and immediately hit the lock button. I check my mirrors just in case, but I'm not exactly sure what I'm looking for. "Get it together, Eve. It's just a note. No one is out there waiting for you. This is real life, not some horror flick." After my brief encouragement to myself, I wad the note up and toss it into the back seat. My drive home is clouded by thoughts of who could have left the note. My gut tells me it's Thomas, but for some reason I can't get the idea of Bridgette leaving me the note out of my head.

Noticing the time as I park in front of the guesthouse, I decide it's best to skip the shower. It's already one thirty and the wake starts at two. How awful of a person would I be, if I couldn't even show up to my boyfriend's grandmother's wake on time? Making a quick change of clothes, I glance at myself in the mirror. I run my fingers through my long brown locks. My hair is still wavy from when I curled it this morning, so just a little hairspray to keep it from frizzing should do the trick. I'm wearing my black slacks, a charcoal gray silk sleeveless dress shirt, and a black short sleeved cardigan. I slide my feet into a pair of black ballet flats and head out the door. Thankfully, when I pull into the parking lot at the funeral home, I notice that not a lot of guests have arrived yet. I take a deep breath in and brace myself for the worst, as I head inside to find Theron.

I'm sitting with Kayla in the lounge at the funeral home. It's a little after six and guests are starting to leave. The minister from Isa's church gave a lovely speech, followed by a sweet farewell from Theron. I'm tired, and my feet hurt from standing and moving back and forth between Theron and Evan. Theron stayed in the front with me beside him, as everyone said their goodbyes. Evan stayed in the back of the room. He sat in a chair he pulled into the corner, with his face buried in his hands during most of the wake. When it was time for the service, Evan abruptly left the room, causing some people to whisper, but they were quickly hushed when the minister began to speak.

I hear a shrill laugh, as the front doors are propped open to allow everyone to exit comfortably. My fists clench, my jaw locks, and my entire body tenses, as the voice I recognize walks into the entryway. She can't see me from where I'm sitting, but I can see her through the small doorway off the lounge. I don't know what she's trying to pull, but I'm not going to stand for it. Kayla grabs my wrist, distracting me from the evil thoughts playing through my mind.

"Eve, this isn't the place."

"I know." Squeezing the bridge of my nose, I take a deep breath trying to ease the tension. "I just can't believe the nerve she has to show her face here."

"I know. If it was any other time or place, I would let you at her. However, this isn't the right time or place. Just go find, Theron. He's going to need you when he sees her."

She's right. I make my way into the viewing room, excusing myself as I quickly rush by a couple of the guests, but I'm too late. She's beat me into the room. I quickly take my place by Theron's side. Sensing my discomfort, he wraps his arm around my waist and places a kiss on the top of my head before he gives her any recognition.

"Theron." Her voice is sweet like honey, but I know what kind of treacherous snake she is. Her venom is definitely not sweet it has more of a bitter, vile taste to it.

"Bridgette, do not address me so formally. You act as though you know me, or if you have a right to be here. Which, in case you weren't aware, you don't." His voice is smooth and sharp like the edge of a knife blade. Any pleasantries she wished to offer are shredded, as his words cut into her.

"I have a right as your ex-fiancé. I was a part of this family, once."

I bite my tongue, holding back my words of contempt for her. Theron pulls me into him, eliminating any space between us. I lay my hand on his chest, softly tracing the design in his tie. He glances down at me, giving me a soft smile. As his gaze moves back towards Bridgette, all the light in his eyes fades. His stare is cold, angry, and murderous. Theron opens his mouth to speak, but I beat him to it.

"That's it though, isn't it? You used to be a part of his family, but you no longer hold any position even closely related to be an acquaintance with Theron now. So, why are you here, Bridgette?"

Her eyes narrow, as she sneers at me. "Why are you speaking to me? I'm not here for you."

I can feel Theron's heart pounding in his chest. He doesn't want her. It's obvious, so why won't she go? Theron moves his hand to my back, pulling me against his body, shielding me from her. I use this second to revel in his touch, knowing she's not going to get what she wants.

"Bridgette, you need to leave. You are not wanted or needed here. In fact, you were never wanted or needed. I have despised you since the first lie fell from your lips. Don't try to better yourself in my eyes by showing up with some lame excuse of sympathy. Please, see yourself out before I have you escorted out." Theron's voice is flat and full of disdain. Her gaping mouth opens and closes like a fish. We turn away from her, leaving her floundering in waves of our disgust. Theron looks down at me. I return his gaze, with a corner of my mouth sneaking into a spiteful smile. He shakes his head at me as we walk away. "No, Eve."

"No?" Looking up at him with confusion, I stop walking.

"No, Eve. I know that felt good. I know you feel like you've won against her. That feeling is addicting. You are sweet and pure. I don't want you tainted by her. Don't darken your soul because you are reveling in her demise." Theron gently lifts my chin with his fingers. Beautifully colored eyes look back at me. I hate that they are dull with only a few specks of light left. I don't want to be the reason they go out.

"I'm sorry. I was just so angry. I don't want her anywhere near you. She's vile. I wouldn't be surprised if she's plotting against us as we speak."

"She probably is. It's what she does best, but I can't handle losing you. I wouldn't make it through the pain this time." Theron's eyes darken as he looks at me.

"Hey. Stop. I've already told you. I'm not going anywhere."

"You say that, but I'm afraid it won't be under your control."

"Baby, just stop. Okay?"

An older couple approaches us. Knowing they want to give their regards to Theron, I step away. I'm sitting outside on the bench getting some fresh air, when Kayla sits beside me. She lays her head on my shoulder. I know this move. She is going to turn into my mom.

"Hey."

"Hey, yourself."

"So, how are you handling all of this? I swear your life has gone from ordinary to crazy over the last couple of months."

"I'm okay. I'm not worried about me."

"When's the last time you ate anything?"

"I had a banana this morning. Oh, I had coffee and a muffin in the lounge."

Kayla sighs, rolling her eyes. It might not be the response she wanted, but it's the one she got. "You need to take care of yourself first, or you won't be able to take care of him."

"I know." I stand to make my way inside when I notice another note on my car. "You've got to be fucking kidding me. Seriously?"

"What?" Kayla follows me over to my car. I snatch the pink note from underneath the wiper blade. I cannot believe she had the balls to leave another note on my car at a funeral home. Who the hell does that? I'm fuming, as I read the note.

The game isn't over yet. This won't last between you. I've made it my goal to separate you. Just wait.

Shit. I don't need any more stress. I already feel like a rubber band ready to snap. I start pacing back and forth, but Kayla stops me with her hand, grasping my shoulder. She spins me around to look at her. She must think that I've lost my mind. "What the hell are you mumbling about? What's on that note, Eve?"

"Bridgette. God, I hate her. She keeps leaving these little snarky notes on my car." I hand Kayla the note. Her cheeks redden, as she reads it.

"Are you sure this is from her?"

"Who else would leave a note threatening my relationship with Theron?"

"I don't know. Maybe it was his dad. He seems devious enough to do it."

"I thought about that, but he's running a business. If he's going to destroy us or me for that matter, it's not going to be by a pink note stuck to my windshield. It has to be her. She was the only one that was here tonight."

"Okay. Yeah, that makes sense. What I don't understand is why leave the notes?"

"I don't know. Maybe she thinks if she can scare me enough, I'll leave. She's wrong, you know. I won't leave him again. I can't. I tried and every day I felt like I was dying inside. I don't want to feel that empty again." I lean against the hood of my car, burying my face in my hands. I try to hold back the tears, but a few sneak down my cheeks.

"Ssh. It's alright. I'll go with you so you can give the note to Theron and see what he thinks, okay?"

I'm shaking my head back and forth before she even finishes her thought. "What? No, that's not an option. Have you lost your mind? He's been through so much, he's already broken, and you want to try and tip the scales by giving him a note that may or may not be from his ex-fiancé? No. Nope. Not happening."

"You can't keep this from him. What if it's not from her? What if it's from someone else? Have you even thought of that?"

"Yes, I have. I'll tell him eventually, if they keep happening, but for right now he doesn't need the added stress."

"God, you are so stubborn."

"The same goes for you! I'm not giving him the damn notes."

"Fine. If you need me, I'll be inside." Kayla spins on her heels, stomping back to the front doors. I watch her blonde curls sway back and forth until she disappears through the doorway.

Theron is holding my hand in his, as we say goodbye to the last of the guests. Tomorrow is the funeral. It's going to take so much out of him. I look around for Evan, but I can't find him. "Babe, where's Evan?"

"He left a little bit ago. He's going to stay at his sister's place tonight. I think staying at the house is too much for him. I don't blame him. It's almost too much for me."

I have no words to offer him, so I gently stroke my fingers up and down his arm. I give Theron a few minutes alone with his gram. The other rooms are now dark and locked. The hair on my neck stands on end and I shiver. Funeral homes are incredibly creepy in the dark. The doors open and I watch Theron walk towards me. He looks exhausted. His eyes are swollen and puffy, with dark circles under them. He looks so defeated. The drive home is short, but quiet. The thought of telling him about the notes enters my mind a couple of times, but I push it back. It's not something we need to deal with right now.

CHAPTER 4

EVE

I'm sitting on the edge of Theron's bed watching him pace back and forth in his flannel pajama pants that hang so perfectly on his hips. I'm enjoying my view, but I swear he's going to wear a hole in the carpet.

"I don't understand what the issue is. It has been three days. Surely, he has had enough time to go over the contract. He's intentionally doing this just to piss me off!"

My shoulders sag, as I let out a deep sigh. After Isa's funeral, Theron took a week to himself. We mostly laid around the house. He was too depressed to eat, let alone go anywhere. I finally got him to eat a full meal after I threatened to stay the night at Robert's. Thank goodness, my threat worked because there was no way I would have actually gone through with it.

On Monday, he went into Isa's office to get the files she had on Rowe Inc. He looked everything over in detail before setting up meetings with the last three remaining board members at Rowe, who had not signed contracts with GILF, yet. His first meeting was Tuesday morning with Howard. It didn't take much convincing for him to sign the contract Theron presented him with. By three that afternoon, the contract and non-disclosure agreement were not only signed, but also properly filed away. That afternoon, Theron also met with David. He was turning out to be quite the hard sell. He was extremely loyal. After all, Thomas had made him millions over the years. Who wouldn't be loyal? Theron is an excellent chess player. He knew every move David would make. Even before he touched his first pawn, David was outmaneuvered. However, he is proving to be difficult. He refuses to go out easily.

Nothing I say is going to make a difference, but I offer my thoughts anyway. "Maybe, he just wants to make sure of every possible outcome before he signs. He's probably just being cautious."

"Cautious? He signed the non-disclosure without hesitating. He didn't even care to read it. It's Friday. He's not being cautious he's fucking with me! My final meeting is with Anthony on Monday. I swear, if I don't have his signature by the time I have Anthony's, he's going to find me waiting in the parking lot for him. It would be rather difficult for him to walk his fat fucking ass around without any kneecaps."

My eyes widen at his harsh words. Normally, I would roll my eyes at anyone being so dramatic, but I'm not a hundred percent sure he's not serious. Theron is a broken man, and broken people can become desperate. I need to distract him. "Orange isn't your color."

Theron abruptly stops pacing, as he looks at me. "What?"

"Orange isn't your color. Prison life wouldn't work out well for you, babe. I love you, but I'm not sure you could handle being someone's bitch." I raise my eyebrows at him, as he stares me down. The darkness that had taken control of his features just seconds ago fades, as he looks at me.

"Oh, beautiful, you have it all wrong. They would be my bitch."

"So, you'd rather have a prison bitch than me?" My words provoke him. I want some kind of reaction out of him. I want him to show some kind of emotion towards me. Anger has consumed him, except when it comes to me. I've gotten nothing from him since the funeral. No kisses. No touching. He hasn't even given me the slightest glimpse of the man that I fell in love with. I know if I can distract him from all of this, even if just for a second, he would come back to me. Maybe it wouldn't bring him completely back, but it would be a start.

"Are you fucking kidding me right now? Everything is hanging on the decision of one man, and you make a fucking prison joke. Then, you question whether I want you or not. What the fuck, Eve?" His words are hard. He's so incredibly pissed, perhaps provoking him wasn't my best idea. I wanted an emotion from him and I got it. It's just not the one I wanted.

My anger towards his words turns to anger towards myself. Hot tears run down my cheeks, as I turn my head away from him. Screw him. This is not at all, what I wanted.

"Oh, beautiful. What have I done?" Theron's soft fingers lift my chin to look at him. He lowers himself to the floor, kneeling in front of me. Using his thumb, he brushes away my tears. "Please, don't cry."

His words don't help. They only cause me to cry harder. Climbing onto the bed, he pulls me with him. I bury my face in his chest, as my body shakes from my sobs. I feel so out of control. I'm upset, but this is ridiculous. I can't stop crying. Trying my best to calm down, I take a couple of deep breaths.

"Eve, please stop. I didn't mean to yell at you."

"No, it's not that. I mean, yeah, you probably should reign your anger in a bit, but that's not why I'm crying."

"Then, why are you?"

The heat from his hands moving up and down my back, send goosebumps racing across my skin. This is what I've wanted. "Because I need you."

"You have me."

"No, I need to feel you."

"Look at me." He tilts my chin up, as I wipe my face and stare into his beautiful green and brown eyes. "I always need you. I always need to feel you. I've neglected you in all of the craziness. I'm sorry. Let me make it up to you."

"How?"

"For starters, how about this?" His soft lips gently brush mine. A moan escapes me, as I open my mouth to him. His tongue sweeps across my lower lip before it tangles with mine. I arch my body into him, my breasts pressing against him as my nipples turn to hard peaks, and my panties are already wet with desire. I need him so bad. My hands wrap around his neck and grip onto his hair, pulling him on top of me.

He disperses his weight by pushing himself up onto all fours with me beneath him. Dragging my bottom lip through my teeth, I take in the sight of his perfectly fit body hovering above me. The muscles in his arms and chest are enough to make someone drool, but it's his perfectly cut stomach that makes me hot all over. I know where that 'v' leads to, and I can't wait to feel it send me into utter bliss.

"Do you like what you see?" He chuckles, raising an eyebrow at me.

"God, yes. I need you so bad." I dig my fingers into his shoulder trying to pull him back down, but his arms are locked straight.

"Patience."

"No, not today. I need you to fuck me, Theron."

He seems happy, as he rears his head back with a loud booming laugh, but when he looks back down at me his eyes are dark and hungry. My sexy gorgeous man is licking his lips as if he's going to devour me. "Be still."

I know better than to question his motives. I lie very still, barely breathing, waiting for his next move. His hand slides into my black yoga pants and my breath hitches, as his fingers skim the inside of my panties. Desire tugs at the knot between my legs, wanting to break free. "Please," I whisper, begging for his touch.

"Ssh, be still." His hands roam underneath my shirt, lifting me just a little, as his fingers undo the clasp of my bra. "Hmm. What shall I do to you? Gentle or rough?"

"Rough. Oh, God, please rough." My back arches, as he pulls hard on my nipple, twisting it between his fingers, sending sparks flying through my body.

"You are not very good at following directions tonight. Be still." Grabbing the hem of my t-shirt, he pulls it over my head. With one quick grasp, he pulls my bra off, throwing it behind him. "I don't want to leave any marks on your perfect skin, so I'm going to improvise. Don't ask any questions." He takes my shirt, pulling it tightly, and wraps it around my wrists, so that I can no longer move my arms. His fingers brush against my legs, as he slowly pulls off my pants, then my panties.

I am squirming. I can't control it. If he doesn't touch me soon, I'm going to die. "Please, Theron."

"Ssh. I bought you something the night before you walked out on us. I think now would be a good time to give you that present. Close your eyes." Drawers slide open and close. I can hear his feet pad along the soft carpet, and his breaths are calm. He's so relaxed, and I'm a ball of exposed nerves, ready to explode from the slightest touch. "I want you to feel these first."

Something cold and metal brushes between my breasts, causing a chill to creep up my spine. "Cold." The words escape my lips, before I can even finish processing the thought. Smack! My nipple stings and burns from the pleasure of his slap. I moan, from his rough touch.

"Do not speak." His voice is calm, and collected, but I know something dark lies just beneath the surface. "I originally bought these beautiful clamps for your delicious nipples, but you want me to fuck you. You want me to take my pain out on you. I don't want to give you pain, I want to give you pleasure, but sometimes they come hand in hand. Pun intended."

I feel the cold medal of the clamps swirl around my nipples. There's a slight pinch, but it doesn't hurt like I thought. It's more like pressure, constricting my blood flow, causing my nipples to plump. He slides a finger through my wet folds, circling my clit before thrusting it deep into my pussy. "Yes. More!"

"I wanted to taste you, take my time with you, savoring every little bite. I don't think I'll be able to last that long. I want to watch your body claim me. I'm going to enjoy this." With a slight tug on the clamp, my nipple is released and blood rushes to my hard peaks. It feels incredible. A harsh breath escapes me, as I feel a clamp grasp one of the outer lips of my pussy. It squeezes me, pinching me, it's rough, but I breathe through it. "Good girl. Take another breath." Breathing deep, I feel another clamp clench onto the other side of my pussy. He gives a soft tug on the chain "Open your eyes."

Instantly, my eyes spring open, staring down at his hand holding tightly to the chain between my legs. He hooks the chain over his thumbs, pulling it taught, spreading my pussy open for him. My eyes roam his body. To my surprise, he's completely nude. Disappointment fills me, knowing that I wasn't able to watch him shed his clothes. It's quickly replaced with anticipation, when I feel the tip of his cock rub against my clit.

"You are so fucking wet." He slowly slides himself deep into my pussy. Closing my eyes, I let out a deep moan. "Open your eyes, Eve. I want you to watch me fuck you. I want you to watch how badly your body needs me, craves me, as I slide in and out of your slick cunt."

Holy hell. His words alone send my nerves shooting off in all different directions. I watch, as he slowly and steadily slides his hard cock in and out of my wet pussy. Our breaths are ragged and strained. My toes curl, as he leans down, sucking one of my nipples into his mouth, as he lightly nips at me. "Oh, God! Theron!" His name is a strangled cry, as my body explodes around his hard cock.

"Yes, baby. Come for me." He rocks harder into me, pushing my body deep into the bed. His eyes roll back, closing tightly.

"Open your eyes, Theron. I want to see them when you come." His eyes fly open, staring straight into mine. His one eye is a bright and explosive green, showing me the excitement running through him. The other one pools into darkness, exposing the danger lurking under his surface. Chills spread across my body and my pussy clenches his cock, while he thrusts deeper into me. I can't take my eyes off of him. Watching his body strain, as he tries to hold himself back is such an amazing sight. "Yes, Theron!"

"Eve!" My name is a harsh cry, as he loses himself in me, filling me with his release, triggering my body to explode around him a second time. I feel a slight pinch, followed by a release of pressure, as Theron removes the clamps. He collapses beside me, freeing my arms from my shirt. I curl into him, laying my head on his damp chest.

"Eve?"

"Hmm?"

"Eve? Did I break you?"

"Mmmm."

He chuckles, placing a kiss on my forehead, his hands softly stroking my back.

Closing my eyes, I drift to sleep. Movement wakes me, and I roll to the side when I feel him slide out from under me. My body is completely, drained. I don't want to move. The bathroom door closes and I hear the water in the shower turn on. I was hoping he would lay with me for just a little longer. Stretching my muscles as best as I can, I untangle myself from the sheets and make my way to the bathroom. The door softly clicks, as I push it closed. Theron is standing under the shower, letting the hot water pour down over him. I slip into the shower, wrapping my hands around his waist. His head and shoulders drop, as he lets out a deep sigh.

"I thought you were sleeping? Didn't I wear you out?"

"I was and you did."

"I see, but you aren't now?"

"I'm not tired anymore, but I'm definitely worn out." I smile, as I place a soft kiss between his shoulder blades. I'm not sure when he's working out his body, but it's so obvious he does. I start to slide my hands up his stomach, but he pulls out of my grasp.

Turning to face me, Theron lets out yet another sigh. It's obvious I'm bothering him. I don't know why I thought this was a good idea. He probably just wanted to be alone with his thoughts, but me being the selfish person I am, invaded his space. "Beautiful, what are we doing?"

"I don't know. I just want to be near you."

"I'll make you a deal. I'll order us some dinner, and after you are done with your shower you can lay with me on the couch, while I go over some more files. Okay?"

Disappointment flutters into my stomach, causing a small knot to form. I shouldn't expect everything to be back to normal with us. We've both lost so much, him more than I. We haven't even discussed the night he left me. The knot in my stomach grows, as I think about that night. I felt so loved when I fell asleep in his arms, but I woke up alone, only to find out that he left me, after reading a note on the fridge. One day, I'll ask him about it, but for now, I'll leave it.

"Yeah. Okay." I nod my head and step into the water. I have a tight hold on my emotions, but once he closes the door, my tears blend with the water now streaming over me. I want to take away the weight that's on his shoulders. It's apparent my distraction, was exactly that; it distracted him, but not long enough for me to help him. I finish with my shower, while trying to decide on my next move.

Walking into the living room, I notice that Theron isn't anywhere to be found. There's a sticky note attached to a pizza box on the counter.

Beautiful,

I'm over at the other house, looking through some more files. Go ahead and eat without me. Evan might stop by. I'll be back as soon as I can.

Love,

Theron

Figures. Grabbing the pizza box, I plop down on the couch. I turn on the television and make myself comfortable, while watching the Food Network. I only manage to eat one slice of pizza. With all of the stress I've had lately, my stomach just seems to be in knots. I'm watching some guy demonstrate how to grill the perfect steak. One would think after watching so many of these shows, my cooking skills would be greatly, improved, but they are far from it. I love eating food, but if it came to me being able to cook it to survive, I'm afraid I would not live very long.

There's a light tap at the door. Standing, I stretch out my muscles and slowly walk to the door. I open it and find a very distraught looking Evan looking back at me. He looks worn and exhausted. At least two days' worth of stubble lines his jaw, his eyes are sunken and dark, and I am pretty, sure that he's wearing the same suit that he wore to the funeral.

"Evan?" He doesn't move. I step back, thinking that maybe I'm too close. "Sweetie, you coming in?"

He barely moves, but I register a slight nod of his head. He shuffles into the room, crashing onto the couch. "Nowhere to go." He starts mumbling, but I can't understand him. He's struggling to take his jacket off, so I walk over to help. That's when I notice the smell. He reeks of alcohol no wonder he's mumbling. He's drunk. My past, experiences that I obtained during college come in handy. I know better than to move him around too much.

"All right, big guy. I think you've had a little too much to drink tonight. I'm going to help you get this jacket off and then lay you back on the sofa. I'm going to put the trash bin right next to you, so use it if you need to. Theron should be back soon. Okay?"

Slipping his jacket off, I roll him onto his side, and prop him up with pillows. Hopefully, he will be okay. I am not sure what I'm supposed to do now, so I send Theron a quick text letting him know that Evan is here and passed out on the couch. No sooner do I hit send, I hear a vibrating sound coming from the kitchen counter. Glancing down at the counter, I grab Evan a bottle of water from the fridge. "Of course, Theron forgot his phone. Could this night get any better?"

I should have never said those words because I completely jinxed myself. Taking a deep breath through my mouth, I grab some towels out of the guest bathroom. Evan is throwing up all over the floor, completely missing the trashcan that I put beside him. I cringe, as I walk over to him and throw the towels over his vomit. There's no way I can clean this up tonight, I would end up using the trash can myself. I hand Evan a washcloth for his face, and he lays back down again. I'm done. I've hit my limit of shit for the night. I leave Evan in the living room, hoping he stays asleep, and head to bed.

"Hey, beautiful." Theron whispers in my ear, his breath tickles my neck, waking me up.

"What time is it?"

"It's only ten, babe. What time did you come to bed?"

"I don't know. I had a piece of pizza and then Evan came over. Please, don't wake him. He's drunk. I threw towels over his vomit. I'll scrub it in the morning."

"I noticed as soon as I came in. It smells awful in there."

"That's why I'm hiding in here under the blankets." Theron stands and starts to walk towards the door. I don't know why, but I start to panic, like he's going to leave. "Wait. Where are you going?"

"Nowhere, babe. I'm just getting ready to join you in bed. Everything okay?"

"Yeah. I just…I thought maybe you were going to grab some pizza or something."

"Nope. I lost my appetite when I walked in the house."

I nod my head at him, while chewing the inside of my cheek. He lays down beside me, circling his arm around my waist, pulling me to him. "I love you, Theron."

"I love you, too. Is everything okay?"

"I just feel off. You know? I can't explain it. Maybe I just need some sleep."

"Well, I had other plans, but I'll let you sleep tonight."

I close my eyes with his body wrapped around me. I feel so safe in his arms, but I still can't shake the knot of nerves in my stomach.

CHAPTER 5

EVE

"Wait, are you serious? He just left you to clean up after his drunk friend. Who does that?"

"I didn't really have to clean up after him. Poor Rebecca was stuck with that job; I just sort of covered it up. Anyways, is doesn't matter. We barely spoke all weekend."

Kayla is circling the park bench I'm sitting on. I really wish she would just sit down. She's making me dizzy. "So, what's going on with you guys?"

Resting my elbows on my knees, I drop my head into my hands. "I don't know. He seems so distant. When we have sex, he is right there with me. I can see how much he loves me in his eyes. But no sooner do I think I have him back again, his eyes are dark and my

Theron is gone again. I know he's going through so much right now. I just wish he'd let me help him."

Kayla sits down beside me, softly rubbing my back. "It's okay, sweetie. He is hurt right now. I'm sure he doesn't realize that he's distancing himself. It will all work out, I promise." She hands me a napkin and I wipe away my tears. Maybe she is right. I just need to give him some more time. "How long of a break do you get today?"

"I don't know. I normally take about a half an hour or so. Olivia doesn't really seem to mind."

"Okay. Well, we will get you a cup of coffee and then head back to the bookstore. You look like you could use a cup."

"I could use a whole pot. I am so tired. I feel so off lately, my stomach is a ball of nerves, and for some reason I feel so anxious when Theron leaves, or is working on files from GILF."

"I'm sorry. I need to stop you right there. What the hell is a GILF?" Kayla jumps up from the bench and pulls me to my feet.

"Okay. Don't laugh, but it's the name of Isa's company."

"Tell me my mind is in the gutter and it's not what I think it stands for."

"Nope, it is. Grandma I'd Like to Fuck."

"Oh, my God! That's great." She can barely contain her laughter. "That woman just amazes me." Her excitement over the name makes me smile. "Wait, are you smiling? This just keeps getting better. We can get our coffee and then dish some more on our walk back."

We both order two large coffees, cream, no sugar. I like to add my own because they always tend to put too much in it. I open the lid to my coffee, and the strong smell assaults my nose. This doesn't smell good at all. Glancing over at Kayla, I notice she is drinking hers without a problem. Great, now my nerves are affecting my coffee intake. No way am I going to let that happen. By the time we reach the bookstore, I have finished more than half of my coffee, but I am starting to regret it.

"What are your plans for the rest of the day?"

"Um, I'm working. Do you mean after work?"

"Nope. I mean, like, right now. Can I hang with you for a bit?"

"Don't you have to go to work?" The little bells rings, as I open the door to the bookstore, alerting Olivia to my return. She peeks around one of the shelves with a pile of books in her arms, towering over her face, and gives me a small wave with her fingers. "Kayla, hold that thought. That woman is going to hurt herself." I rush over towards Olivia, grabbing some books off the top of her pile. "What are you doing? You could have waited. I was coming back."

"I know, but I needed something to do. You do so much already—"

"Olivia, stop. I am your employee. I am here to do work and to help you. Please, stop trying to kill yourself with work. Harold would never forgive me."

"Fine. Have it your way."

"Thank you."

"I'll just be sitting behind the desk, all alone."

"Nice try. It won't work. You and I both know you will be busy checking the inventory and sales reports."

"Alright. You have me there. Do you girls need anything before I sit down?"

"Nope. Kayla is going to help me for a bit. We will be in the back."

"Okay, sweetie. Let me know if there's any good gossip, though."

I laugh, handing some books over to Kayla for her to carry. We walk into the backroom and plop down on the makeshift mats I made out of flattened boxes. Setting the books down beside us, we both lean against the wall. "Why don't you have to work today?"

"Because I quit. Bridgette may not be there anymore, but I don't want to work for Thomas either."

"Wait, Bridgette quit?"

"I guess. One day Bridgette was there. Then the next day Sharon was back. Supposedly, the deal fell through, but it's just a rumor. I don't want to take my chances, so I talked it over with Paul. It's not like it will hurt us moneywise, if I don't work for a bit. So, I quit. Now, I'm just bothering you."

I have no idea why, but tears start falling from my eyes. By my reaction, you would have thought she proposed to me, or something. I'm a blubbering mess and Kayla is staring at me like I have lost my freaking mind, maybe I have. How can you tell if you've lost your mind or not? Does the crazy part let you know or does it just happen?

"Eve, what on earth is wrong with you? Damn, girl, you're crying like I just ran over your dog or something."

"I know. I know. I think I'm losing my mind. I feel so closed off from Theron, but it's not justified. He's not ignoring me, he's just busy. Then, Evan came over and he was just so broken. It was awful. We set him up in the spare bedroom again. I took all of the alcohol out of the house. He was pretty, bad on Saturday, but yesterday he seemed better. Tired and grouchy, but not drunk. Plus, Theron is having a hard time finishing whatever Isa's plans were with the company, and I'm just so tired. I can't fucking eat. There's a huge knot in my stomach. I just don't fucking know, you know?"

"No, sweetie. I don't know. All I know is you are a mess. I mean, yeah, things have been overly fucked up, but I think you're having a breakdown. Here finish my coffee and I'll get us some more. You always function better with coffee."

I take her cup from her and gag from the smell. At least, I thought I was going to gag. I end up retching so hard, I slap my hand over my mouth to keep from throwing up everywhere. Kayla jumps back as if I have a horrendous disease and runs to grab the trash can in the corner. I'm bawling my eyes out, while puking into a trash can in the back room of a bookstore. What the hell is going on with my life right now?

"Hey, take a breath. Just breathe, Eve." Kayla, who is being a complete saint, is softly rubbing my back, while holding my hair. I finally catch my breath, and sit back against the wall again. She brings me a wet paper towel and I wipe my face. I'm shaky and my hands are clammy. "Eve, just listen for a second. I'm going to say something, but I don't want you to lose the rest of your sanity, okay?"

First of all, I hate being approached as though I am some fragile person who shatters whenever someone says something. I also hate when people start conversations like that. Obviously, it's not going to be good news, so why not just come out and say it? "Say whatever you need to say, Kayla. Just get it over with. I'm not a fucking child."

"No, sweetie you're not, but has the thought that you may be having one, crossed your mind?"

Wait. Hold everything. What the hell is she talking about? We may not use condoms every time, but I'm on the pill. I am not stupid. I know how babies are made. I can't be. "No. No. No. Nope. Not happening. This is not happening. Kayla, I've been on the pill since I was sixteen. I never miss. Hell, I have an alarm set on my phone."

"Okay. So maybe you're not. Maybe I'm just jumping to conclusions. We could check though, right? Tell you what. Come home with me, and I'll pick up some tests. At least, we will know one way or the other, right?"

"Yeah, okay. Um, can I drop my car off at home first? I'm not sure I'm going to want to drive home later." I cannot believe I am agreeing to this. We do not need this right now. I do not need this right now. Kayla helps me stand and follows me to the front of the store. Olivia is going through some papers, but looks up when I lean against the counter.

"Eve, you look awful. What happened?"

"I think she has food poisoning. She just got sick, so I'm going to follow her home. Sorry she has to leave like this." Kayla to the rescue. Thank goodness, she knew what to say. I can't put any rational thoughts together right now.

"Oh, it's no problem. Eve, sweetie, please get some rest. Take tomorrow off and I'll see you Wednesday, if you are feeling up to it."

I cannot form words. Kayla grabs my arm and follows me to my car. Mother fucker. There is another pink note on my car. I am not in the mood for any bullshit right now.

"Another note? Eve, how many is this now?"

"I don't know. I don't keep track, Kayla. I just throw them away."

"You throw them away? Have you even told anyone else about this, yet? Does Theron know?"

"No, he doesn't and he doesn't need to. They are just harmless notes."

"Harmless? This one says 'I'm watching you. It's my turn next.' What the hell, Eve? That's not harmless."

I snatch the note from Kayla's hand and toss it into my back seat. "Stay out of it, Kayla! I have enough going on. Don't create problems where there aren't any."

"Damn it. I'm going to drop this for the time being, since we have other problems to address, but we are not done with this conversation. We are leaving. I'll follow you home."

"Done with this conversation? You are not my mother, Kayla."

"No, I'm not, but since you are deciding not to tell anyone about this I'm going to act like it until you pull your head out of your ass."

"Fine. Whatever. Let's just go." I slide into my seat, slamming my door. Who the hell does she think she is?

I pull up in front of the guesthouse and Kayla is right behind me. My intentions were to jump straight into her car, and just shoot Theron a text, but my plan goes out the window, as I rush inside to the bathroom. I pass Evan on my way, but I don't have time to explain.

I've thrown up everything I had in my stomach for the entire duration of my life in the last fifteen minutes. I am lying on the bathroom floor, absorbing the feeling of the cool tile on my face. I roll over to allow the other side of my face to rest on the tile. I never thought I would enjoy tile flooring so much in my life. Thoughts are crashing through my mind right now. A tear slips from the corner of my eye, rolling over my nose and down my other cheek. My hands immediately cover my stomach. I don't need a test. I have no doubt in my mind that Kayla's right, but I'm going to take one anyway. I think I need to see it for the idea to really set in.

Taking a couple of deep breaths, I sit up on the floor. I pull a towel down from the sink and dry my face. I couldn't even make it to our bathroom, I'm sitting in Evan's, completely grateful he's a messy slob, so I don't feel so awful about any mess I made. I make my way to the living room, but stop just short of the entranceway. I can hear Kayla and Evan talking in low whispers. Great. That's all I need is Theron to find out, before I can figure out for sure what's going on. I tip toe a little closer, trying to keep my body as flat to the wall as possible. I am eavesdropping and I don't care.

"So, he doesn't know?"

"No, she's never said anything to him. Look, I know you all have a crazy amount of *Days of Our Lives* drama going on, but someone is watching Eve. The note I saw today is the final straw. I assumed she told someone, or she stopped getting them because she hasn't mentioned them to me. But today, I saw that note on her car and she just tossed it in her backseat like it was nothing."

"What do you want me to do? He's going to flip shit because she didn't tell him."

"I know. That's why you can't tell him. I'm going to make sure she tells him, but in the meantime, someone needs to keep an eye out for her."

"Okay. I'll keep my eye out, but if she doesn't tell him soon. I will."

Shit. Kayla just told Evan about the notes. I swear if she told him about the pregnancy test, I'm going to kill her. I've had enough of being the topic of conversation, so I walk into the room. Of course, all conversation ceases, but I act like I don't notice.

Evan's expression is nothing but pure pity. "Everything okay?"

"Um, I think I might have some food poisoning. Have you seen, Theron?"

"Not today. He texted earlier and had me email him some documents, but I think he's in meetings."

Tears spring to my eyes. I really need him and he's not here. I can't be mad at him though. It's not like he knew. Right? Right. Shit. Did I just ask and answer my own question? I'm losing it. "Okay. I'll just text him. I'm going to go with Kayla for a little bit. If I need a ride later, can I call you?"

"Sure. No problem. You have my number?"

"Yeah, from when you called me from the hospital."

"Okay. So, just call me if you need me." Evan stands, giving Kayla a knowing look before walking out of the room.

"I swear, Kayla, if you told him I'm pregnant…I'm going to kill you."

"I didn't. I take it that you've accepted it as a possible outcome?"

"I don't know what I'm doing. Let's just go get the tests."

"Okay, but there's been a slight change of plans. I can't do this at my apartment. Paul will flip shit. He will think it's me. So, I kind of called your mom."

"Have you lost your fucking mind? What the hell, Kayla?"

"Stop. Don't freak out. She doesn't know. I told her I needed a mutual meeting ground, and she didn't ask why. She just said she'll make us some snacks. Now, we have to go there because you know her version of snacks is going to be some incredibly delicious cookies or something."

Chewing on the inside of my cheek, I shoot Kayla a look that could kill. "Fine. Can we please go now?" I send Theron a text that I'm spending the afternoon with Kayla, since it was slow at the store. It is not a complete lie. It's just a little omission. I follow Kayla to her car and we head to the store. I had no idea how many different kinds of pregnancy tests there are. I hand the clerk my credit card and she raises her eyebrows at my purchase. Don't judge me. I make a mental note never to shop here again.

"Down, killer."

"What?"

"You looked like you were going to kill that cashier. Just relax." Sliding into Kayla's car, I get an incredibly bad gut feeling. I don't see this going well.

Kayla is sitting on my mom's bathroom floor. I'm lying at her feet. Her floors aren't as cold and smooth as mine, but the tile still feels great on my cheeks. "How many more should I take?"

"Honey, I don't think you need to take anymore. I think we bought every kind the drug store had. You've taken seven already. The results aren't going to change, Eve. What are you going to tell him?"

"I don't know. What if he freaks out? What if he doesn't want a baby right now? What am I going to do then, Kayla? Fuck. It's not like this was planned. I don't know what to say or think. My head is swimming right now. Just let me lie here on the floor, I'll be fine."

"I would totally be okay with that if this was my house. However, we are at your mom's. She already knows we are up to something. She's not an idiot. We've been hiding out in here for almost an hour now."

"I know. I just don't want to move. The floor is so cold, it feels great."

"Oh, sweetie. That's just so sad. Come on. If you don't want to say anything right now, I'll just tell your mom you're sick. Come with me and I'll get you a cold rag for your face. You'll feel better."

"Promise?"

"Sure. It's worth a shot, right?"

"I guess." Kayla stands and pulls me up off the floor. I follow her into the kitchen where my mom is sitting at the table with three different kinds of freshly baked cookies in front of her. I guess we were really in there for a long time. She pats the chair beside her. I plop down in the chair and almost gag when she offers me a cookie. I've never been able to lie to my mom. She has always seen right through the webs and plots I've tried to construct. I give up trying to pretend nothing is wrong. I lay my face down on the kitchen table, taking turns laying each cheek down for a few minutes. The tabletop feels so cool against my face.

Kayla gently places a wet washcloth across my neck, as I lay there looking at my mom. She doesn't say anything, but she pulls the cookies away. Kayla opens a can of ginger ale pop and sets it beside me. My mom watches Kayla's movements and raises her eyebrow at me. "Are we going to pretend this isn't happening?"

"What?"

"Don't 'what' me, Evelyn Davidson. You damn well know *what* I'm talking about. How long?"

"Mom, please, less riddles."

"How far along are you, Eve?"

My eyes go wide when she guesses my secret. I don't know why I'm surprised. I know I can't lie to her. "I don't know."

"Okay. So, what's the plan?"

"Plan? My plan right now is to stop throwing up every five minutes. I also want to stop crying all the time. I want to feel like myself again." My eyes water and I refuse to blink. I'm not going to cry, damn it.

"Evelyn, you won't ever feel like you did before and that's okay. You are going to grow and change with this baby. You are going to experience and learn things you never knew were possible. Now, for the sickness you can either take some ginger pills or drink some rosemary tea. The tea always helped when I was pregnant. The crying, I can't fix. Your hormones are all over the place right now, and you are under a lot of stress. My suggestion would be telling Theron as soon as possible."

"I know. I will. I just…I'm afraid I'll lose him. What if he leaves me?"

"I don't know what has happened between you two, but I know he loves you. I can tell by the way that he looks at you when you are not paying attention. He's completely aware of you at all times. Someone doesn't search for someone they met over fourteen years ago because they just want to be friends, Evelyn. That's what you call love."

I sit up and take the cup of tea that Kayla has made me. This girl is a fucking saint. My drama keeps spilling over into her life and she doesn't even bat an eye. She's right there with me, taking on everything as it comes. I love her so much. She's such an incredible friend. Kayla sits down across from me, and eyes me over her cup of tea. I know she has questions too, so I don't hesitate to go first. "Mom, how did you know Theron and I met before."

"I had a hunch because I recognized his face from somewhere, but I couldn't place it. That night his grandma came over with her gentleman friend, asking for your number so she could call you, put all the scattered puzzle pieces together. I recognized her instantly. I remember sitting off to the side, reading my books in my lounge chair, and watching you guys play on the beach. When Theron came around, you were so enamored with him. You looked at him as if he walked on water. I knew then, he would be someone special to you, but then his dad sent him away." She wrings her hands in her apron, and tucks a few stray strands of my hair behind my ears. "You were so heartbroken; you couldn't understand why he wasn't coming back. After he left, you sulked in your room for a couple of weeks before Matt came and forced you to go back to the beach. You were so young, and your life was in front of you. I told you to forget about him. I just didn't think you would actually forget. Do you still dream of him?"

"How did you know about the dreams?"

"At first, you would cry in your sleep, but then you started waking up talking about a boy in sunglasses. I convinced you it was just a dream, and you would fall back to sleep. I never thought you would see him again. I think after a while, you blocked it out of your memory, so you wouldn't feel the pain anymore." She sweeps her hand across the table, wiping away imaginary crumbs and completely avoiding eye contact.

"Wait, I remember him now. He always wore those black sunglasses and board shorts. He used to show us tricks on his skateboard. I had no idea that was him. Did you know, Eve?" Kayla watches me intently, making circles with her fingers along the edge of her cup, waiting for my answer.

"No, well not at first. I started figuring things out, but then I found out about him and Bridgette. I kind of flipped shit and ran."

My mom stands and sets her cup in the sink. She looks over at me, as if this is all my fault. "Like you're doing now?"

Not being able to ignore her accusing look, I fire back at her. "I'm not running. It's not running if no one knows you've left or notices you're gone."

"Eve, that's all in your head. Don't let your emotions create a problem that isn't there." Kayla pipes up, but I shoot her down with a glare.

"You know what? Right now, I feel like shit. Right now, all I want to do is lay down on something cold and not cry. Right now, I just want to be alone." Knocking my chair back, as I stand up, I grab my purse and head outside. I need some fresh air to cool down. I can't handle anymore of Kayla or my mom's accusations. I send a quick text to Evan letting him know that I need him to come and get me. It's not long before he pulls up into the drive. I don't bother going inside to say goodbye because I know they are watching me from the window.

CHAPTER 6

EVE

Evan walks around the car to open my door for me. "Miss Evelyn."

"Really, Evan? I think we are past the stage of you calling me, 'Miss Evelyn'. Just take me home."

"Is everything alright, Eve?"

"Yes, no, I don't know. I just want to go home." Tears slip from my eyes and I take a steadying breath. I slip into my seat. Laying my head against the car window, I close my eyes, trying not to focus on the motion of the car.

"I know."

My heart slams in my chest. Fuck my life. "You know?"

"About the notes, Eve. Kayla told me."

"Oh." Thank God, he only knows about the notes. My heart calms down, just not entirely. I want to be the one to tell Theron about everything that's going on. I just want to make sure I do it right.

"I know things aren't going as planned right now. I know more than most, but you can't keep it from him, Eve. If you don't tell him soon, I will. His dad is a crazy motherfucker. If he's behind this, you could be risking your life. It's not something I can just sit by and watch."

"I know. I will."

"Thank you."

"You're welcome."

"No. Thank you for helping me the other night. I was in an awful place—"

"Evan, stop. I don't need an explanation. You lost your other half. You're allowed to fall to pieces after something like that."

"You knew?"

"Theron told me. I'm sorry, Evan it must be hard. You seem better today, though."

"I am. Theron slapped me around yesterday. He made me wake up and see the bigger picture. Isa wouldn't want me laying around drunk, she'd want me to keep going. She left Theron the business because she wanted to protect me from Thomas…he offered me a partnership."

"Who, Thomas?"

"No, Theron. I don't think he felt right taking over, since Isa and I worked so hard for everything. I told him I can't do it."

"Why? He said you started it from scratch?"

"I did with help from her, but without Isa being here, it just feels wrong."

"Oh, Evan. I don't know what to say. Sorry doesn't seem to be good enough for all of this."

"Don't worry. I took another offer from, Theron. I'm going to be his head of security, which is where I feel more comfortable. So, as of now, I am taking your safety very seriously. I don't know who's leaving the notes, but I'm going to find out. In the meantime, it will be your job to tell, Theron."

"Fine, Evan. I already said I would."

"I know, but I'm just making sure, Miss Evelyn."

Great. Now we are back to Miss Evelyn again. We are almost to the house, when I get a text from Theron.

Hey, babe. How was Kayla's? You coming home soon?

Yeah. On my way now.

Is she bringing you back?

No. Evan is.

Why?

Because I asked him to.

I realize that I am being a complete bitch. I just can't stop myself from feeling pissed off at him. Putting my phone on vibrate, I drop it back into my purse. He will see me soon enough. I have no idea what I'm going to tell him. We pull up and I don't wait for Evan to open my door. Stepping out of the car, I head straight inside. I plop my purse down onto the dining room table. Badass is parked outside, so I know Theron is around here somewhere. I start heading for the bedroom when Evan stops me, grabbing my shoulder.

"You will tell him."

"I said I would. Let me go. Do not ever touch me again!" I pull myself from his grasp and slam our bedroom door.

"What was that about?"

Looking over at the bed, every emotion, every thought I had scatters. Theron is leaning back against the headboard, with a book in his hand. I have never seen anything so sexy in my life. Dragging my bottom lip through my teeth, I run my eyes over his body. He's only wearing a pair of flannel pants, even his feet are bare. Why do I suddenly find his feet attractive? One arm is bent behind his head, his muscles flexed. My eyes meet his, and I am drawn to him. I start taking off my clothes before I even make it to the bed.

"Beautiful, what are you doing?"

I crawl up onto the bed in only my blue lace bra with matching panties. I need his touch right now. Making myself comfortable, I straddle his lap, my fingers tracing his tattoo. "This."

"I see and what is 'this' exactly?"

"It's me needing you."

He tosses his book onto the nightstand and runs his fingers up my arm, leaving a trail of goosebumps in their wake. I shiver, and swirl my hips, grinding into him. I need him so bad. I want him to take away all of this confusion.

"You need me?"

"Always."

"Well, then. I'm not one to turn down the love of my life. What shall I do first?" His hands cup my breasts, rubbing his thumbs over my nipples through my bra. My breath stutters as I arch my back, pushing my breasts into his hands. With a quick movement of his fingers, he has my bra unclasped, sliding the straps down my shoulders. My breasts are free and feel heavy in his hands. His touch is just added heat to my flame.

"Ahh." I moan, as he rolls my nipples between his thumbs and forefingers.

"Maybe I'll move onto this." His fingers skim the lace edging of my blue panties. The heat from his skin is burning me. I'm going to explode and we haven't even done anything yet. "Take them off."

I stand using Theron's hands to steady myself. Hooking my thumbs in the blue lace, I slowly slide my panties off, making sure to wiggle my hips for added affect.

"You are so incredibly sexy."

My face flushes at his compliment. I know I don't have a perfect body, but he doesn't notice the few extra pounds on my waist or thighs. I walk to the edge of the bed, and run my hands up his pant legs. Fisting the material in my hands, I yank them down his legs as he lifts his hips.

"Fuck, baby. You're not messing around." I'm rewarded with a very naked, Theron.

"No boxers?"

"Nope. Now there's nothing between us. Climb back up here."

I do as am I told. Being with Theron like this is probably the only time I don't question anything. It always feels right, like it's where I'm supposed to be. I straddle his waist; his erection is hard against my back. "Theron, I need you so bad."

"I know, beautiful. Come here." He motions me towards him with his finger. My lips softly meet his. Our kiss is slow and passionate at first, building into something greedy and hungry. We are starving for each other. His tongue crashes with mine. I moan into his mouth, as I slide my hips back and forth, trying to release the building pressure between my legs. His teeth clamp onto my bottom lip, as his hands grip my ass. Taking me by the waist, he leans me back, as his fingers find my clit, pinching it and rolling it. I'm on the brink of climax. He lifts me by my hips, and I slide down his hard cock. I am completely filled by him, there's no room between us. Our breaths are ragged; his eyes are so alive. He lifts me again, holding my hips firm above him and he slams back up into me.

"Yes! Again." A delicious grin spreads across his face. He lifts me again, but this time he pulls me down crashing onto him. A throaty moan escapes my chest. Damn. I think I might have even growled a little. This is so intense. His arms wrap around my waist and he pulls me to him. I lay my head on his chest, as one of his hands hold me to him and the other steadies my hips. He thrusts into me, over and over. It's hard, fast, and rough.

"Shit. Eve." The moan that follows his words is my undoing. It is such an incredible feeling to know that I'm causing him to lose control. My pussy clenches around his cock, as he pounds into me. My body spasms and I fall apart in his arms. My upper body goes limp in his hold. His breaths are ragged and I can hear his heart pounding in my ear. "Fuck!" His cock throbs inside of me; filling me, making me shutter against him. I lay on his chest, while his hand strokes my damp hair. I feel light and calm, like I am floating, without any care for anything else around me.

He rolls onto his side, taking me with him, and slowly pulls himself out and I'm immediately filled with dread. I don't want him to leave, I want to stay right here in his arms. My stomach starts to knot and I roll onto my back. Nope. Not now. I take a couple of deep breaths in through my nose, and close my eyes. I can smell Theron wrapped around me. I take comfort in it; relaxing my mind, I drift to sleep.

"Eve. Come on, beautiful, I need you to wake up. You've got me worried, baby."

Theron brushes his hand over my face, tucking my hair behind my ears. I start to sit up and then nausea hits me. Hard. My feet are tangled in the sheets, and I'm trying to kick them loose. I end up almost falling out of the bed, but I catch myself on the nightstand, as I make a run for the bathroom.

"Eve! Eve!" I can hear Theron yelling for me, but it is hard to answer with my head in the toilet. "Babe. What's going on?"

I am sitting next to the toilet laying with the side of my face on the seat. Do not judge me. It feels great, and I'm currently not puking. Theron opens a drawer, and then I feel his hands run through my hair. He starts combing my hair, pulling it back into a ponytail. It's such a simple gesture, but it means more than he knows. I love him so much.

"Is this why you had Evan come get you? You should have called me."

"I'm sorry, babe. I wasn't feeling well after lunch. Kayla and I got some sandwiches and when we got back to the store, I wasn't feeling right. It has just gotten worse throughout the day."

"Why didn't you say something? We shouldn't have done that when you got home. I can't imagine how badly that had to have shaken up your stomach. Tell me if you aren't feeling well. I'll take care of you."

"I'm sorry."

"Don't be. Let me get you some clothes, and I'll send Evan out for some soup." He gently places a kiss on my forehead, and walks out of the bathroom. I gather my strength and stand in front of the sink. Catching my reflection in the mirror as I wash my face, I notice how pale I am. Guilt is staring at me from the corner of the room with its arms crossed over its chest. I know I should tell him, but I don't think when I'm getting sick is such a good time. Later. I'll tell him later. Theron stands in the doorway with clothes in his arms. "Come here. I'll help you."

Theron walks me over to the bed and helps me slip into some of his sweats and a t-shirt. Exhaustion starts to take over me and I scoot back onto the pillows. He sits beside me, brushing his fingers across my forehead. "Beautiful, I want to run something by you before I say anything to Evan." I don't want to talk, so I give him a small nod of my head. "Evan doesn't have anywhere to go right now. He lived with Isa, but he doesn't want to stay in the house. It's too painful for him. So, I was thinking, since Gram left everything to me, then I could say where everything goes. Right?" My brows furrow with confusion. Where is he going with this? "What if you and I move into the big house, and I sign this one over to Evan. It would give us each our own space."

"But, I don't want my own space. I want my space to be with your space."

Theron lets out a soft chuckle, turning onto his side, and pulls me to him. "That's what I mean, babe. You and I in the big house and we will give Evan his space. If you want, you could redecorate."

"No...I mean, no I don't want to decorate. I love that house. I just have one question."

"What's that?"

"Can I live in the library?"

I feel his body vibrate against mine, as he lets out a deep, loud laugh. "As long as you're with me, I don't care." The smile on Theron's face is ear to ear. I think I just won the lottery. I'm glad I could make him smile, even though I know it will fade. Grasping my hand, he brings it to his lips, kissing it softly. "Evan should be here with your soup soon."

"Babe, why did you wake me?"

"You were moaning in your sleep and your hair was soaked from sweat. I got nervous that something was wrong."

"Oh. I'm sorry."

"You have to stop apologizing all the time. I'm going to go see if Evan's here. I'll be right back."

I got nervous that I would feel alone again when he left the room, but I was okay. I knew he would be back. I need to get better control over my emotions. When they are in check, I feel so much better. I close my eyes and breathe in Theron's scent, lingering on the pillow.

It's so hot in here. I'm sweating. I sit up and pull the sheets off me. There's a bowl of soup, a spoon, and a glass of water sitting on the nightstand. I take a sip of the water and I can feel it slide down into my stomach. I wait a few seconds, but nothing happens. I decide to make a go with the soup. The first bite is warm and it rushes down my throat. Oh. My. God. This is so good. I have no problem eating the entire bowl.

"Was it good?" Looking up, I notice Theron sitting at the end of the bed. I didn't even notice him come into the room.

"So good."

"I thought as much. I've never seen anyone eat soup so fast in my life. Are you feeling better?"

"A bit."

"Kayla and your mom called. You didn't answer your phone, so your mom called mine. She was really, worried about you. I told her you were fine and that I had you tucked into bed with some soup. She wants you to call her back."

"Okay. Thank you."

"No need for thanks, it's what I'm here for. I have some papers I have to go through for a little bit. Is it okay if I go over to Isa's office, or do you want me here with you?"

"I'm just going to lay in bed, so go ahead and go to the office...I completely forgot about your meetings today. How did they go?" Once again, I was selfish and focused totally on me. I feel awful about not remembering his meetings.

"I got every signature that I need. Now, I just have to file everything and set up a meeting with the board as a whole. That's when I'll announce the purchase of Rowe Inc. There's a good chance, I'm going to be swamped for a bit, but I promise it won't always be like this. I'm going to head the company, but I'm going to stand back and let the board do most of the work. They've been doing it long enough they don't need me. I have a couple of changes that I'm going to make, but that's it."

"What kind of changes?"

Theron takes the bowl out of my hands, and I lay back down on the pillows. "For starters, there will be no more buying companies and then selling them off piece by piece to the highest bidder. If we can't make the company work for us, or we won't earn a profit with them under us, then we won't buy it. I'm not ruining other people's lives for my monetary gain. I'm not sure of any other changes yet, but I know I will start with that one." He pulls the sheet up loosely around me. Placing a kiss on the tip of my nose he whispers, "I love you, beautiful. Your phone is on the table if you want to call your mom. If not, it's okay. I'll let her know you're sleeping."

A smile spreads across my face, warming me from head to toe. "I love you, too." Watching him walk away, I wait until I hear the front door shut, before I pick up my phone. I decide to call my mom first.

"Evelyn, are you okay?"

"Yeah, I'm alright. Theron got me some soup."

"I take it you told him."

Shit. She's not going to like my response. "Not exactly."

"Evelyn! You need to tell him. This isn't just about you anymore."

She's right and I feel like shit. I wipe the few tears that have escaped off my cheeks, as I listen to her yell at me over the phone. "I know, mom. I'm sorry. I just—"

"Eve, please don't cry. I don't understand why you're so scared. He loves you. If you don't tell him soon, there's a good chance this is going to blow up in your face."

"I know. I was thinking I could go to the doctor first, you know. Then I could show him one of those ultrasound things when I tell him."

"Eve, be honest with yourself. Don't you think he would want to be there?"

I don't answer her question, of course he would want to be there. I want him there. Why is this so hard to do? "Look, mom, I got to go. I'll call you later." Without waiting for her reply, I end the call. I might as well call Kayla, while I'm at it. She must have been waiting because she picks up on the second ring.

"How are you feeling?"

"Better. I was able to hold down some soup. I need some advice. Please, be nice."

"On? Have you told him anything?"

"No. I don't know how. I was thinking of making an appointment and having him come with me."

"Hold that thought."

"Why? Do you have a better idea?"

"Yes, I do. I am sending my aunt a text. You remember my Aunt Helen, right?"

"Yeah. She's the one that lives in Chicago. The doctor your mom always brags about."

"Yep, and not just any doctor. She is the exact kind of doctor that you need. She's an obstetrician. Tomorrow, I'll pick you up and we will drive over to her office. You can do your pee in a cup test and she can give you all those lovely pamphlets they hand out to pregnant moms. Then you have an official result, right?"

"Yes, but I don't get why that's going to help."

"While we are there, you can schedule your first ultra sound. That way, Theron won't miss it and you will have the physical proof you are so desperately wanting."

"Kayla, I love you so much right now."

"I know. When are you going to tell him about the notes?"

"Can we just focus on one thing at a time? Evan said he will look into it. Can we just drop the notes for a little bit? My plate is full."

"Okay, sweetie. Don't get upset. It's probably not good for the baby, Eve."

"Yeah?"

"Eve, you are having a baby! Oh my, God. This is so awesome! I'm sorry. I shouldn't be excited with you all stressed out, but I am."

Kayla is squealing into the phone. All I can picture is her bouncing around her place like a little pixie who has had way too much caffeine. "It's okay. I'm excited, too."

"You are?"

"Just a little. Listen, I'll see you in the morning. I'm going to try to get some sleep before my dinner comes up."

"Gross. Some things I just don't need to know. Night, sweetie."

I end the call with Kayla, and set my alarm for tomorrow morning. She didn't say what time, but I know her. She is going to want to go first thing in the morning. I am not sure what I'm going to tell Theron, but I'm sure I'll think of something by morning.

CHAPTER 7

EVE

"*A*re you sure you feel up to shopping today?"

"I am. I feel so much better."

"I don't know if it's such a good idea. Just be careful, okay?"

"Okay. I love you."

"I love you, too."

I keep replaying my conversation with Theron this morning repeatedly. My shoulders are still heavy with guilt from lying to him, and now that all familiar knot is starting to grow in my stomach. Of course, that could be from all of the water Kayla had me drink before we got here. She wanted to make sure I would have 'reserves' for the bathroom. I tried arguing, but it was a lost cause.

Kayla is sitting beside me, flipping through some tabloid magazine. I don't know why reading lies about other people excites her, but to each their own. I have tried crossing and uncrossing my legs, absolutely nothing is helping, and now I've resulted to knee bouncing. If I pee in this chair, I am blaming Kayla.

"Miss Davidson?"

I look over at Kayla when the nurse calls my name. She squeezes my hand and offers me a smile with a side of pity. Grabbing my purse, I follow the nurse. She leads me to a room, and I take a seat on the exam table.

"Dr. Knox will be in here shortly. We were lucky to be able and squeeze you in today. Our schedule is full, but she insisted. So, here we are."

Condescending bitch. Whoa. I've known this lady for a whole thirty seconds, and I already hate her. Taking a deep breath, I try to calm my nerves. It doesn't matter what anyone thinks, I'm just here for a pregnancy test.

"Have you had any pregnancies or health issues in the past?"

"No. This is my first." I'm not sure if she senses my nervousness, or if maybe I was just jumping the gun a little bit earlier, but her demeanor seems to change at my response.

"Well, this is exciting then, isn't it? I'm going to have you take this cup with you down the hall and into the bathroom. I need you to urinate in the cup. Make sure you secure the lid, and then just set it on the metal ledge in the wall with the sliding door. While we wait for your results, I'll go ahead and get your weight and blood pressure. Okay?"

My mouth is so dry that I swallow a couple of times before I can answer her. "Sure." Grabbing the cup, I hop down from the table and head towards the bathroom. I am in my own little world, while I walk down the hallway, not really paying attention to anyone else. Suddenly, I walk right into something. I look down, and I realize that I have just completely knocked someone over. I feel like such an ass. I help them up from the floor, but I am not prepared for when they turn around.

"Eve?"

"Bridgette?"

"What are you doing here?"

I hide my cup behind my back, as I circle around her so I am closer to the bathroom. "Oh, you know. That annual visit. Got to love those."

"Yes, I guess someone might. Look, we should talk soon—"

"No." I cut her off with a wave of my hand. "There will be absolutely no talking between us. In fact, I'm going to pretend I never even saw you. My contempt for you has no boundaries right now, and it's taking everything in me not to lay you flat on your ass." With the last words leaving my mouth, I feel the knot in my stomach twist and turn. No, no, no. Not right now. I swallow trying to prevent myself from throwing my breakfast up in front of her.

"You have some nerve!"

I don't stand around waiting to hear what she has to say. I need a bathroom and I need it now. I find the door, and kick it shut with my foot. At least I made it to the toilet, before I got sick. It takes me a couple of minutes to gain my composure back. I shouldn't have come here without Theron. He would make me feel so much better right now. I set my cup on the ledge like the nurse said and wash my face. My reflection deceives me. Even though I am trying to hold back my emotions, my face is displaying everything. My complexion is pale and ghastly looking. My eyes are red and puffy, and the messy knot on my head only emphasizes the mess that I am. I open the bathroom door and slowly step out; making sure that Bridgette is nowhere to be seen. Keeping my head down, I walk back to the room.

The nurse takes my blood pressure and my weight. She marks all the measurements down in her notes before leaving the room. I feel like I have been sitting here for hours, but it has only been three minutes. I know this because I haven't stopped watching the second hand on the wall clock above the door. Hearing the latch on the door click, I look down to see Kayla's aunt walk into the room.

"Eve. It has been a while since I've seen you, at least a couple of years now. How have you been?"

"Okay, I guess."

"And your parents?"

"They're okay."

She washes her hands, and tosses the paper towel in the trash bin next to the sink. "Not really revealing anything, are we today?

That's okay. I know how nervous you must be. Shall we get this over with?"

Swallowing hard, I nod my head. She says something, but I can't hear her. It's like everything has gone silent and all I can hear is my heart thumping in my chest.

"Eve, are you alright?"

"I'm sorry, what did you just say?"

"I said you're definitely pregnant. Are you alright? I thought you were going to faint there for a second."

"I'm okay. Just kind of out of it, I guess."

"Do you have someone here with you today?"

"Kayla is in the waiting room."

"Okay, good. Here are some general pamphlets for you. Basically, what to do and not to do. Tylenol is safe if you need some and you should start a prenatal vitamin, just make sure it has some folic acid in it. Carrie, my nurse, will set you up with an appointment for your first ultrasound. It looks like your last period was almost ten weeks ago, is that correct?"

"Yeah."

"Well if I had to guess, I'd say your anywhere between six to eight weeks. Carrie will be right in to help you set things up, and your next appointment with me will be in about four weeks. It was nice seeing you, Eve. Oh and congratulations." She smiles and shakes my hand, and leaves the door cracked open a bit. I hop down off the exam table, and quietly walk over to the door. I swear I can hear Bridgette's voice, but I brush it off as being in my head. No sooner do I close the door, the nurse walks in. She hands me a bunch of papers and we set up a time for the ultrasound on Friday. I take relief in knowing that I have three days to tell Theron, but I dismiss it because I know I have to tell him today.

Kayla is scrolling through her phone when I walk back out into the waiting room with my stack of papers in hand.

"Hey."

Kayla looks up from her magazine, trying her best to give me a soft smile, but all I see is pity. "Hey. How did it go? What did you find out?"

"I'm definitely pregnant."

"Honey, we knew that already. Did she say anything else?"

"She said that I'm most likely six or eight weeks pregnant, but I don't see how that's possible. I just moved back in with him. Before that, we hadn't had sex since…Oh. You've got to be kidding me." I squeeze the bridge of my nose with my fingers, inhaling deeply through my nose.

"What? Why do you look like you've seen a ghost?"

"The night Theron left me. We had sex and then he left in the middle of the night, leaving me a stupid fucking note. Kayla, that was almost eight weeks ago."

"Okay?"

"Kayla, he left me when I was pregnant." Blood. Why do I taste blood? Shit. I am chewing on my cheek again. I can't believe this is happening.

"Oh, no. I'm not letting you go there. Neither he, nor you knew anything about your little bump. You cannot use this against him."

"Fuck my life."

"Um, sweetie, Theron already did and look where that got you."

"Kayla! You are not helping right now."

"And neither are you, all you are doing is causing a scene. Come on, let's get you home." She links her arm in mine, dragging me along with her.

Poor Kayla had to pull over twice on the way home. Perhaps toast, orange juice, and all the water I drank, wasn't a good idea after all. I feel like crap when we pull up in front of the house. I shove my papers and pamphlets in my purse and say goodbye to Kayla. She has already done enough for me today, so I turn her down when she offers to stay with me.

I go to open the door, but then I remember Theron saying we were going to give Evan the guesthouse. Crap. I don't know which house to go into. I call Theron, and of course, it goes to voicemail.

"Hey baby. It's me. I don't know which house I'm supposed to go into. You and Evan are both gone, so I'm just going to go into the guesthouse and lay down for a bit. Love you. I'll see you when you get home." Hitting the end call button, I head into the guesthouse. It still looks the same and our clothes are still in the closet. I shed my clothes and throw on one of Theron's t-shirts. I am physically and mentally exhausted, sleep sounds really, good right now. Pulling back the covers on the bed, I make myself comfortable, close my eyes, and drift off to sleep.

"Eve, I need you to wake up and I mean really wake up."

I open my eyes and find Theron pacing back and forth. Sitting up, I rub my face with my hands. "What's going on?"

"We need to talk and I need your full attention."

"Okay." No, it is not okay. The knot in my stomach tightens, and my mouth fills with warm spit. I jump off the bed and push him out of my way, as I run to the bathroom. Theron doesn't leave. He just stands in the doorway, watching me throw the entire contents of my stomach up into the toilet. I lay on the floor and curl up into the fetal position, pressing my cheeks against the cold tiles.

"Eve. What is this?" I don't have to look at him to know what he's asking. Tears stream down my face, and I try my best to hold back the sobs so desperately wanting to come out. "Eve. You need to tell me what this is right now!" His voice booms echoing around the room, causing me to jump. This is exactly what I was afraid of. He is not going to want anything to do with me now. "Damn it, Eve. I am giving you a chance to make this right and you're not using it."

"Make what right, Theron? I'm fucking pregnant. Is that what you wanted to hear?" My voice is nothing but strangled cries.

"I know."

"You know? What the hell is that supposed to mean?"

"I got a text about thirty minutes ago, congratulating me on knocking up the gold digger. Their words, not mine. I had no clue what they were talking about, or who it was from, though I'd place all my bets on it being, Thomas." He runs his hands through his hair. His gaze never drifts from me. I swear I can feel his eyes burning into my skin. "I decided to come home and check on you since you were sick yesterday, and I find the contents of your purse spilled out on our bedroom floor. Do you know what I found, Eve?"

Once again, I am speechless. Of course, I know what he found. I put the damn papers in my purse. "I was going to tell you, I just wanted to make sure."

"Right. I'm guessing this is why you spent the day with Kayla yesterday. This would also explain you feeling like shit yesterday and right now, wouldn't it?" I can't respond. I sit up and grab some tissues to wipe off my face. If he is going to be an ass about this, then I am going to be a bitch about it.

"I planned on telling you when you got home. I had no idea someone was going to text you, nor do I know how they found out. I've only had it just confirmed today."

"Do you know how bad this hurts, Eve? You should have told me when the first thought crossed your mind. I should have been there with you yesterday. Hell, I should have gone with you today. That's my baby. I have a fucking right to know what's going on with you and you hid it from me!"

"I didn't mean to hide anything from you! I didn't know how to tell you, I just wanted to know for sure. That's why I went to the doctor without you today."

"How am I supposed to know you're telling the truth?"

I look at the paper in his hand and recognize it immediately. It is the paper that I got from the nurse confirming my pregnancy. "Turn the paper over, Theron." He looks at me confused, as if he can't understand what I'm saying. "The paper in your hand, Theron. Turn it over." Theron slowly turns the paper over and his eyes drift over to me in shock.

"I didn't…I didn't see it."

"What does it say?" Theron sits beside me, and pulls me into his lap, kissing the top of my head. A kiss is not an answer to my question. "You still haven't told me what it says."

"I'm so sorry. I was a complete dick. I didn't even give you a chance to explain things. I thought you were going to run again. God, I'm so sorry."

"Damn it, Theron. What does the paper say?"

"It says, 'Congratulations, Daddy. We love you.'"

"Like I said, I was planning on telling you when you got home. I'm sorry I didn't tell you about the tests I took yesterday. I guess I needed to come to terms with it."

"Tests? As in more than one?"

"Kayla and I didn't know which ones would work better, so we bought every kind they had. I had to have taken around seven of them yesterday."

"And between the puking and the tests, that wasn't enough proof for you?"

I shrug my shoulders. They are extremely lame excuses, but at the time, they made sense. "I just wanted to have everything together when I told you. I wanted to be able to give you something I could show you. I was so scared you would leave me."

"Beautiful, that's never going to happen. Come on lets get you off of this floor. It can't be comfortable."

"To be honest, it is. It's really cold and it feels so good against my face. I think I've fallen in love with this tile."

"It will be fine. I'll take care of you now, you won't need the tile." He scoots me off his lap and stands. "Can you walk?"

"I'm pregnant, Theron. My legs work perfectly fine."

"Right. Sorry, I was just worried you might feel sick or something." He pulls me up from the floor and leads me out of the bathroom. I crawl back up onto the bed and Theron plumps up the pillows behind my back, propping me up so I can sit comfortably. He is hovering over me, asking me a ridiculous amount of questions that all end with me responding, 'I'm okay'.

"Are you sure there's nothing I can do."

"Stop it. I've said I'm fine. If I gave you something to do, would it make you feel better?"

"Immensely."

"Fine. Stop hovering over me. Just lay with me and hold me for a bit."

"That I can do."

Theron slides in beside me. He lays back on his pillows, pulling me to him. At first, he draws small circles on my shoulder, but then he moves his hand to my back. My stomach starts to knot, but I refuse to let it ruin this moment. Rolling over, I lay flat on my back with Theron's arm under my head. He turns onto his side and splays his hand across my stomach.

"We made this. This tiny little thing you are carrying, we made it."

"It's not a thing. It's a baby. It's our baby."

"Our baby. Beautiful, I love you so much. What are all of those other papers you had in your purse?"

"Just a list of do's and don'ts. The doctor wants me to start taking some vitamins, but other than that, it's just general information."

"Hmmm. This list you have, what does it say about sex?"

"Were not allowed to have sex for at least a couple months." I bite my tongue to keep from laughing at Theron's expression. He looks absolutely, horrified. I can't contain myself anymore. I lose it.

"Tell me you're joking. Eve, this isn't funny."

"Oh my God, you should see your face. It was fantastic…I should have recorded it…It was pure horror." I am laughing so hard that I can barely catch my breath. "Your face—" I can't even finish my thought, before I snort. Damn it. I had the upper hand until that happened.

"Did you just snort? You're laughing at me and you're the one snorting? You are incredible."

I use my t-shirt to wipe the tears out of my eyes. It felt really, good to laugh like that. Theron places a kiss on the top of my head, and draws my attention back to his hands, which are now sliding under my shirt and up to my breasts. Electricity cracks in the air and the mood of the room changes instantly.

"You're mine." Cupping my breasts, he pulls and softly tugs at my nipples. "Say it."

I hesitate for a second because the urge to be a smart ass and repeat him word for word is great, but when I look into his eyes, I see light dancing in dark green seas and amber flecks sparkling in the chocolate pools, I know he needs to hear those words. "I'm yours."

Soft kisses trail down my neck, across my jaw, and back to where they started just below my ear. I shiver from his touch. He leans over me, grasping my face in his hands. My eyes sweep over this man beside me, and I fall deeper in love with him. His touch, his taste, his words wrap me up and send me away to a place where it's only just him and me. Nothing else matters.

His fingers barely graze my skin, as I bend my legs to help him slide off my panties. Theron crawls over me and kneels between my legs. "Sit up." His hands slide under my shirt, skimming my back as he grabs the hem, pulling it over my head. My long brown locks fall down my back, leaving a couple of strands resting on my shoulder. He wraps them around his finger winding them tightly, as his other hand wraps around my waist, holding me close to him.

"I have loved you since the first moment that I saw you on the beach. The sun was so bright behind you that all I could see was the silhouette of a beautiful girl wrapped in light. You looked like an angel. When you smiled at me, the wall around my heart cracked, but the sound of your voice was what completely knocked it down. I knew in that moment you were going to save me. You were the reason for my smiles that summer and every smile since then. I love you, Eve." He presses his lips to mine. His tongue brushes my lower lip and I open to him. Our tongues collide in a feverish rush. He pulls away from me, dragging my bottom lip through his teeth. "Now lay back, I'm going to worship your body like you deserve. I'm going to make love to you until neither of us can walk."

I lay back, my head resting on a pillow. Theron lifts my left leg and kisses the arch of my foot. He slowly works his way up my leg, leaving a trail of soft kisses up to my stomach. He stops between my hips and whispers, "You pay no attention to what I'm about to do to your mom. It's between me and her only."

I laugh as he looks up at me with a huge grin. God, I love him. Kissing my stomach, he works his way back down my other leg. Taking my foot in his hands, he starts massaging it, making sure to get every muscle. This feels so good, but now I am feeling way too relaxed. "Theron, you're making me sleepy."

"Is that so?"

"Mmhmm."

"I'll have to wake you up then." His hands slide up my thighs, up to my pussy, spreading it open with his fingers. His lips are soft at first, but soon his tongue takes over and any sense of taking this slow is out the window. I am desperate for his touch. He is my drug and I am his addict. My fingers scrape his scalp, as I tighten my grip in his hair. I am rewarded with a growl and a soft bite to my clit. My back arches, as I grind onto his mouth. His hands grip the back of my thighs pushing them back and to the side, spreading me open for him, his fingers digging into me.

"Ahh." My muscles protest as they stretch, but they are easily forgotten when the familiar warm feeling creeps up my spine, spreading over my body. "Don't stop. Please, don't stop." Sucking my clit into his mouth, he thrusts two fingers into me. He curls them up, hitting and stroking my wall. My legs are shaking, my back arches, pushing my breasts into the air. He flicks his tongue over my clit, as he swirls it in his mouth and I come completely undone. "Theron!" His name leaves my lips, as I soar higher than I ever have before.

Opening my eyes, I can see his face glisten from my orgasm, as he crawls up my body. Leaning down, his lips crash into mine. His tongue sweeps into my mouth and I can taste myself. I have never been so turned on in my life. He pulls back, taking my lower lip with him, dragging it through his teeth. His mouth moves to my neck, nipping and licking as he goes. My skin is alive and his breath is hot in my ear. "I'm going to fuck you now. Wrap your arms around my neck and don't let go."

Wrapping my arms around his neck, I tuck my head against his shoulder. He pushes me down with his upper body, pushing my legs back as far as they will go. His arms wrap around my neck and hold onto the back of my head, as he pounds into me. It is hard, rough, and animalistic. We groan and grunt as our bodies slam together. It's so deep that it's almost painful. I can feel his grip tighten and I know he is holding back. I moan, as I lift my head just a little before sinking my teeth into his shoulder.

"Fuck!" He rams into me one last time, as I feel his cock throb inside of me, triggering me to lose myself once again. My orgasm is soft and wraps around me, floating me back down to Theron's arms. "Baby, I'm so sorry. I don't think I can do slow with you, beautiful. I can't control it and I lose myself in you."

"I never said I wanted it slow. That was your idea, babe, not mine."

"I don't deserve you." Placing a kiss on the tip of my nose, he pulls himself from me and softly lowers my legs to the bed. "I love you. Please, don't keep things from me."

The guilt that had escaped me when I told him I was pregnant now finds itself back into the pit of my stomach. I close my eyes and curl up next to him, ignoring the small knot reminding me of my secrets. I push away the thought of the notes. We don't need any more problems right now, and sheets of paper are just sheets of paper.

CHAPTER 8

EVE

"Oh. My. God. Why is this so good?" I am sitting at the island, licking the last bit of my dinner off the spoon. Theron laughs and takes my bowl from me, setting it into the sink.

"It's just soup."

"I know, but it's so good and I don't feel like puking. That makes it even better."

"I'll let Evan know to keep the ingredients on hand for Rebecca."

"So, when you said you were going to send Evan out for soup, what you really meant is that you were going to have Rebecca make me some and have Evan bring it over."

Taking a seat next to me, he grabs my stool and pulls me closer to him. A soft smile forms on his face, but it seems forced. I can see the worry in his eyes. "Something like that. Listen. Tomorrow I have my meeting with the board to announce my purchase. I'm going in expecting the worst. The board doesn't need Thomas anymore to meet with me, since I now own majority, but he may show. I can't stop him either. He's going to figure out what I'm up to eventually, and I'm worried about what he will do when he does."

"Whatever he does, we will just have to deal with it. Legally, he doesn't have a hold anymore, right?" I run my fingers along the top of my cup of tea. So far, between the soup and rosemary tea, I am feeling great. I just wish the business with Thomas would be over and done with.

"He still has a small hold, but I control the majority. I want to buy him out as well. He doesn't always do things legally either. Thomas is a crook. He's a villain of a businessman, think Lex Luther meets the Joker. Nothing is ever what it seems with him."

"Just be careful. I need you. We need you." Looking down, I glance at my stomach. I try to picture what I am going to look like soon with my belly swollen and huge, but it still doesn't seem real. The front door opens and Evan walks in carrying two huge boxes, as if they weigh nothing. I swear I can feel him looking at me, but I avoid his gaze.

"I assume you are feeling better, Miss Evelyn."

"I am."

"Good."

"Yep."

Theron is going to get whiplash if he doesn't quit whipping his head back and forth between us. Evan sets the boxes down on the floor before walking back outside.

"What was that?"

"What?"

"Why do you do that?"

"Do what?"

"That. It's so fucking frustrating. You try to avoid giving a real answer, so you answer me with a question."

I try to play it off by being cute. "Can you give me an example?"

"Not cute, Eve. What is going on?" Obviously, that just backfired. "I swear if you don't tell me what's going on; I'm going to lose my fucking mind."

The door opens again and Evan drops another box to the floor. "I can tell you what's going on."

Fuck. I haven't told Theron about the notes, and Evan knows it. "Evan. Stop."

Theron silences me with a hard stare. "No, Evan, don't stop. Tell me what's going on."

"I'm sorry, Eve, but secrets shouldn't be kept."

"Wait. You knew? Eve, how the fuck did Evan know before I did."

Now, I am completely caught off guard. Perhaps, this was the exploding in my face part that my mom warned me about. They both know I am holding secrets, but they each only know of one. "Um...I didn't. He doesn't really know." My response is half-assed. What the hell am I supposed to say?

Theron spins around and points his finger directly at Evan. "You knew she was pregnant?"

Evan's eyes are huge. Surprise! I guess he didn't know my secret after all. His shock turns into anger and his face darkens. I swallow trying to keep my composure. Theron can't see me with his back to me, so I plead with my eyes for Evan to go along with this.

"I didn't know exactly. I mean, I guess I just, kind of guessed. I asked her about it, but she wouldn't give me an answer. She was sick one minute, but fine the next. Then she seemed to be sneaking around behind your back with her friend, so I figured she was hiding something from you. I made a point of letting her know that if she didn't tell you what was going on, I would soon. Very. Soon." Evan glares at me, but to my relief he doesn't mention the notes. If looks could kill, I would probably be six feet under. Shit. I know I have to tell him, but I don't want too. I am going to add to his stress over nothing.

Theron spins back around and stares right at me. I don't want to lie to him, so I just opt to leave out a couple of small details. "I didn't tell Evan, babe. The only ones that knew were my mom and Kayla. They only knew because I took the tests at my parents."

"Evan, was this why she yelled at you in the hallway?"

"She yelled at me because I told her not to keep secrets from you. It wasn't my place, Sir."

Theron stands and walks into the living room. He leans against the fireplace, running his hands over his face. I glance away to see guilt staring at me from the corner of the room again. Tomorrow. I'll tell him tomorrow. Theron sighs and my gaze meets his eyes again. "I feel like I'm missing something here, but I'm going to drop it for now. Also, Evan knock off the 'Miss' and 'Sir' shit. You are family and I expect you to act like it."

"If that's what you want."

"It is. Go set your boxes down. I have Rebecca and some of the other staff coming over tomorrow to gather our things and move them over to the other house. Are you okay with everything here?"

"I wish you'd let me pay you."

"Yeah, well, I wish you and Eve would really tell me what's going on, but it's clear none of that is going to happen. I'm going to go hit the gym, I need a break." He slowly walks back to the island where I am still sitting. Lifting my chin with his fingers, he looks deep into my eyes. "No secrets. If that's what's going on here, I need it to stop. I'll give you a couple days, but that's it. Now get some rest. I don't know how long I'll be. I love you." His lips softly brush mine, and I pull him in closer. I lightly nip at his lip, as his tongue invades my mouth. Goosebumps spread across my flesh. Fisting his shirt in my hand, I moan into his mouth. My nerves are lit up and I could really use some release. His hands grasp my neck, as mine move under his shirt, my fingers tracing his abs. He pulls back from the kiss. I am left on the brink of something, but I'm not sure what.

"Baby, please."

Placing a kiss on my cheek, he whispers into my ear, "I bet if I checked you would be wet right now. Wouldn't you?"

"Yes." My voice is husky and full of need.

"Good. You are mine. I'm keeping you and right now I rather like the idea of keeping you like this. I want you waiting for me like this. I want to come home later, and know this is the reason you can't keep your hands off of me." With those last words, he turns and walks away from me. He is so incredibly sexy.

I stare at the door, as it closes behind him. Damn that was hot. My cheeks flush, when I notice Evan is still in the room. Standing, I grab my tea, taking it with me, as I head to the bedroom. "Goodnight, Evan."

"Goodnight, Eve. I'm sure I don't have to remind you that you need to speak to him about the notes."

I stop and look over my shoulder. "No, you don't, but it seems you did anyway."

"Just covering my bases. Eve?"

"Yes." My tone is curt and flat. I am not in the mood for his guilt trips right now.

"Congratulations on the baby."

I don't say anything. I just continue walking into my bedroom. I am sure he probably thinks I did this on purpose. I slip off my jeans and long sleeve shirt. Digging through Theron's drawers, I find an old college t-shirt. University of Chicago is printed proudly across the chest of the shirt. What are the odds of us going to the same college? Of course, with it being Theron, I am sure he knew that I was going there. How long has he looked for me? He couldn't have been looking for the past fourteen years. At some point, he must have given up on me. After all, he was engaged to Bridgette for some time. Bridgette. Her name alone makes me want to spit nails. I should have laid her out on her ass when I saw her earlier. Who knows when I am going to have an opportunity like that again? I am not sure if it was Thomas that sent the text, but I know Bridgette is most likely the reason he found out. How the hell did she find out my test results? Someone who works for Helen is a snitch.

You know you are tired, when you dream of sleeping in your dream. I dreamt that I was sleeping and woke up to the bed being wet. It was so odd. I roll over to try to shake off the feeling and the dampness on my pillow brings me out of my dream. I'm hot and sweaty. I try to fix my pillows, but I notice it really is damp from my sweat. Why am I so hot? I try to sit up, and that is when I notice the leg wrapped around me. That man is like a furnace. I push his leg off me, and glance at my phone. It is four fifteen in the morning. I didn't even notice him come to bed. As I head to the bathroom to splash some cold water over my face, my stomach lurches.

I wake up lying on the cool tile. My back is screaming at me for my obviously idiotic choice for a bed, but my face and nausea are thanking me. I try to move, but my body is so stiff. Closing my eyes, I take a couple of deep breaths. When I open them, I am greeted by a very handsome man staring at me, while I lay on the floor.

"That looks painful. Let me help you up." He holds out his hands and I gratefully take them. "I woke up and you weren't in the bed with me. I came in here to see if you were okay, and I find you laying on the bathroom floor."

"I'm okay. My back doesn't like me right now, but it will get over it. I woke up around four and I was so hot, I was sweating. I came in here to wash my face, and my soup decided it didn't want to stay down anymore." He pulls me to him, wrapping me in his arms. I sigh, as my body melts to him. I never feel as good as I do when I am in his hold. He kisses the top of my head. I look up and take in his handsome features. My heart quickens at the thought of the things he could do to me before he leaves. He gives me a dazzling smile, as if he knows where my thoughts are starting to stray.

"Will you be okay if I leave you today?"

"Yeah, I'll be fine. I'll call Kayla. Maybe we can go shopping or get some lunch. I could use some fresh air."

"Okay. I'm going to hop in the shower. Go lay down, babe. I'll bring you some toast in a little bit."

I am sitting on our bed while a thousand thoughts are running through my mind. I can hear the shower turn on and my mind drifts to thoughts of Theron naked, water running over him, as he takes me up against the wall. It only takes me a second to decide that I need to make this a reality, not a day dream.

Opening the door, steam escapes, as I step into the room. Theron is standing under the shower with his head tilted back. The water runs down his chest and over his stomach. I am practically panting in heat, as I watch him wash his body.

"Are you coming in, or are you just going to keep watching me?"

"Coming in." I pull my t-shirt over my head and drop it to the floor. I wiggle out of my panties, as I walk towards the shower. I barely open the door before Theron grabs me by my waist, pulling me into the shower with him.

"I need to feel you." He looks at me, waiting for permission.

"Do it." His hands slide up my waist, as his mouth finds my nipple, swirling it with his tongue. I moan, thrusting my breasts up towards him. His hands roam my body; every touch is like lightening to my core.

"I need to be in you. I can't wait." His hands grip my hips, lifting me by my waist. I wrap my legs around him, as I slide down onto his hard cock. He pushes my back against the wall and rocks into me.

"Ahh. Theron!" My pussy is so tight around him. He feels so incredible.

"This is going to be fast, baby. You ready?"

"Yes!" His mouth finds my neck, nipping at my skin, as he slams into me. I have nowhere to move or go. He has me pinned. His teeth graze my ear and move down along my jaw, seeking my mouth. Our tongues crash together, wrestling and fighting for control. I suck on his bottom lip. He moans and it sounds so incredibly sexy. I love making him lose control. His mouth moves lower to find my nipple, dragging it between his teeth before flicking it with his tongue. I let loose a moan, but it is more of a demand for more. "Yes!"

"Beg."

Beg? For what? He picks up his pace, thrusting in and out of me. My hands claw his shoulders, as my head falls back hitting the shower wall. I can't hold onto him. I am so close, but he pulls back.

"Beg."

I need to come so bad. "Please, Theron. Please."

"You want to come, baby?"

"Oh, God, please!" His body braces me against the wall, as he continues his relentless movement. He holds onto me with one hand, while the other slides between us finding my clit, pinching and rolling it between his fingers. "Oh, God. Right there. I'm, I'm...Ahh, Theron!" My orgasm rips through me, shredding me with waves of pure bliss.

"Fuck. Eve!" My name leaves Theron's lips, as he loses himself in me. I can feel his cock throb inside of me, filling me. My head lolls forward, resting against his shoulder. I can't stand, I can't move, and I can't speak. Theron turns off the water and carefully holds me, as he steps out of the shower. He wraps a towel around us, and carries me to bed. Lowering me to the mattress, he starts to dry me with a towel. I feel a sheet cover me and I drift to sleep.

"Beautiful, open your eyes for a second."

"Hmmm."

Laughing, he places a kiss to my forehead. "I'm sorry for breaking you again, but I have to go to work. Text me if you go anywhere with Kayla. Okay?"

"Okay. I love you."

"I love you, too." He places another kiss on my forehead and I close my eyes once again.

When I wake, I find a cup of tea and some toast waiting for me with a little note tucked between them.

Eve,

I made you some more rosemary tea. I hope it helps. Text me before you leave.

Love you,

Theron

Most people send text messages or leave voicemails, but not him. I like my little notes, well most of them anyway. After finishing my little breakfast, I send Kayla a text to see if she wants to go shopping or get some lunch. Opening Pandora on my phone, I hook it to my Bluetooth speakers, and jump into the shower. I am rinsing conditioner out of my hair, when my phone rings over the speakers. I figure its Kayla, so I take my time and finish up with my shower. That's odd. I check my missed calls and the last number who called me came up Unknown. Thinking it must have been some kind of sales call, I push it out of my mind.

I slip on a pair of jeans, a lavender blouse, and my black chucks. As I am combing out the knots in my hair, there's a knock on the bedroom door. I open it to find two men with tape and boxes in their hands.

"Can I help you?"

"We are here to box everything up, per our instructions, Miss."

Just great. I haven't even finished getting ready. "Start in here. I'll finish up in the bathroom." I quickly pull my hair into a braid and grab my phone. I don't like being here with these people packing up and moving things around, so I send Kayla another text letting her know that I'm coming over. I am almost out the door when Evan catches me.

"Where are you off to?"

"Just Kayla's. Don't worry. Theron knows."

"Have you told him?"

"You know what, Evan? I haven't. I'll make sure to let you know when I do."

Fuck him. I am not in the mood for the reprimand. My phone beeps, as I slide into my seat.

Evan says you're leaving?

Yeah. I just got in the car. I was going to text you, but I don't think I need to now. Going to Kayla's. We might get lunch.

Ok. Love you.

Love you, too.

Tossing my phone into my purse, I make a mental note to have a talk with Evan. He is not my babysitter.

CHAPTER 9

EVE

I pick up Kayla and we head out to lunch. We are sitting at the Fifth Street Bistro. I am moving the lettuce around on my plate, doing my best to look interested in whatever Kayla is saying. The truth is; I feel like absolute crap. I just want to lay down, but I can't. There are people moving stuff around at the house, and I feel weird there by myself. I haven't addressed that yet with Theron, but I'm going to have to soon.

"And then I stabbed him. I'll tell you where I hid the body if you promise to keep it a secret."

"What?" Did she really just say that?

"I knew you weren't listening. I was telling you about the new furniture Paul and I ordered, but you weren't listening. So, I started telling you a story about how he lied to me, and I stabbed him. Apparently, murder gets your attention."

"Sorry. I'm being such a horrible friend. I was trying, but I feel like crap. I just want to go to bed, and I can't because we are switching houses."

"Switching? Does he have more than one house?"

"Not really. Isa left everything to Theron and he didn't want Evan to be alone. So, Theron gave Evan the guesthouse because the main house reminded him too much of Isa. Now we are switching houses. Theron has people moving everything for him, and I just felt like I was in the way. You know?"

"Kind of. I've never had people move things for me. Also, doesn't the main house have a library?"

A huge grin spreads across my face. "Yes, and it's all mine."

"He's never going to get you out of there."

"I already warned him."

My phone starts buzzing in my purse. It's another call from Unknown, so I ignore it. "New furniture, huh?" Kayla opens her mouth to answer me, but my phone buzzes again.

"Maybe you should get that. It might be the movers." She has a point, I never thought of that.

"Hello?"

"Eve? Thank God, I got a hold of you. Do you know how hard you are to track down?" Red. All I see is fucking red.

"Bridgette?" Kayla spits her drink across the table; at least I'm not the only one in shock.

"Eve. I know after what happened between us I shouldn't be calling you, but I don't know who else to call."

"You intentionally lied to me, befriended me, and then used your past relationship with Theron to tear me and him apart. Why should I care even the slightest about you?"

"I'm pregnant. That's why I was at the office. Thomas is the father."

Attention daytime Emmy winners, you now have competition for this year's award. "And you're telling me this because?"

"I don't know whom else to talk to. My family will disown me. Thomas doesn't want the baby. He wants me to have an abortion. He's offered to pay for it and pay me to keep quiet."

"Again. Why are you telling me?"

"I thought you could talk to Theron. After all, it is his sibling and he doesn't have any family left now."

Is she serious right now? If I could reach through my phone, I would strangle her until her face turned blue. She didn't succeed the last time when she tried to get back in his life, so now she's going to use his family as an angle. She has another thing coming if she thinks I am going to let her within one hundred feet of Theron. Breathe. I need to breathe. "Listen here, you manipulative bitch. I know you are the reason Theron found out that I was pregnant, before I told him. You have the audacity to call me, and ask me to speak to him for you after everything you've done? Have you lost your mind?"

"I didn't tell Thomas you were pregnant. I told him I ran into you at the office. He just presumed you and I were both there for the same reason."

"Am I supposed to believe that? I don't feel sorry for you at all. You put yourself in this situation. The only person I feel sorry for is that baby you are carrying. For once in your life, do something selfless and give the baby up for adoption." I hit end call, and throw my phone into my purse. My day just keeps getting better and better.

"What was that all about?"

"Long story or short?"

"I'll take a summary."

I take a big gulp of my tea, and wipe my palms on my jeans. It is getting really warm in here. "Okay, so when I was at the doctor's office I ran into Bridgette. She just called to inform me of why she was there. She's pregnant."

"Why would you care?"

"Because the baby is supposedly Thomas', so that makes it Theron's sibling. Thomas offered to pay for an abortion and to keep her quiet, but she doesn't want one."

"Wow. I don't even know what to say to that. Do you think if we wrote it all down we could sell it as a daytime drama?"

"The thought did cross my mind." Why is it so hot in here? I take a napkin and wipe the back of my neck. My stomach lurches, as I take another sip of my tea. Scanning the restaurant for restrooms, I notice one is right next to the entrance. I push my chair back from the table and head to bathroom trying to draw as little attention as possible to myself.

After washing my face in the sink, I start heading back to the table, when I notice Kayla sitting on the bench outside. I walk outside to join her. Tapping her shoulder, I motion for her to hand me my purse. "Sorry."

"Don't be. It's alright. Do you want me to take you home, or do you want to come back to my place?"

"You can take me home."

As we get closer to my car, Kayla grabs my arm. "Strike that. You can take me with you. I'm done waiting. You are telling Theron tonight." Following her index fingers, my eyes find what she is pointing to. There is another pink note on my car. Grabbing it, I sit on the curb, as I read it.

Did you have a nice lunch? I rather enjoyed the conversation I overheard. I knew of your bundle. I didn't know of hers. This changes things. Don't go far. I'll know.

Fear over takes me, as my heart slams in my chest. If they didn't know Bridgette was pregnant then the notes aren't from her or Thomas. My hands instantly wrap around my stomach, as I rock back and forth. Who the fuck has been watching me? They were close enough to hear my conversation. Oh my God, they were close enough to touch me if they wanted.

"Theron. Kayla, I need Theron."

"Ssh. Eve, hand me the note and I'll call him." She takes the note from me and I hear her start to cry, as she talks to Theron over the phone. He is going to be so pissed. This isn't a little fuck up on my part, this is huge. I put both of our lives in jeopardy all because I didn't want to upset him. I wish I could take it all back and tell him sooner, but it is a little late for that now. Kayla ends the call and sits beside me. "He's pissed. To be honest he almost sounded crazed. Evan is coming with. I am going to have Paul come and pick me up. I wouldn't want to be in your shoes." She sits beside me softly rubbing her hand up and down my back, as we wait. I need him, but I am so scared of what he is going to do.

Tires screech, as Theron pulls into the parking lot. He slams on the brakes, throwing the car into park. He doesn't even bother shutting his door, he comes straight for me. "Kayla, thank you for calling me and bringing this to my attention. It seems someone doesn't value their life like I do. Evan can take you home."

"Would it be alright if he just waits with me? Paul is already on his way."

"Sure. Evan!" Evan appears like magic from behind Theron. "Stay with Kayla. Her ride is on the way. Then I want you to take a drive. Empty Eve's gas tank before you bring it home and bring me her keys. She won't need them anytime soon."

"Are you kidding me? I'm not your prisoner. You can't just lock me up because you see fit."

"I will and I am. I cannot believe you have kept this from me. I'm so fucking pissed right now. We will talk when we get home. Get in the car, Eve."

"No." I don't know why I won't do what he says. All of this is my fault. I know I should get in the car, but I still can't do it.

"Eve. Get in the fucking car! Now!" I jerk, as his voice booms across the parking lot. I don't know if it's from fear or maybe I've gone crazy, but I just sit there staring at him. "That's it. I'm done. Get up." He puts his hands underneath my arms and yanks me to my feet. Grabbing my purse from my grasp, he digs through it until he finds my keys and tosses them to Evan. Theron leads me to the car and I slide into my seat. Leaning over me, he fastens my seatbelt and drops my purse back into my lap. Tears slide down my cheeks, and my hands wrap around my waist, as he slams my door shut. Sliding into the car, he slams his door and starts the engine. I can't look at him. I know that I have failed us. Turning my head, I look out the window, letting the tears roll down my cheeks, as he drives us home.

We pull up in front of the house and Theron steps out of the car. "Get out, Eve." Grasping the handle, I slowly open my door. I feel like a berated child, as I follow him into the house and up the main staircase. To my surprise, the stairs do not lead to a hallway full of doors; instead, I am welcomed with a large sitting area with a fireplace and balcony. It is breathtaking. Theron clears his throat and

I turn to follow him to the left, going down a small hallway with two doors. He opens one and I follow him into the room.

"This is our master bedroom. I was planning to have it redecorated for you, but you will have plenty of time on your hands to do that yourself now. The room across the hall is my office. There are three other bedrooms on the other side of the parlor."

"Parlor?"

"The living area we just walked past. It used to be a parlor and the name just stuck. Are you really questioning me about what the rooms are called?"

"No. I'm sorry."

"Yeah, well I'm entirely too pissed to talk to you right now. Do *not* leave this house. I'm going to have to rearrange my schedule now, since I canceled my meeting today. When Evan gets back, we will be meeting with two detectives from the police department. They are probably going to want to meet with you as well. I'll come get you before they get here. I'm not messing around with this. Thomas is a dangerous man."

Without looking at me, Theron leaves the room, slamming the door behind him. My nerves are shaken, and I feel consumed by my guilt. This is my fault and I need to accept my fate. There is no sense in trying to hide from any of this. Closing my eyes, I take a deep breath, and reopen them determined. I am going to face all of this head on.

I set my purse on our very large, king size bed in the center of the room. There is a very ornate dark cherry armoire with claw feet standing in the corner, next to a matching vanity table with a mirror inlaid in beautifully carved wood. The room is decorated in beautiful hues of grays and lavenders. Sheer silver curtains catch my attention, and I find myself standing in front of gorgeous French doors, which lead to a balcony. My breath catches in my throat, as I step through the doors. There are vines crawling up the brick walls, flowers and stone paths as far as I can see, and a beautiful fountain in the center, surrounded by peonies. I can only imagine the beautiful splendor that must take place when all of the flowers finish blooming. The view is just amazing. I didn't realize how large the garden was.

Stepping back into the room, I notice that the bed with its gray silk bedspread and the dresser, also have claw feet. Everything is so exquisite. White marble floors greet me, as I walk into the bathroom. A double vanity is to my right, and to my left, I find a very large Jacuzzi tub across from a shower that seems just as big, if not bigger. I open the glass shower door and let out a soft sigh. Just when I thought I was used to Theron's shower, I am met with even more levers and handles. There are mounted wall jets and two separate showerheads. The world of indoor plumbing seems to be more complicated than I originally thought.

I desperately want to walk down to the library and let it consume me, but I don't want to push Theron any farther. Emptiness creeps its way into my heart, I feel so alone. I try to call my mom, just so I can hear her voice for some comfort, but it goes to voicemail. My stomach knots and twists, and a wave of exhaustion hits me, but I am too flustered to sleep. It only takes me a minute to figure out the Jacuzzi. I watch it fill, and my mind drifts to the secrets I have kept from him. I left him for keeping secrets from me, and yet I did the same to him. I set my clothes on the vanity, and slip into the hot water, sitting on the ledge and laying my head back against the leather pillow. The jets massage my stress away and I close my eyes, feeling completely relaxed.

"I'm still very pissed at you."

The fog lifts from my mind and I open my eyes to find Theron sitting on the edge of the tub. Tears start to form in my eyes, but I hold them back. I watch, as he stands and starts unbuttoning the front of his blue long sleeve shirt, before removing his black suit pants. He is dressed for his meeting, which because of me, is now cancelled. I wonder how that will sit with the board. My eyes linger over his form, and I squeeze my legs together. How is it with everything going on, my mind still drifts to sex whenever he is in the room?

Sliding into the water, Theron sits across from me. "Lift your legs." My body complies and he takes my feet into his lap. His thumb starts massaging the pads of my left foot. "Why didn't you tell me?"

"I don't know." My voice is a whisper and I cast my eyes down, as I start chewing on my cheek. I can't even make eye contact with him.

"Bullshit. Tell me or I leave."

"What do you mean by leave?"

"Does it matter? Tell me."

I take a deep breath and try to compose myself, as I gather my thoughts. There is no easy way to explain this, so I just spit it out. "The notes started showing up on my car after I found out about you and Bridgette. I assumed they were from her because they were all little digs, reminding me of what I didn't have anymore. The first one, wanted to know where my pretty car was. I got a couple more after the night you left me, reminding me of how you weren't mine anymore. I just assumed it was Bridgette; the notes were even pink. There was one on my car after my doctor appointment for my hand, and then on the day of Isa's wake. Bridgette was there and the note wasn't there until after she left. Kayla told me to tell you, but I couldn't. You were already so upset and I didn't want to add fuel to the fire."

Theron's jaw clenches and I expect him to yell, but he doesn't. Instead he lets go of my foot and moves to my right foot, massaging deep circles with his thumb. "How many were there?"

"I don't know. I tossed them into my car. I just ignored them."

"Evan told me you got one the other day. What did it say?"

"It said they were watching me, and their turn was next. I have no clue what they meant. Kayla was mad that I wouldn't tell you, so she told Evan."

"So, when Evan said you were keeping a secret, he thought you meant about the letters on your car."

"He only knew about the letters. He didn't know I was pregnant."

"It seems you are getting good at keeping secrets. How is that working out for you exactly?"

"Stop it! I didn't mean to hurt anyone. If I would have thought I was in danger, I would have told you sooner. I just thought it was Bridgette or your dad."

"People who are ruthless when it comes to getting what they want."

We sit there quietly for a minute. Theron holds my feet in his lap, as I lean back against the jets letting them massage my back and shoulders.

"What do you mean you assumed it was Bridgette? What makes you think it isn't?"

"The note I got today, said they knew about my bump, but not hers. Thomas knows about Bridgette being pregnant. It couldn't have been from either of them."

"She's pregnant? I feel awful for whoever had the pleasure of knocking her up. She's going to make their life a living hell."

I swallow hard. There can't be any more secrets between us, so I prepare myself for the worst when I tell Theron about Bridgette. "She called me. Kayla and I were at the restaurant and I answered my phone thinking it might be one of the movers or something. It was Bridgette. She wanted me to talk to you for her."

"I want nothing to do with her. Nothing she could say would change my mind."

"She implied as much. She asked me to tell you she was pregnant and to let you know Thomas is the father."

"What?" The look of shock on Theron's face is unsettling. I sit up and move myself into his lap, straddling his thighs. His hands move to my waist, holding me in place. My hand moves to stroke his face, but he grips onto my wrist, stopping me from touching him. "I want so badly to be free of these fucking people, but all they keep doing is bringing me back in. I don't want them. I don't want any of them." He drops my hand back into the water and looks away. I don't understand how people can be so malicious and thrive on hurting others.

"I know. I'm sorry."

"Stop apologizing for other people's mistakes."

I softly press my hand to his cheek. Holding his gaze, I let him know how sorry I really am. "I'm not apologizing for their mistakes. I am apologizing for mine. I should have told you when I got the first note, even if we weren't together at the time. If they have been watching me this entire time, they could have been watching you, too. I can't lose you. It's not a matter of me not wanting to lose you, it's a matter of I can't lose you. I won't make it next time. It hurt so much when you left me. My heart went cold and ice shredded the inside of it. It stopped beating, Theron. I can't do that again. Not now, not ever."

"Beautiful, I may be upset with you, but I won't leave you. I left you that night because I thought that was what you needed. I heard you talking and your words cut me." His hands slowly move up and down my back.

"What do you mean you heard my words? I didn't say anything to you. I fell asleep and when I woke, you were gone."

"But you did. You were talking in your sleep to someone. I heard you tell Matt you love him. I thought you were having a nightmare so I whispered, 'beautiful, I love you' in your ear. I was hoping it would wake you, but instead you said 'I'm not your beautiful, I'm his.' Those words cut me. You're my beautiful, you've always been my beautiful, but you rejected me."

"Theron, I was sleeping! You can't hold me accountable for what I say when I am sleeping. I didn't even know you said that to me. I dreamt that Matt was telling me to go with you. I told him I loved him and I still do, just not like I love you and he knew that. He called me beautiful and told me he loved me, but I wasn't his beautiful. I was yours. I've always been yours." A horrible sob rips through my chest. I can't believe I went through all of that pain because he assumed the worst of me. "You left me. You didn't even give me a chance to explain!" I have now gone from nervous, to scared, to pissed in less than a minute. Who the fuck leaves someone because of a dream? I am so furious that my hands are shaking. "You killed me when you left. I didn't understand. None of it made any sense. Every piece of happiness I was desperately holding onto, shattered."

Hot tears slip down my cheeks, and I give up. This stress is too much. I feel way, too hot. My stomach is in knots. I scramble to get off Theron's lap, but he doesn't understand why. I am pushing his hands off me, trying to stand and I get my feet twisted. It doesn't matter now. My attempt at making it out of the tub is futile. I barely bend over the side, before my entire lunch splatters onto the floor. If I could die from embarrassing moments, this would be the one.

"Baby, no!" Theron jumps out of the tub, grabbing towels to clean up my mess. My stomach starts to retch again, and this time I make it to the toilet. I am so over this. Every time I get myself worked up, I get sick. I collapse onto the floor and curl into a ball. I am barely aware of Theron cleaning up around me. The tile is cool on my skin, and I don't want to move.

"Beautiful, you can't lay on the floor."

"Why not? It feels good on my skin and it's convenient."

"First of all, you're naked. You at least need a robe on or something. Second of all, despite what you say, that cannot be comfortable. Let me help you."

"No, I don't want your help. I just want to be left alone. I want all of this stress to end, I want your father to leave us alone. I want to be able to leave the house without worrying about someone watching me. I want to eat without feeling like death afterwards, and I just want to sleep."

"That's quite a list. Come on. We've both hurt each other today, we need to stop while we are ahead. Can you walk?"

"No."

"Shall I carry you then?"

"No."

He doesn't listen. He bends over, scoops me up off the floor, and carries me to our bed. He pulls the covers back and lays me down. "Get some rest, my beautiful girl. I'll be back to check on you in a little bit. Do you need anything?"

"Toothpaste."

Theron laughs, as he pulls the soft sheet over me, tucking me in. "Already in the bathroom, beautiful." He presses his lips to my forehead and my heavy eyes close.

Chapter 10

EVE

The room feels so stuffy. I walk over to the window and crack it open, just a tad. There is a nice breeze this evening, and my skin instantly cools, as I lean against the window frame. We are all sitting in the downstairs living room, going over every detail. Evan collected all of the notes that I tossed into the back of my car. For once, being a slob and not cleaning out my car has worked in my favor.

Detective Hallow and Detective Markz are taking notes of everything Theron is saying, and I have already been grilled several times. I am not sure what else they could possibly need to know. They lost interest in me when Theron mentioned his father might possibly be involved, and they started talking directly with him. I wish they would leave. I am tired and hungry. Tomorrow, I am supposed to go back to work, and I haven't even approached Theron about that, yet.

"Miss Davidson. We will be in touch."

I give one of the detective's a simple nod of my head, without moving from my spot. I love that Theron has become my mantra over the past two hours. If it wasn't for him, I would have walked out by now. This has to have been the longest meeting that I have ever had with the police. When they interviewed me after Matt's death, it didn't take this long. The thought of Matt, stirs in my mind. I wonder what he would think of this predicament that I have gotten myself into. I am sure that he would side with Theron, as well. Matt was always looking out for me. They would probably both be pissed with me. My skin feels flush again, so I lean down in front of the window and let the breeze blow on my face.

Strong hands grasp my hips and I stand up, my back coming flush with Theron's front. Brushing the hair off my shoulder, he whispers in my ear, "Are you hungry?" His breath is hot and tickles my ear.

"Mmmm."

"That's not an answer." Goosebumps spread across my skin, as I think of what I am hungry for.

"I could eat."

"What would you like, beautiful?"

Thoughts of Theron taking me here, or in the library cross my mind. "You."

"I can't think of why that is. Shouldn't we feed you two soon."

"I'm not hungry for food. I'll eat later."

His mouth runs up my neck, nipping me with his teeth. My pulse is racing. His mouth finds my ear. "Is that so?"

"Theron, shut up. Don't toy with me. Either fuck me so I can't walk, or quit taunting me."

He laughs and spins me around in his arms. "You have such a lovely way of speaking sometimes."

"It's an art form."

A throat clears in the room, and I turn to find Evan standing in front of the couch. "I'm going to call it a night. Let me know if either of you need anything. Eve, please don't leave the house without me or Theron with you."

My cheeks flush at the realization that we aren't alone. Theron and I watch as Evan leaves. As soon as he is out of sight, Theron picks me up in his arms and playfully tosses me onto the couch. I prop myself up on my elbows and watch him, as he crawls over me.

"I love you."

"I love you, too. I need to feel you."

"Don't worry, beautiful I've got this. Are you mine?"

"Yes." There is no hesitation. I have always been his.

"I'm keeping you. There's no more running away. There's no more secrets. There's only you and me from now on."

"You and me for a little while."

Theron looks at me confused, and I can tell that he starts to get mad, before he realizes his error. "I meant you, me, and our little family."

"Okay."

"Damn right, it's okay. No more talking. I want you screaming." His words crack the air around me and just like that, my Theron has turned from sweet and loving, to dark and dangerous. I love this side of him.

His mouth crashes into mine, our tongues collide and chaos ensues. He is pulling my shirt over my head and I am desperately trying to get to his. We are pulling and tugging at each other until we are both left naked in each other's arms. He leans over me and our eyes meet. The dark desire in his eyes, lights up all of my nerves. His mouth finds my neck, licking and sucking, as he works his way down to my stomach where he plants a soft kiss. He wraps his arms around my thighs, spreading me open for him. Sparks shoot through me, as his tongue massages my clit.

My back arches and my hips raise off the couch, as I try to get closer to his mouth. Theron thrusts his fingers into me, curling them up to hit all the right places. I am squirming. I can't keep still. Grasping for him, I pull his hair. His mouth leaves my clit and I moan in protest. I gasp, as I feel his teeth bite into the inside of my thigh. "Mine. You are mine." Oh my God, he has marked me. I was desperate before, but now I am frantic for his touch.

"All yours." Theron grabs my waist, flipping me over. Smack! My ass cheek protests from where his hand has been, but my body loves it, as I let out a moan. He grabs my hips, pulling me and spinning me. I am now kneeling on the floor with my waist bent over the cushions and my ass displayed before him. Smack! "Ahh!" Brief pain, followed by pleasure. My head pulls back, as he wraps my hair around his wrist.

"You are so fucking gorgeous with your ass red and marked by me." Theron spreads my legs apart with his knee, making sure he has me where he wants me. My breath leaves me, as he suddenly slams into me. My pussy welcomes him, clenching around him. He slowly pulls out and rams back into me. This is a brutal onslaught to my nerves and I won't be able to last long with him doing this. His pace quickens, and my grip tightens onto the cushions beneath me.

"Theron! Don't stop. Oh God! Please don't stop." My body is a frenzy of exploding nerves, as my orgasm rips through me.

"Fuck, beautiful. You feel so good wrapped around my cock."

I gasp, as I feel something that I have never experienced before. I feel his hands spread my cheeks and his fingers softly push and circle where I have never pictured anyone ever going.

"Ssh. I got you. Eventually, you'll beg me for this, but we have to work up to it." His cock slides in and out of my pussy, as he rubs his new conquest. Softly pushing, he slowly slides one finger into me, while keeping his pace. My body burns and stretches, as it accepts the intrusion. I feel tight and full.

I find myself pushing back onto him. "Oh, my God."

"Fuck. Eve." His cock slams into me again, filling me completely, and igniting another orgasm, as my pussy clenches around him, milking him for every, last drop of cum. I have never felt so stretched and full before. It is definitely something that I will be doing again. He has definitely helped me accomplish my goal of not being able to move. I glance at him over my shoulder, as he leans back on his knees. "Don't move, my beautiful girl."

My head falls onto the cushions and my eyes start to close, as I watch his glorious ass walk into the kitchen. I am startled awake, when I feel something warm sliding between my thighs.

"Don't worry. I'm just taking care of you." He runs the washcloth up and down both of my thighs, making sure to wipe every inch between. His arms wrap around my waist, gently moving me so that my entire body is now laying on the couch. "You are absolutely breathtaking. You're glowing, and you look so incredibly satisfied."

"Mmmm."

"No words, again?"

"Mmmm."

"Baby, I know I've broke you, but I at least need to get you dressed. What will the staff think if they find us in here like this?"

"No."

Theron laughs as I watch him pull his slacks on. "At least, put on my shirt."

"No."

"Come on. Arms up." I don't want to move, but I comply with his request and slide my arms into his gray polo shirt. He pulls it down over my head and I am rewarded with a kiss on the tip of my nose. "Thank you."

"Mmmm."

"Food. You need food. What would you like?"

"Nothing."

"Nothing isn't food, Eve. You really need to eat. It's not just you anymore."

"I know, but it makes me feel like crap. I don't want to get sick anymore. I just want to lay here, and pretend everything is okay. There's no drama, no stress, and no puking."

Theron lets out a sigh, before he starts roaming through the very large pantry in the kitchen. He disappears behind the doors and I think he may have crossed over into Narnia. I can hear things moving around, but there is still no sign of him.

"Theron, if you find a lamp post in the middle of a forest full of evergreens, you've gone too far."

It is quiet for a couple of seconds and then I hear an "Aha!" coming from the pantry and I assume that he has found what he is looking for. The door opens and Theron steps out with a box of crackers, and a small box of tea in his hands.

"I thought you got lost."

"Nope. Sadly, I do have to report there is no lamp post in the back of the pantry."

"Well, that's just disappointing."

"I'm going to make you a cup of tea, while you nibble on some crackers. The pantry is fully stocked, so if you wake up hungry later, I'll make you a snack then."

"Okay, but can we take them with us? I'm so tired." I stand and stretch my muscles, I feel as if I have been hit by a truck.

"Beautiful, I don't think you'll make it up the stairs. Let me help you."

As we head upstairs to our bedroom, I mentally go over everything I want to discuss with Theron. The first being, me working tomorrow. With everything going on, I can see him being hesitant, but I don't want to be a prisoner. I haven't told him about the ultrasound on Friday, either.

We walk into the bedroom and my attention is drawn to the balcony. The moon looks so big tonight. Theron says something, but I keep walking. Grasping the handle to the French door, I pull it open. I step out onto the balcony and I am in awe. The moon is shining brightly with the stars tonight and it is casting on the garden in a beautiful shade of blue. A hand gently clasps the back of my neck. His touch is so warm and inviting. I move, wrapping my arms around his waist and gaze at the night sky with my head on his chest.

"You are supposed to be eating."

"Yep."

"But you're not."

"Yep."

"Eve, please eat."

"I want to talk to you."

"Why? What's the matter? If it's about the police, I won't apologize. I'm still mad that you blew those notes off as if they were nothing."

"It's not about the police or the notes, per se."

"I don't play games. Tell me."

I drop my arms and walk back into the bedroom, so I don't have to look at him. "I'm going to work tomorrow. I know it's not going to sit well with you, but I'm not a prisoner."

Theron follows me into the room. I can see him out of the corner of my eye. He is pissed. "What? The hell you are! You're not leaving this house."

"Damn it. Don't fight me on this. Send Evan with me, or drop me off yourself if you have need for your idiotic control. You can't keep me locked up. I'm not a fucking criminal."

"Idiotic control? Why don't you feed me some more bullshit? This mess is your fault. You lied to me. You hid shit from me. First, the pregnancy and now someone is following you, leaving threatening notes on your car. You want me to ignore that? No, Eve. That's my final word."

Now, I am pissed. Surely Evan coming with me, or Theron dropping me off would have been a compromise, but instead he thinks he can keep me locked up. Nope. Not happening. "I may have held things from you, but it doesn't give you the right to dictate my fucking life. You don't own me. I'm not your property. I will be going to work tomorrow. I suggest you figure out whether you or Evan is coming. I'm not asking for permission. I am telling you what

I am doing. That's *my* final word." I slam our door behind me, as I leave the room and head down the hallway. I need some time to myself.

I have gone off the deep end and completely lost my mind. I know this because I am currently complaining about mistakes that I have made to an empty library. This is not my proudest moment, but I am not ready to admit it. I should be agreeing with Theron. I am turning down this library for a bookstore. I want both. I really like helping, Olivia. It feels like I have finally found my niche.

My fingers are grazing the spines of the books, as I walk. There are so many choices. I find one that looks worn by love and pull it out to inspect it. *Alice's Adventures in Wonderland by Lewis Carroll.* The pages are soft under my fingers, as I carefully flip through them. I have always loved Alice's blue dress. I know this isn't a first edition, but I know it's after nineteen eleven because that was the first time Alice was printed with her blue dress. I hold the book firmly to my chest, as I make myself comfortable in front of the chairs. Alice only sees the rabbit once or twice before my eyes become too heavy to open and I fall into a dream of my own.

"What's your favorite kind of pizza? I like ham and pineapple the best. Want to know why?" I look over at the boy in the sunglasses next to me. He doesn't say anything. He just keeps drawing pictures in the sand of flowers. "I always ask for ham and pineapple because no one else in my family likes it, so I get the

whole pizza to myself. Sometimes I let my brother have a piece, but he doesn't really like it. What kind of things do you like to do?"

"I don't know. I can skateboard. I can grind pretty good. I could show you."

I am stunned into silence. He rarely ever talks. I give him a smile and shrug my shoulders. "That's cool. If you want to, that is."

"I said it. Why wouldn't I? You're my friend, right?"

"Yeah, I'm your friend."

"Will you always be my friend?"

"Yeah, I'll always be your friend."

"I'm going to keep you."

I am not sure what to say. No one has ever said anything to me like that before. It makes my stomach flip and I think I like it. "Okay."

"I'll show you some tricks another day. I should go before my dad finds out that I'm here. Bye, beautiful."

Kayla and Matt walk over, as I watch him walk back towards the parking lot.

"So, how's your mute?"

I shoot Matt a look. He can be such an idiot. "He's not mute. You guys are never nice to him, so why should he talk to you?" I look back out over the lake and watch the white foam scatter, as the waves hit the shore. I like the boy in the sunglasses talking just to me. I like when it is just us.

CHAPTER 11

EVE

The sun wakes me. It's peeking playfully through the curtains, teasing me with promises of a good day. I open one eye and then the other. I am back in our bedroom. Theron must have found me at some point and carried me back up here. Damn his sweetness. I still wanted to be mad at him for keeping me locked away like a criminal. After glancing around the room some more, I decide I am more like a princess locked away in a tower. It is a really, nice tower, but I'm still locked away.

I peek into the bathroom to see if Theron is in there, but he must have already went downstairs or maybe into his office. Either way, he obviously didn't want to talk to me. I take a long hot shower to relax my muscles. Slipping into my robe, I start picking out some clothes for the day, when I hear a voice in the hall. Trying to make as little noise as possible, I softly walk across the room and hide just on the other side of the door. I can barely make out what he is saying, but I don't hear anyone else. He must be on the phone.

"I'm not thrilled with this idea, either. You know she's right. I can't lock her up...Do the perimeter first...That's your call. If you need more people, just let me know. I'll let you know what time. She's still sleeping...I found her in the library. Next time I'll check there first...Evan, do not let her out of your sight."

I cover my mouth from screaming with excitement. He is not going to fight me on this. I hear his footsteps on the hardwood floor and I run back into the bathroom. I am doing my best trying to look like I was in here the whole time by sitting and combing my hair, but I'm a horrible liar. He steps into the bathroom and I give him a soft smile. He crosses his arms across his chest. Shit. I've been caught.

"What are you doing?"

"Getting ready for work."

"And who says you're going?"

"Me. I know you already talked to Evan about it."

"I knew you wouldn't stay here. You're too stubborn for your own good. Please, don't go anywhere without Evan today."

"I won't."

I throw my hair up into a bun and rush around the bedroom, as I get ready. I have thrown on a pair of jeans, a navy blue tank top, and my chucks. It is the beginning of June and it's finally getting warm out. I thought I was going to be stuck in sweaters for the rest of the year. I check myself in the bathroom mirror. The circles under my eyes are fading and my face isn't red from crying. It's about time.

Theron is already sitting at the dining room table when I come down stairs.

"Rebecca is making us breakfast."

"Oh. I was just kind of hoping for something light." Pulling out a chair, I take a seat next to Theron. It is odd eating in this beautiful dining room when there's only two of us. I suddenly feel underdressed.

"What?"

"I didn't say anything."

"You didn't have to. I could tell something was wrong by your face. Do you feel okay?"

"I'm fine. I just find it odd that we are eating in the dining room. Couldn't we have eaten breakfast in the kitchen? I don't mind."

"Rebecca asked where we would like to dine. I just assumed the dining room table would work. It's what it was made for."

"I guess I feel out of place. I'm not used to this."

"Ok. Tomorrow will be breakfast in the kitchen. We can save the dining room for dinner, okay?"

"Thank you."

Rebecca places a plate of toast, yogurt and granola in front of me. My stomach rumbles, as I glance from my plate to Theron's. He has toast, eggs, bacon, and two links of sausage.

"I thought you might not feel well. Is your food okay?"

"It's fine. It's just that you have bacon."

"You want my bacon?"

"Yes."

"Not happening."

"What? Why not?"

"I don't share."

"I call bullshit. I'm pregnant. I claim all rights to bacon within five feet of me."

"Fine." Theron hands me a piece of bacon, grabs his plate, and heads into the kitchen.

"What are you doing?"

"You said within five feet. There's no way you are getting the rest of my bacon. I'm eating in here."

I let out a loud laugh. This man is crazy protective over some bacon. I have just finished my toast, as he takes his place back at the table. "How was the bacon?"

"Delicious. Thank you. I want to talk to you about tomorrow. When I went to the doctor, she scheduled me for an ultrasound tomorrow morning at nine. Do you want to come?"

"Does she think something is wrong?"

"No. It's just to see how far along I am."

"Do you want me there?"

I slip my hand into his and stare deep into his colorful eyes. My heart flutters in my chest. I wonder if I will always feel this way when I look at him. "Yes."

"Okay, then I'll go. Evan is ready for you whenever you are. Promise me that you won't go anywhere without him."

"I said I wouldn't." I lean across the table and softly place a kiss on Theron's lips. "I love you."

"I love you, too. Have a good day, beautiful." I stand and push my chair back from the table. As I walk towards the front door, I can't help but be thankful for how agreeable he is being this morning. I have a huge smile on my face, as I approach Evan's car.

"Are we not taking my car or Theron's?"

"I thought it would be best if we went in my car today. It's most likely less recognizable to whoever is leaving the notes."

"Oh." I slip into the back seat and buckle my seat belt. I thought this was Isa's car. Maybe it was and it is Evan's now. I don't bother asking because it doesn't really matter anymore since Isa is gone. Evan hasn't said anything more about her. Although with everything going on, I haven't taken the time to ask. "How are things, Evan? I worry about you."

"You don't need to. I'm just working on breathing right now. Besides, you've definitely kept me busy the past couple of days."

If you were going to look at the positive side of things, at least I have kept Evan distracted. The drive is quiet. There is no music, no conversation, but lots of room left for thoughts. When we pull up to the bookstore, it starts to rain. Evan opens my door and holds an umbrella over my head. It's not necessary, but I don't bother arguing.

"Eve, I'll just be outside."

I stop, as I open the door. He can't be serious. "You are going to wait all day in the car? Don't you think that's a little extreme?"

"I'll be close." He slides into his car and shuts the door. I would hate to be anyone going up against him. He is huge and grouchy. That cannot be a good combination.

"Olivia?" The doors open, but there are no lights on in the front of the store. Where is she? "Olivia?"

"I'm in the back!"

I walk into the backroom to see Olivia surrounded by boxes of books, tools, and something that is supposed to resemble a bookshelf. "What is all of this?"

"Well, I ordered some new shelves, but I have to put them together. There are instructions in the box, but I was trying to wing it. I think I need the instructions."

"You definitely need something. Let me turn the lights on and I'll help you."

It doesn't take long for me to figure out the instructions. Olivia watches me, as I start taking apart the shelf and start organizing the pieces. Wiping sweat from my forehead, I look to check the clock and notice that it's almost noon. Kayla should be here for lunch soon. Olivia and I have already put together three bookshelves. I am sure we could have gotten a couple more done, but taking apart the first one took a little bit longer than I wanted. "Olivia, do you mind if I take a lunch? I was going to wait for Kayla, but I'm starving."

"Sure, dear. Go ahead. Are you going to one of the food trucks?"

"Yep. You want something?"

"Just bring me back a sandwich of some kind. Take a twenty out of the cash register. Lunch is on me."

I love this woman. My grandparents on my dad's side live in Florida, and I hardly see them. My mom's parents are retired in Arizona. What is with old people and warm weather? If I could choose Olivia as an adoptive grandparent, I would. As I leave the store, I look for Evan, but I don't see him anywhere close. It catches me off guard. Knots form in my stomach, as I walk towards the courtyard where the food trucks are parked. I order Olivia and me each a sandwich and I grab a bag of chips for me. The hairs on the back of my neck start to stand on end, as I pay for our meal. I turn around and slam into a large broad chest. "What the hell?"

"I should be asking you that." I look up to see Evan glaring at me. He is pissed. I have never noticed before, but when Evan is mad, his nostrils tend to flare out like a bulls. He grabs my elbow and pulls me alongside him, as we walk back towards the store.

"I was hungry. I looked for you and you weren't around."

"I was around. I was across the street. I watched you come over here. You could have texted me or even called me. I would have brought you lunch."

"Olivia sent me for sandwiches. I don't want to freak her out by having some big brute deliver us lunch because I'm afraid to leave the store. That would look *so* normal."

"Next time, you let me know." He drops my arm and stomps off in a hurry back towards the store, leaving me trailing behind him. He is so frustrating.

When I get back, I see Evan through the window talking with Olivia. This is exactly what I didn't want to happen. The bells chime, as I walk through the door. Olivia greets me with a big smile.

"Eve, why didn't you tell me you had such handsome friends?"

"Because I don't. Evan feels the need to follow me around." I quickly walk past Evan, hoping that if I ignore him, he will go away.

"I'm just doing my job, Miss Evelyn."

I quickly turn around on my heel. "Knock off the *Miss* bullshit, Evan. I agreed to you taking me today. I didn't agree to you following me into my workplace, and harassing my boss."

"Calm down. We were just discussing how much of a help you are. She tells me you were building shelves this morning. Should you be doing heavy lifting?" Evan leans back across the counter with his arms crossed over his chest, and raises an eyebrow. I hate playing chess with him.

Olivia's gaze travels back and forth between Evan and me with a worried look in her eyes. "Eve, is everything okay?"

"Yes, it's fine."

"Actually, Olivia, it's not. My friend, Theron is Eve's boyfriend. I'm sure you've heard his name mentioned."

"Once or twice. I over hear Eve and her girlfriend gossip sometimes. Not that I'm listening, Eve, it's just your so loud."

The needle in my bullshit meter is all the way in the red. She overhears my ass. I have caught her snooping before. "Evan get to the point. Why are you in here?"

"No. I'm talking with Olivia, not you. Olivia, did you know Eve shouldn't be doing any heavy lifting?"

"I wasn't. They are bookshelves made from composite wood, Evan. It's not like they weigh all that much."

"Okay. Everyone stop. You two are making my head swim. Evan, why are you here bothering my sweet, Eve? Shouldn't you be off doing something else?"

Ha! I knew she loved me. Olivia stands at the plate ready to take on whatever Evan throws at her.

"Well, at first I came to see if she was hungry, but it looks like she has that taken care of. She really should eat, and quit moving heavy things. Especially in her condition." Evan winds his arm, and throws the first pitch across the plate. It looks like this is going to be a fast one.

"Quit trying to lead this discussion, just tell me what you want to say. Do not play chess with me, boy." Olivia hits it, but it is a foul ball. Strike one.

Evan winds up again. You can see the look of determination written on his face. "Okay. Eve is pregnant. She hasn't been feeling well the past couple of mornings so Theron, her boyfriend, who also happens to be my employer, sent me to keep an eye on her today." He has just thrown a curve ball.

"Eve, you're pregnant?" Olivia swings at the pitch, but spins around completely missing it.

"She is. I'm her body guard. I'm here to protect her and she left the building without me." There it is folks the very last pitch. It sneaks in right over the corner of the plate. Olivia doesn't even have time to swing. She stands at the plate, as the ball rushes past, unable to respond.

"Bodyguard? Eve, just who are you dating and why didn't you tell me about the baby?"

"Evan, this is exactly why you were supposed to stay outside. You want to play the employer card then fine. You are to leave this store at once. You will wait for me in the car for the duration of the day. If you cannot abide by those simple tasks, I will call Theron, letting him know I had to fend for myself and get lunch on my own. You left me unattended and alone, as I walked to the park, and had to carry everything back by myself. There's no possible way I could have defended myself against anyone or anything with my hands full." Check Mate. I cross my hands over my chest and tap my foot. I dare him to challenge me. Instead, his face turns completely red and he slams the front door behind him, as he stomps off towards his car.

"Olivia, I'm so sorry. I didn't know he would be coming into the store. It was not my idea."

"Wait!" Olivia yells for me, as I walk into the back of the store. "Wait. Evelyn, didn't anyone ever tell you it's not nice to make an old woman run?"

"No, they haven't." Laughing, I turn around to find Olivia all out of breath. I sit on the floor, pull out my sandwich and take a bite. "Here." Handing Olivia her sandwich, I take another bite of mine. So far, today I haven't felt nauseous at all. I am going to take full advantage of it while I can.

Olivia sits beside me, opening her sandwich. "Today was interesting."

"Yep." The bells chime on the front door and I go to stand, but Olivia shakes her head at me.

"If you need something we are in the back!" She yells out into the store. She is so trusting. Anyone could steal from her, and she wouldn't be any wiser.

"You got lunch without me. You're such a hooker, Eve."

"Hello to you too, Kayla. Have a seat. We are having an interesting day today."

Kayla joins us on the floor, stealing my bag of chips. "You guys should invest in a table and chairs. This eating on the floor is for the birds. Also, what's with the mess?"

"We are building shelves. Want to help?"

Kayla has never used a tool in her life. She looks at me like I'm speaking a foreign language. "No, I don't want to help. Is that why there's an angry Sasquatch in the parking lot? He seems pretty, pissed off. What did you do?"

"It was nothing. I didn't see him, and yes I did look, so I went to get lunch from the food truck."

"By yourself? Theron is going to be pissed."

"Can someone please explain to me what is going on?" Olivia looks over at Kayla, when I won't give her an answer.

Kayla looks way, too excited to be able to tell someone all of this. "Okay. This is crazy, but here it is. Eve is dating Theron. They met when they were younger, but she didn't remember him at first. His dad, Thomas is the owner of Rowe Inc., or was until recently, but he doesn't know that yet. Someone has been leaving notes on Eve's car and she thought it was Thomas, but it turns out that it wasn't him." Kayla takes my drink from me, and takes a huge sip. First my chips and now my drink. I love her, but she needs to back off my food.

"By all means, go ahead and take a sip of my drink."

"I did and it was refreshing. Anyways, back to what I was saying. Thomas knows that Eve's pregnant because he knocked up Theron's ex-fiancé, Bridgette, who ran into Eve at the doctor's office. Bridgette was also our boss for a couple of days, when Thomas purchased the company we worked for, so that he could separate Eve from Theron. He hates Theron, like really, really hates him. Anyways, we know it's not Thomas because whoever it was followed us to lunch the other day and left a note saying that he knew Eve was pregnant, but he didn't know that Bridgette was." Kayla grabs my drink again, taking another sip. She goes to hand it back, but I just shake my head at her. She obviously needs it more than I do. "In the meantime, Eve found out that she was pregnant and hid the notes and the pregnancy from Theron. To be fair to Eve, she did plan on telling him, but Theron got a text telling him congrats on knocking up the gold digger. Which we believe was from Thomas. Evan is Theron's head of security and I'm guessing he's now Eve's babysitter."

"Wow…I just…wow. I feel like I just sat through a recap of a soap opera."

I finish the last bite of my sandwich and wipe my hands on my pants, standing up from the floor. "Well, now that we have a detailed summary of my life, can we please get back to work?"

"Eve, does Theron know you are building shelves?"

"No, Kayla, he doesn't and since you seem so concerned that I am leaving you back here with Olivia. You can help her with the shelves, and I'll go man the front of the store. The Allen wrench is next to the box of shelves."

"The *what* wrench?"

"Good luck!"

I leave the ever, stunned Kayla in the back with Olivia. I spend the rest of my day, dusting and reorganizing shelves in the front of the bookstore. I have only had to help out a few customers. It really ended up being a pretty, easy day. At five o'clock, Olivia and Kayla call it a day. I stay behind to sweep the floors and lock up the cash register. When I get outside, Evan is waiting for me. He opens the rear passenger door and I slide into the car. Beautiful music is playing through the speakers. I smile softly, when I recognize the song. It is from Simply Three. Theron loves this band.

"Thank you for not leaving the store this afternoon."

"Let's not talk, shall we? I looked for you. How was I supposed to know you were watching me from across the street? If you were watching me, obviously I was still safe. I didn't need you coming into my work, making me look helpless."

"Is that what you think I did?"

"Yes, it's exactly what you did."

"That's not how I see it at all."

"Of course you don't. Can we just go, please?"

"No, we aren't going anywhere until you hear me out." I let out a loud sigh, and cross my arms over my chest, staring pointedly at him in the rearview mirror. "This is how I see it. Theron loves you, completely, and with everything he's got. You make his world move. I know what it's like to lose someone like that. I loved Isa with everything I had to offer. She accepted my love graciously and returned it only in a way that she could. No one else will ever love me the way she did. I would do anything in my power to bring her back, if only for a moment, just so I could tell her how much I love her." My heart sinks, as he continues with his sharp words. "If Theron loses you, he's going to snap. That man is going to break, and no one, and I mean no one, will be able to bring him back. So, I see this as me protecting my friend's world. I see this, as me protecting the one thing that he can't live without. I see this, as me protecting someone who isn't just dear to my friend, but dear to me. Someone who opened a door for me and took me in when I was broken and falling apart. Now let me ask you this, how do you see it?"

Shit. That was one hell of a guilt trip he just laid out for me. I drop my stare and turn to the window. A tear rolls down my cheek, as I whisper, "Take me home, please."

Chapter 12

EVE

We pull up to the house and Evan comes around to open my door. Taking his hand, I step out of the car. My heart breaks for him, as I replay his words in my head. Leaning up on my toes, I place a soft kiss on his cheek. "Thank you, Evan."

"No problem, just doing my job."

I head into the house yelling out for Theron, as I slip off my shoes, but I don't get an answer. I make my way upstairs, so I can change out of my clothes. I softly bite my lip, as I reach the top of the stairs. Rose petals are sprinkled along the hallway leading me to our door. As I push it open, I notice even more rose petals covering our floor and our bed with some trailing to the bathroom. The balcony door is open, and I can see Theron sitting in a little chair by a small table. Those are new.

"Theron, what is all of this?"

"Do you like it? I wanted to surprise you. Come out here. I want to show you something."

I step onto the balcony, and I am speechless. Lanterns have been hung around the garden, lighting up the pathways with a beautiful amber glow. Theron is sitting in a black wrought iron chair next to a small table with a beautiful stone mosaic design in the center. He gestures to the chair across from him. I take my seat and stare into the garden with awe.

"I wanted the garden to be ours now. Do you like it?"

"I love it. Is this what you did today?"

"No, this is what I had the gardener do today, but the table was my idea. My mom used to have a set like this in her garden. I searched all over and I finally found one that I liked. So, I went and picked it up. You would have liked the lady I bought it from. She was very sweet. She smelled like cookies."

Isa smelled like cookies. I am not sure Theron put the two thoughts together, but I can tell he is happy either way. The garden is incredible. "This is beautiful, thank you."

"I know you liked the balcony, so I thought you could use somewhere to sit."

He stands and pulls me to my feet, leading me back into our bedroom. "I did this, too." I follow the petals into the bathroom. He ran me a bath and there is pizza on a tray next to the tub with a pitcher of water and two glasses. "I thought we could eat in here tonight. I got ham and pineapple. Is that okay?"

"It's perfect." I turn around and smash my body against his. Our mouths crash and our tongues collide until we are left breathless. This is so much more than I imagined coming home to.

"God, I want you so incredibly bad, but our dinner is getting cold. Go slip out of your clothes and come join me."

"Pizza in the bath?"

"I know you love both, so why not enjoy them together."

"I love you."

"I know. Now go." He smacks my ass, as I walk back into the bedroom. Shedding my clothes, I grab my robe and walk into the bathroom. Theron is already in the tub with the jets on, waiting for me. I slip into the water, sitting between his legs. He hands me a glass and I take a huge sip. Bubbles tickle the back of my throat.

"Ginger ale?"

"I didn't know how well your stomach would handle the pizza."

"Thankfully, I haven't felt sick at all today."

I only eat two pieces before I feel way, too full. Theron is gently running his fingers up and down my arm. He seems so content. I am a little nervous about the ultrasound. "So, tomorrow at nine o'clock you and I will get to see how far along I am. Are you nervous?"

"A little, but it's more along the lines of me being afraid I'll turn into my dad."

I spin, wrapping my legs around Theron's waist. Taking his glass out of his hand, I set it next to mine on the tray. I gently grab his wrists and place his hands on my belly. His eyes meet mine, as his fingers brush circles on my skin. I take his face in my hands, and ever so gently place a soft kiss on his lips. "You are not your father. You are two completely, different people. Please, don't ever compare yourself to him."

"My father loved my mother with all of his heart. He changed after I was born and he became jealous of me. How do I know that won't happen with me?"

"Because I won't let it. Do you love me?"

"I always have."

"Then don't doubt yourself, especially when you have my heart and all my faith is in you. It's like you are doubting me."

"Never." He kisses me, butterflies flitter around in my chest. I love this man. His lips leave mine, and begin to trace my jaw, down my neck and back up to that spot just below my ear. My body shivers from his touch, electricity coursing through my veins. I lean back and circle my hips against him. I can feel his hard erection between my thighs. Positioning myself just right I circle my hips again, but this time I make sure to focus on my clit.

My insides clench at the knowledge of what is going to come. His hands slide up my waist, cupping my breasts with his thumbs, teasing my nipples into hard peaks. I moan, as he pulls my breast into his mouth, his tongue circling my peak before lightly nipping it. His hands move up my body, grasping my face and he kisses me like this may be his last. Every ounce of love and passion he has for me is behind this kiss.

I feel his hand move under me. Positioning his hard cock, he slides into my pussy. My body wraps around him, clenching him. I grip onto his shoulders, as I slowly raise and lower myself onto him. I wrap my arms around his neck and lean back. I continue a slow torturing rhythm, as his cock slides in and out of my pussy, hitting every nerve.

Theron bites his lip and I watch his eyes glaze over. He is going to lose it soon, but I try to hold out. This time, I let out a long deep moan, as I grind myself back down on him. His fingers dig into my hips, as he tightens his grip. "Fuck, baby. I can't hold out much longer."

I shake my head, as I keep up my momentum. "Wait. Just wait." My nerves are building, my skin is warming and the familiar feeling spreads over my body. I am so close. Raising my hips, I slam myself down on his thick, hard cock, hitting exactly where I need it. "Fuck!" My thighs tighten around his waist, as my orgasm spreads through my body. It's not rushed. It is slow and blissfully sweet. Opening my eyes, I find his gaze. His eyes are dark and full of lust.

"I'm not waiting anymore." He stands in the tub, lifting me with him and he spins us around. He sets me back down on the edge of the seat and pushes me back, so my head is resting against the bath pillow. He bends my legs, spreading my thighs far apart. "Hold onto your thighs. Keep them open. I'll hold onto you."

I do as he says, and I grasp the back of my thighs with my hands. He grips my waist and slams into me, rocking me to my core. "Ahh!"

"There's my girl." He does it again, but this time, he pulls me towards him, as he pounds into me. Water splashes onto the floor, as he continues to rock into my body. My fingers are digging into my thighs, as I try not to lose my hold.

"Ohmigod!" My moan comes out as one word. He is relentless. I am going to rip apart underneath him.

"You're mine!" Theron's words undo me. He owns me and he knows it. My orgasm rips through me, sending my body spiraling out of control. One of my hands slip, and my leg falls lose into the water. "Hold on, beautiful. Fuck. Hold on." His jaw clenches, his eyes squeeze shut, and his head tilts back, as he calls my name, "Eve!" I can feel his cock jerking inside of me, filling me. I let go of my other leg and my body goes loose. He is the only thing holding me from sliding under the water.

Theron falls to his knees and slides his hands up my back, pulling me to him. He moves my body, so he is cradling me in his arms. I lay my head on his chest and close my eyes.

"Beautiful, I love you, but you can't fall asleep on me in the tub. I don't trust myself carrying you with both of us being wet. I'm afraid I'll slip."

"No."

"Let me up and I'll dry off. Then I'll carry you to bed."

"No. I just want you to hold me."

"And I will. Just let me out of the tub first, okay?"

He laughs when I refuse to move, but he slides me off his lap anyways. He does as he has promised and soon I am dry and warm, sitting on our bed. He lets my hair down and runs his fingers through it. I am sure it looks crazy since it's been in a bun all day, but he doesn't care. Theron slips one of his t-shirts over my head, and kisses the tip of my nose.

I lay back against the pillows and watch him move about the room. He pulls on a pair of flannel pants, before walking over to the balcony door, latching it shut. I watch him, as he walks into the bathroom and cleans up our mess. He has such an amazing body. I love the way his pants hang just right on his hips. I smile, as he walks back into the room and I am blessed with one of his. His teeth are so perfectly straight. I haven't found a flaw yet.

He pulls the covers back, as he looks down at me. "Rebecca, can fix it tomorrow. I'm too tired. It seems someone has worn me out."

"You do realize it's only a little after eight, right?"

"Yes. You do realize someone wanted me to hold her."

"Oh." My cheeks blush and Theron slides in behind me, wrapping me in his strong arms. Rolling over, I push him onto his back and lay my head on his chest. I drape my leg across his and my arm around his waist. My body is completely relaxed. I feel as if I am floating on clouds as I drift to sleep.

CHAPTER 13

EVE

Nothing and I mean nothing is more annoying than waking up from a dead sleep to a horrible sounding alarm. I lay there for a minute, just letting it go. I know I need to turn it off, but I don't have the energy to move, yet. I shut off the alarm and notice that it is only seven. Why the hell am I waking up this early? Then, I remember our appointment today. I immediately feel wide awake and alert. Jumping out of bed, I hastily fix the covers before grabbing my clothes. I turn the shower on and let it warm up. Just before I step in, my stomach knots. The warm, gross feeling creeps into my mouth, and I dash to the toilet. I was hoping I was past this, but no such luck.

I can hear Theron calling for me. He walks into the bathroom and stops mid-sentence when he sees me. "Hey, beautiful, what kind of—"

"I just wanted to shower." A tear slips down my face and I wipe it away with the hand that is not gripping the toilet seat.

"Baby, I'm so sorry. I guess pizza wasn't such a good idea after all."

"I don't think it would have mattered. My stomach hates me."

Theron squats down, handing me a towel for my face. "Come on. I'll help you up off the floor." He holds his hands out for me and I gladly take them. He doesn't let go until he is sure that I am standing securely on my feet. "Take a shower, beautiful. It might make you feel better." He kisses my forehead and another tear rolls down my cheek. No words are said. He leans in and kisses my cheek where my tear landed. I close my eyes, reveling in his touch. His touch and scent wrap around me. I inhale deeply, breathing him in.

Everything about him makes me feel more relaxed and calm. He eases my nerves and makes my heart rush at the same time. Opening my eyes, I find a bright green emerald and a golden chocolate pool staring straight back at me. His eyes are full of light. I don't know when the shadows disappeared from his eyes, but I'm glad that the light is back.

He helps me step into the shower and closes the glass doors. I wait for him to leave, but he just leans back against the vanity.

"What are you doing?"

"This is my bathroom, too. Am I not allowed?"

"Why are you watching me?"

"Because I like watching you. You are beautiful, and so incredibly sexy. I'm going to watch your naked body move under the water. Why?"

My cheeks flush at his words. I have never thought of myself as beautiful, let alone sexy. My thighs jiggle. My stomach isn't taught or tight, it's soft. I have stretch marks on my breasts from when Mother Nature decided I needed them overnight. I don't resemble anything close to what magazines and the media tell me is pretty, yet there is this unbelievably gorgeous man telling me that I am incredibly sexy. To hell with what sexy is supposed to look like. If he tells me that I am sexy then damn it, I am sexy.

I turn so that my back is facing the glass doors, and give Theron a little swivel of my hips. Grabbing my body scrub, I bend over, working the soap up my legs, starting with my toes. I have a huge grin on my face and I hear him laugh. "Naughty, naughty girl. Finish up with your shower. You need breakfast and I don't want to be late to our appointment."

"What? I'm just washing up."

"Sure you are."

"Theron, you're a perv."

"Yeah, but I'm your perv."

"Yes, you are. Now get out, so I can finish."

When I meet Theron downstairs, I find him in the kitchen with my breakfast waiting for me. Theron's gaze never leaves me, as I get closer to him. He shakes his head, as if he is snapping back to reality and pulls my chair out for me.

"You look beautiful."

"Thank you." I am wearing a pale, yellow sundress, with soft, red flowers on it. I have left my hair down, and dried it into waves. It is hanging loosely around my shoulders. I can't shake his words from this morning, and I feel absolutely radiant sitting beside him. I didn't even put lip gloss on. He has seen me at my worst, and he still loves me.

"A few things came up this morning. Thomas found out about the buyout. I'm not sure who leaked it, but it doesn't matter because officially at three o'clock yesterday afternoon, I owned majority of his company and now retain full assets to the company. So, his opinion no longer matters. I plan on having him forced from the board this afternoon, and I will give him the option to sell to me. If he chooses not to, I will prove that he is unfit to run the company. If I have to, I'll smoke him out, but he will be done with Rowe Inc. I hope to have the name changed to GILF by Monday morning. My lawyers are already working out the details with the banks."

"Wow. Did you know that it was going to happen this quickly? I mean, I know this is what you have been working for, but I didn't think it would be that easy."

"Neither did I. My gut is telling me that he isn't done with this, yet. That's why I'm worried about those notes. I know you don't think he has anything to do with this now, but who else would be out to hurt us, to hurt you?"

"I don't know, babe. Are you not coming with me then?" My eyes drop to the plate in front of me. I have barely touched my breakfast. I am so afraid that if I eat, I am going to puke. Theron takes my hand, his thumb brushing over the skin of my knuckles and raises it to his lips. A soft gentle kiss graces my skin.

"Of course I'm coming with you. I'll come to every appointment. I'm not going to miss any of this."

I try to hold back my grin, by biting my lower lip. I hear him gasp and our eyes meet again.

"Those are my lips. Bite them again, and I'll have to mark you before we leave. We don't have time for what I will want to do to you, so finish your breakfast, Eve."

I drop my eyes back to my plate, and cross my legs. Holy shit. He knows exactly what to say to set my nerves on fire. I finish my breakfast in silence. Rebecca clears our plates and we stand from the table. Theron waits for me, as I rush upstairs quickly to grab a light sweater in case the office is cold, and rush back downstairs so that we can leave for the doctor.

I am in the gown they gave me to put on. I thought ultrasounds were done on my stomach, but the nurse insisted I take off everything below the waist. Theron is sitting nervously in a chair in the corner of the room, taking turns bouncing each of his knees. There is a light tap on the door, and a woman comes in pulling an ultrasound machine behind her. She introduces herself and shakes both of our hands. She instructs me to lay back and has Theron come stand by my head.

"This is going to be a transvaginal ultrasound. Dr. Knox wants us to determine how far along you are, and since she thinks that you're only a couple of weeks, this will be our best option. I'm going to have you scoot down to the edge of the table and put your feet in the stirrups. Make sure you bend and relax your knees, letting them fall to the side." I follow her commands, and Theron grabs my hand. "Okay, here we go. This may feel a little weird, but I promise that it won't hurt." The ultrasound tech puts a little gel on the wand in her hand, and my first instinct is to close my legs. It is cold and intrusive, but she is right. It doesn't hurt. I look over at Theron and all of his attention is focused on the black and white screen. There it is. I can see my little bump on the screen. It is so small, but I can see a little flutter.

"That's the baby's heart. Your baby is very strong. I'm going to take a couple of pictures for Dr. Knox. I would estimate you being around eight weeks. If you give me a couple of minutes, I'll get all of this cleaned up and put away. Dr. Knox will be in to speak with you shortly."

"That's our baby." Theron speaks. Glancing at his face, I think that he is in shock. He has a euphoric look in his eyes. "Beautiful, we made a baby."

"We did." My hands find my stomach, and love that I never thought possible, fills me completely. The tech allows me sit up, while she goes to get the doctor.

"Eve, it's a pleasure to see you so soon."

I turn my head and shake Helen's hand. "This is my boyfriend, Theron."

"Doctor." Theron shakes her hand, and she walks around the table and takes a seat beside me.

"First of all, I'd like to say congratulations to both of you. Eve, I've known you since you were younger. You are going to make a wonderful mother. Now, my tech gave me the report. It looks as though you are right around eight weeks. So, we can try this, but don't stress out if it doesn't work. Obviously, the baby is doing just fine, as we just saw him or her nestled all warm and cozy. I'm going to put a little gel on the tip of this, and rub it around your stomach. Let's see if we can hear your little one's heartbeat. Shall we?"

Theron grabs my hand again. It is hot and sweaty. Is he really that nervous? At first, I don't hear anything, but my heartbeat. She must notice something that I don't. She moves back and forth, pushing down on my lower stomach in the same spot, and then I hear it. It's so fast. It is incredible.

"Is that it? That's the baby?"

"Yes, Sir it is. Congratulations again. Eve, you can go ahead and get dressed. I'll need to see you for a checkup in about four weeks, so if you don't have one scheduled, the receptionist will set you up with one." Helen hands me a little white folded card. When I open it, I see my ultrasound with the words Baby's First Picture printed on the edges. She leaves and Theron helps me get dressed.

There is a permanent smile on my face, as we leave the office. Absolutely nothing can ruin this day. I am in complete and utter heaven.

CHAPTER 14

EVE

We park in front of the bookstore and Theron's phone starts ringing before he can even turn the engine off. I start to get out, but he grabs my wrist and motions for me to wait a minute. I lean back in my seat, as he answers the phone.

"Theron…what? Damn it. Did he tell you why? Fine. Fuck, I'll be right there. Keep him in that room until I get there."

I grab Theron's wrist, giving him a questioning look. What's going on? I really hope whatever it is, doesn't deal with Thomas. Theron looks at me and shakes his head.

"Shit. That will leave Eve here by herself."

"Babe, it's okay. I promise I won't leave the store. Olivia's with me. I'll stay in the back and order in. Okay?"

He covers the phone with his hand and I can see the thoughts of concern bouncing around in his head. "I don't like the feel of this, at all. Come to the office with me."

"Who's in the room? Who do you need to get to?"

"It's Thomas. He is refusing to leave until I get there, and he's threatened the board if I'm not there soon."

"See? It will be fine. You are so worried about Thomas, and you already know where he is. It'll be fine."

"But we aren't sure it's him, yet. Please, come with me, Eve. I won't be able to get anything done worrying about you."

I lean over and place a kiss on his temple. "I'll be fine. I promise. I'll call you if I'm the least bit suspicious of anything. Okay?"

Theron lets out a deep sigh, and leans his forehead against mine. "Fine, but you call me if you need anything. I don't care if it's for a bottle of water, you call me."

"Absolutely. I love you. Will you be here when I get off?"

"Yes ma'am. Badass and I will be waiting right here for you. I love you."

"I love you, too."

I give him a soft kiss on his cheek, and head into the store. I call out for Olivia and she pops out from behind a shelf, nearly giving me a heart attack.

"Don't do that!"

"Well, hello to you, too. How are we feeling this morning?"

"Better, I was little ill earlier, but it seems as if it's left me for the day. Would you like to see the baby?" Laying my purse on the counter, I reach into it and pull out the white envelope with my ultrasound tucked neatly inside it. I hand it over to Olivia and her face is already beaming with excitement.

"Has anyone else seen this yet?"

"Nope, just you and Theron. I'm hoping to have my family over for dinner this weekend, so that I can show them. I'm so excited."

Olivia pats my hand and beams at me. "I can tell. You are absolutely glowing. We will have to find you a more comfortable chair to sit in. These wooden ones are going to start hurting your back soon."

"Don't put yourself out. I'll be fine. So, what's our plans for today? Anymore shelves to be built?"

"No, Kayla and I finished the last one up yesterday. Today we are stocking the shelves. We are going to move your lovely organized boxes onto the shelves. Harold's nephew came by earlier and helped me push them against the walls, so now all we have to do is fill them."

"Well, that should be easy enough."

I follow Olivia into the back and make my way through the maze of boxes she has set up. The shelves are tall, but I should be able to reach all of them. We start with the books sorted by age group, then sort through genres, and finally alphabetically. I am sweaty and my feet are tired by noon. We decide to take a break and I sit in the chair that Olivia has insisted that we keep in the back for me. I send Kayla a quick text asking if she will be by for lunch today. While I wait for her response, I order some salads for Olivia and me from the diner up the street. Since we are so close, the girl agreed to walk them over. I think me offering a big tip might have persuaded her just a little bit. The bells chime in the front of the store and Oliva walks out to see who is here. She comes back with the salads in her arms, along with our drinks. We have just started eating when my phone goes off.

"Heplo." Note to self, swallow food first and then answer the phone. I am not even sure of what I just said. I clear my throat and try again. "Hello?"

"Beautiful, I miss you."

"I miss you, too. How is everything going?"

"Surprisingly well. It's odd."

"Okay. Are you going to elaborate?"

"I will when I see you tonight. I'm still processing everything right now. Did Kayla come by for lunch?"

"No, I texted her, but I haven't heard back yet. If I don't hear from her soon. I'm going to call her. It's not like her to not text back right away."

"All right. I have to get back to the boardroom. Let me know if you need anything, okay?"

"I will. I love you. I'll see you when you get here." I set my phone down beside me and look over at Olivia. "Do you think it's odd that Kayla hasn't texted me back, yet? I mean, I texted her almost thirty minutes ago."

"Oh, I wouldn't worry. She's a grown woman. I'm sure she's fine."

We finish our lunches and get back to shelving more books. I have just finished the top shelf of the third bookcase, when I hear my phone ringing in my purse. I grab it and it lights up with Kayla's name.

"Where have you been?"

"Jeez. That's an incredibly rude way to answer the phone."

"Well, you didn't text back. How was I supposed to know what was going on. You always text back."

"Yeah, I always text back, except when my fiancé takes me out to lunch at a fancy restaurant and proposes to me in front of a bunch of strangers."

"What? Oh. My. God! Did you just say fiancé?"

"Yes, I did. I'm sorry I passed up lunch with you today, but Paul never asks me to go to lunch with him. I couldn't turn him down and I'm so glad that I didn't."

"I'm so happy for you. This is so exciting! Yeah to bachelorette parties!" As the words leave my mouth, I realize that I most likely won't be able to partake in the fun. Even, if I am not pregnant, I will have a baby to take care of. I am not going to rain on her parade, though. This is her moment. I won't ruin it.

"I know what you're thinking, and I've already worked it out. We are going to get married next fall, so you will have plenty of time to recoup after the baby."

"You don't need to do that, Kayla. It's your day, not mine."

"I know and I want you there without worrying if you are going to go into labor or not."

"I love you, bitch."

"Right back at you, skank. Now, I got to go. Paul is coming back from the bathroom and I want to give him *my full attention*."

"Gross, Kayla, you make everything sound dirty. I'll talk to you later." I smile, as I hang up the phone. Who knew today would be such an exciting day?

"Did I hear you correctly?"

"Yep. Kayla got engaged! I'm so happy for her. Paul is perfect for her. I know he's going to make her so happy."

The afternoon flies by. At three o'clock the store phone rings. Olivia goes to answer it, but I stop her. I have been sitting for too long, rolling between shelves. I really need to stretch my legs. The phone rings again before I make it to the front of the store. We really need to get a portable phone. I'm surprised that she still has a corded one. "Harold's Book Emporium can I help you?"

"Hello, this is Doctor Michael Kohler. I am trying to reach an Olivia Wolf."

"I'm sorry. I'm just an employee, just give me a second and I'll get her for you." I lay the phone on the counter and run to the back room. My heart is pounding in my chest. "Olivia." She turns to me and her face pales.

"What's wrong?"

"I don't know. There's a Dr. Kohler on the phone for you." She furrows her brow, as if she doesn't recognize the name. I follow her to the front of the store. My heart hopes that this is nothing serious. I know Harold is at home resting, I just hope nothing has happened to him.

"This is Olivia…Yes, he's my husband…Oh…oh…when?" Her face pales, as her hands start to shake. I help her into the chair behind the counter. Please, God, let him be okay. I can't watch another person break. "No, it's fine. I'll be right there. Yes…that's fine. I'll be there soon."

"What is it?"

She sighs, as she hangs up the phone. "My dear, sweet Harold decided today would be a good day to cut the grass. It seems he got overheated. He passed out in the yard, and the neighbor found him. He's at the hospital now. They gave him an IV, as he is dehydrated. One of the nurses were trying to find out how to get in touch with me and he got angry with them. He swore that if they told me, I would be down there yelling at him and stressing him out. Well, they called me anyways and guess what?"

"What"

"I'm going to go down there and yell at him for being so stupid. Then, I'm going to kiss him and hold his hand. I don't want to ever get another call like this."

"I don't blame you. Do you want me to go with you?"

"No, dear. Give your sweet boyfriend a call and have him come get you. We'll close up early today."

"Okay. You get your things ready to go and I'll lock the door behind you. I'm just going to text Theron really quick. I'll see you on Monday."

I give Olivia a quick hug and head to the back of the store. After digging for my phone in my purse, I send Theron a quick text letting him know that Olivia had to leave on an emergency, but I am locking the store up behind her. I also let him know that I am ready to go whenever he can get here. No sooner do I set down my phone that an awful feeling comes back into my stomach. I rush to the bathroom and spend at least the next five minutes with my head in a toilet. This is getting old really, fast. I am washing my face, when I hear the bells chime that hang over the front door. Shit. I didn't lock it, yet. Someone is here and I really hope that it is Theron.

I brush my hands off on my dress, trying my best to dry as I walk over to the counter. I see someone standing at the counter and it is definitely not Theron. It's a man with a short, stocky build. He looks oddly familiar. "Sorry, I was just in the restroom. We are actually getting ready to close early for the day. The owner is in the back, if you just give me a second, I can get her for you." My fingers are crossed that my lie works. If I can get to the back of the store, I can exit through the alley and call Theron. I don't know if this person is dangerous, but I'm definitely getting a creepy feeling from him.

"No need. I know she's not back there. I waited for her to leave. I noticed you don't have a body guard today."

Fuck my life. My stomach sinks, I turn quickly on my heel running to the back of the store. My scalp burns, as the man catches me by my hair, yanking me back to the front of the store. I am kicking and screaming, trying to pry his fingers out of my hair. I can see his feet behind me and I do my best to try and stomp on them. I rear my head back, trying to hit any part of him that I can, but he is too quick. My feet start slipping, as I try to gain my footing. Finally, he stops and drops me to the floor in front of the cash register.

"I assume your purse is in the back. I wouldn't want you calling anyone. How lucky is it for me that the old bird had to leave early? I have to say it was an unexpected surprise, but I'm enjoying it, none the less. I'm sure you've already let your ride know that you're closing early. So, that only gives us a short time together, before we need to go."

His back is facing me. My head is throbbing. I turn slowly, so that my back is facing towards the back room. I start scooting quietly away from him. I need to get out of here, and I know the front door isn't an option, since he's in front of me, but maybe if I'm quick enough, I can knock over some shelves or something. I need to keep him from catching me again. The wooden floor creaks, as I scoot back a little bit more. Shit. He turns to look at me and my mouth hits the floor. What the fuck?

"Ben? Are you kidding me? What the fuck are you doing? Let me go and I won't tell anyone you were here. I'll lie and say it was someone else. Someone I didn't know. You can't possibly know what you are doing."

"I'm not an idiot, Eve. You won't be going anywhere, and in case you are thinking of heading for the back door again, I want you to know that my business partner has it well guarded. So, you see there is nowhere to go."

I scramble to my feet, knocking books onto the floor, as I race to the back of the store. I can see the exit sign just above the door, when a hand grabs my ankle. I fall and my hands slam into the floor, as I try to catch myself.

"Fucking, bitch! I told you not to run. I get my time with you first." He pulls me towards him. I can clearly see his face, as I look over my shoulder. I kick out my other foot, trying my best to connect with his face, but he grabs my other ankle as well. Fuck. He pulls me back towards him. As I try to grab onto the edge of one of the shelves, something slams into my back. I curl into a ball, as he tries to kick me again, this time he gets my ribs. Pain seers through me. I frantically look around, trying to find anything to hold onto. I see a crack in the floor where two slats of wood don't quite meet. Digging my fingers into the crack, I try to pull my legs out of his grasp. His strength surprises me. Ben doesn't let go, but he yanks hard on my legs. I start to lose my grip, but I hold on with one hand. He yanks me again and I scream. My fingernails are stuck in the crack. His hands grasp my calves and pulls hard on my legs dragging me back towards him. Two of my fingernails rip off and a violent scream rips from my throat.

God, let someone hear me. I can see the small trail of blood that my fingers are leaving on the floor, as he drags me back to the front of the store. Grabbing me by my waist, he flips me over, slamming my back into the floor. Pain shoots up my spine, and my chest pinches, as I try to breathe.

"You were always such a tease at the office. Wearing your sexy outfits, but yet, you always turned me down. When the other company took over, I thought my aunt would finally be out of the picture. I could move up, and then you wouldn't be able to say no. Things didn't work out that way though, did they?"

He leans over me and I spit into his face. I am not going out without a fight. He wipes it off. His laughter is cold and evil, causing my hair to stand on end. I wrap an arm around my waist and twist underneath him.

"Ben, stop. God, please stop." I scream for help, but he shuts me up with a slap to my face. It stings, but I can live through it.

"Shut the fuck up. All you keep doing is screaming."

I scream for help again and this time his fist makes contact with my cheek, just under my eye. A white light flashes in front of my eyes, and my face feels like it's on fire. Before I can open my eyes, he hits me again, and this time, the lights are followed by something warm trickling down my face.

"I said shut the fuck up! You stupid bitch. I'm going to have you, whether you like it or not."

His hands reach up my dress, pulling and tearing my panties from my body. His fingers dig into my thighs, as he tries to spread them. I squeeze them as tight as I can and rock side to side, trying to throw him off. I scream again. "No! No!" Ben tries to cover my mouth with his hand, but I bite down, as hard as I can.

"You fucking whore!" He grabs my hair, lifting my head up off the floor and slams it back down. My vision blurs, and I know that I can't hold on much longer. I hear another person talking in the room, but I can't quite make out who they are.

"Benjamin. What the fuck? I never agreed to this. You were to grab her and bring her to me. You've fucked up royally. What happened to the rag? She wasn't supposed to see your face. Now she can identify you, you fucking moron!"

"Here."

All I see is something white coming towards my face. I shake my head back and forth trying to pull away, but it doesn't help. I feel the soft cloth touch my face then everything goes black.

The sun is so bright today. Kayla and I trying our best to get a tan. We are both stretched out on our beach towels. Matt won't leave us alone. He keeps trying to squirt us with his water bottle, but we refuse to give in. I hear Kayla scream and I know that Matt must have finally got her to move. I lift my head to see where they have gone to, when I notice a very tan pair of feet standing in front of me.

"You could say hello. I know you can talk." I watch, as the boy in the sunglasses comes over and sits next to me on Kayla's towel.

"You're going to burn."

"No, I'm not. I put on sunscreen. According to Kayla's magazine we are trying for a healthy glow."

"You don't need it. You are already beautiful and you are going to burn."

"You have to say that because you are my friend."

"No, I don't, but it's true. Walk with me?" He holds out his hand and I slip mine into his. We walk on the beach for a little while. He tries to find me shells. I have a ton at home that I have collected over the years, but I don't try to stop him. He is so excited when he finds them. His smile is infectious and I just want to stay in this moment as long as I can. The boy grabs my hands, and the sky starts to darken. What? I don't remember this being a part of my dream. I look down at the hand that I am holding and I notice that it is bigger and older. Theron's voice startles me.

"Eve. Baby, wake up. I need you to figure out where you are. Come on, baby wake up. I need you to get to me." Water splashes on my face. It's cold. Where is it coming from? I look around for Theron. I can't see him anywhere. "Eve, wake up for me."

I try to move, but my body is stiff and incredibly sore. My tongue wets my lips, and I try to swallow some spit to wet my throat. My eyes won't open. Water splashes on my face again. I can't see anything and I start to panic. I try to kick out my feet and arms. That is when I realize that I am restrained. Shit. Wiggling as much as I can, I try to make sense of where I am. Think. Breathe and think. What do I know? Ben attacked me at the bookstore, but someone else was there. I know that I am restrained, but I'm lying on something soft. I pull on my legs and I can hear metal clinking. There must be some kind of cuffs on my ankles. My arms can move a little, but not much. I don't think there are cuffs on my hands, it feels too tight. Is it rope? I don't know what to do. Being able to see would be really, helpful right now. The last time that I saw Theron plays through my mind. Why didn't I just go to the office with him?

Icy cold water splashes on me again, this time soaking not just my face, but my chest as well. Thoughts of Theron and what our life together were supposed to be, won't stop playing through my mind. Tears slip from my eyes, I can't blink them away. "Stop. Just stop. Please." My voice is hoarse and cracks, as I start to cry.

"There's no point in begging. She thinks she can stop me from having you, but I will. She's not running this show. I am."

"Who the fuck are you talking about? Just let me go. You can leave now. I can't even see to follow you, just go."

I hear the sound of heels clicking against tile or some kind of hard flooring, maybe it is cement. I am not sure.

"I swear if you fuck her up anymore, I will end your life. Benjamin, do not fuck with me."

The female voice sounds so oddly familiar. My mind is racing, trying to figure out who is in here with us.

"Please. I'll do anything. Do you need money? I'll get you whatever you need. Just let me go."

"Eve, don't beg. It's beneath you. What would your family think of you caving in so early? What about Kayla? How would she handle this? I'm sure after Matt, this would break her." Her voice is smooth. Oh my, God. I know her. I fucking know her! At first, the idea of Bridgette helping Ben crossed my mind, but I was way off.

"Anne? What did I ever do to you? We were friends, Anne. None of this makes any sense." My cheek stings, as my head whips to the side. Why do they have to answer everything so forcefully?

"Your boyfriend came into the picture. I was left behind, and then you took my job. I was out on my ass with nothing to show for my years of hard work. Then our friend, Benjamin shows up and tells me that he has been wanting to get back at you for a while. Apparently, you've made things rough for him over the past couple of years. We both wanted revenge. Getting back at your boyfriend for ruining my plans for my career is just a bonus. Now, Ben may have taken it a little bit farther than I wanted, but we are here now. It's not really like we can go back. So…what do I do with you now?"

"We end it, that's what we fucking do."

"Benjamin, shut up!" Her voice shakes and I know that she is flustered. Maybe I can sway her, bring her around to letting me go.

"Anne, please, you're my friend."

"Friend? A friend doesn't forget you exist. A friend doesn't turn her back on you, and then hang you out to dry while she parties with the boss's kid."

"It's not like that."

"No? Your boyfriend's dad buys the business we work for, and then suddenly I was out of a job and you took the position I worked so hard for. Sounds fishy, doesn't it? Did Theron get a kick out of knowing he ruined someone else's life?"

I try to shake my head, but the smallest movements are followed by an intense throbbing. "No. He didn't know. I didn't know."

"What? I got emails, Eve. Emails and messages going between you and Bridgette. You knew. I read them all. Ben, what is she talking about?"

"Don't listen to her, Anne. She's lying."

My mouth is so dry that I swallow and lick my lips. As I take a deep breath trying to gather my nerves, I feel a pinch in my side. "I didn't know. Bridgette and Thomas set it all up—" Before I could even finish my thoughts, my head is yanked to the side by my hair. "Shut the fuck up." Ben's grip in my hair tightens and I can't pull away from him. Fuck him, and fuck her. I never did anything to either of them. Anne was my friend. We hung out and cried over boys together. We rented movies and gorged on Chinese. This isn't my friend, this isn't Anne.

"They will be looking for me. He will find me. Then what will you two do, where will you run?"

A ghastly scream rips from my chest, as something slams into my left knee. White lights flash behind my eyelids. My leg is throbbing. They are talking, but I can't make out their words. The only thought that I can hold onto is knowing Anne and I were never really friends. I feel light, as darkness claims me once again.

I can hear water. The sound of waves washing against the shore and seagulls fill my ears. I know this is a dream. I should wake up, but this is so much better than my reality. Sitting up, I realize that I am alone on the beach. It is serine and peaceful. Contentment fills me. I feel at ease. I watch the soft waves kiss the shore and it is such a sweet greeting. It's gentle and loving. The water kisses the shore, and the shore returns with a sweet kiss of her own, gently giving away a little piece of herself each time they meet.

I can smell him. My body buzzes with electricity, letting me know that he is close. I can't see Theron, but his words are light and heavenly in my ears.

"You've been sleeping for a while, beautiful."

"I know. I don't want to go back. Please, don't make me."

His laughter fills the air around us. "When have I ever been able to make you do anything you didn't want to? If you need to stay here for a few more minutes, it's okay, but don't stay too long. I need you to come back to me. I love you."

"I love you, too. I'll see you soon."

The current running through my body dies out and I know that I am alone again. It's okay. I lose myself in the calmness of my surroundings, once again.

CHAPTER 15

THERON

My phone buzzes. It's Eve. I am not sure what happened exactly, but Olivia is leaving on an emergency. The idea of her being alone, sends a chill down my spine. "Gentleman, I'm sorry, but we will have to reconvene at another time. My lawyer has all of the details, if you have any questions, please deal with him or my personal assistant directly. I have an urgent matter that I need to attend to. If you'll excuse me. Evan, if you'll come with me."

Looks of confusion spread across the boardroom, but I don't give a shit. If Eve needs me, then that is where I need to be. Evan follows me, he knows that something isn't right.

"Sir?"

"Evan, I need you to follow me. Gather who you need to keep a perimeter. Eve is alone at the bookstore, and something feels off. I'm heading over there now to pick her up. Follow me, but stay far enough back, so that it's not obvious. We know that Thomas isn't behind this. With what took place this morning, I know that he isn't involved. He may be an asshole, but he's easy to read. The look of shock on his face this morning when I questioned him about the notes, wasn't fake. Someone else is out there watching her. God damn it!" I slam my fist through the wall. Why didn't I force her to come with me? Why didn't I send Evan over there when I found out Thomas wasn't involved? "I've put her life at risk. If something happens to her, I won't ever be able to forgive myself."

Evan doesn't flinch when I punch my fist through the wall a second time. He nods his head at me and follows me, as I head out to my car. I race through town. He stays right behind me, even when I blow through two red lights. Once we get close to the bookstore, Evan falls back. I park directly in front of the store.

As I get out, everything looks normal. I turn the handle on the door, the lock clicking quietly in my hand, as I push it open. I barely hear the sound of the bells, as I take in my surroundings. There's a shelf knocked over by the cash register. I immediately take out my phone and call Evan. "Evan. Get here now. I don't care what you have to do, but fucking get here now. Bring the police with you. The fucking store is trashed." I end the call before he can ask any questions.

Fear and adrenaline race through me. My heart pumps so hard in my chest, I think I might be having a heart attack. Carefully, I step around the bookcase. I am trying to be as quiet as possible. I don't want to alert anyone to my presence. Books are scattered across the floor. I notice something smeared on the floor, bending down to take another look, I realize that it's blood. Fuck. Fuck. Fuck. I scream her name as loud as I can. Finding my feet, I run to the back of the store, there is a thin line of blood smeared across the floor, leading from the back door. They took her. My knees go weak beneath me and I fall to the floor. Everything that I live for has been taken from me, it was taken through the door.

"Theron! Where the hell are you, man? I got the detectives on the way. Theron!"

I can hear Evan calling for me, but I don't have words to answer him with. Anger, hatred, and guilt seep into my soul like black tar, completely consuming me. I stand, as Evan walks through the door, halting to a stop, as he sees me.

"I know you have connections, Evan. I've never asked about your life before we met. I don't want to know what unholy things you've seen, but I want you to find her. Do what you need to do. Anything you need. Do it. I don't care who you kill or who you buy off. You fucking find her, and you bring her home to me."

"Yes, Sir. I'll leave now. The detectives should be here any minute. I'm sure you don't need me to tell you not to touch anything. They will need everything as it is."

"No you don't. Find her."

Evan leaves me to my guilt. Why is she so stubborn? All that I wanted to do was love and protect her. My head hangs low in defeat. I am vaguely aware of someone approaching me from behind. My body reacts on instinct, as I stand and turn to face the person and make myself known.

Detective Markz, holds both of his hands up in front of his chest. I suppose this gesture is supposed to calm me, letting me know that he is not there to hurt me. It doesn't matter. I have already died a thousand times since I got here.

"I have my team in here. We are collecting all the evidence that we can. I'm going to need you to come with me, so we can clear the scene and let our CSI unit do their job." My stomach rolls and fear eats away at my insides, as I follow him out of the store. I give him a detailed description of everything that I know and what I have seen leading up to the time they got here.

"Her family needs to be notified, but we need to keep things as calm as possible right now."

"They can stay with me. I have room for them. I'd like us all to be together, so that we can all be notified at the same time of any news."

"I'll let them know your wishes. The head of your security is the one who placed the call, but I fail to see him here now. Why is that?"

"He's doing as instructed. I told him to find her. He's ex-military. He's using his skills and connections, just as you are. That's all you need to know."

"I should warn you that anything illegal is ill advised."

"And I should warn you. Money can buy anything. Legalities are not of my concern right now. If you'll excuse me, I need to get back to my place and ready myself for her family."

Fucking cops. I get that he has to do his job, but it doesn't mean that I can't do my own investigation. I ease out of my parking space and take my time driving through town. Once I hit the back roads, my foot finds the gas pedal and I don't ease up until I'm in front of the house.

I had Rebecca turn down the other rooms upstairs. I doubt anyone will sleep, but I want to have the option. I am pacing in my office, when I hear the doorbell ring. My stomach drops, as I try to think of what I am supposed to say. What reassurance can I give them? I have taken their only daughter and played recklessly with her life. I take a deep breath, as the doorbell rings again. Rebecca answers it before I can make it down the stairs.

As I hit the last step, I am greeted with devastated faces. Phillip is holding up Eve's mom with his arms around her waist. She is limp and her face is streaked with makeup. Robert steps in behind them and his face is hard like stone. His eyes are radiating hatred towards me. I don't blame him. I hate myself as well. "I was hoping we could all meet in the library. It's Eve's favorite room and I'd like to be as close to her as possible."

Phillip gives me a nod of his head and her family follows me down the hallway. He sets Linda down in a leather chair by one of the windows. He doesn't leave her side, his hands rest firmly on her shoulders. I can't imagine what they feel right now. Robert won't stop moving. He is pacing furiously back and forth in front of the fireplace. I have no words to offer them. I drop myself onto another leather chair, letting my head fall into my hands. All of my hope lies on Evan. God knows that he will have info before the police do.

The doorbell rings again, and I lift my head looking towards the door.

"I had Robert call, Kayla. It is only fair for her to be here. She's like a sister to Eve."

I nod my head in response and once again, words fail me. Kayla rushes into the room with Paul slowly following behind her. I am surprised when she rushes to me and not to Eve's parents.

"Theron, please, tell me you know something. Tell me you have a lead on this."

I turn my head away from her, I don't know anything. I have nothing to offer her.

"God damn it, Theron! You fucking look at me! Tell me you aren't just sitting here waiting for the police to find her."

"No. I sent Evan for her. If anyone is going to find her, it's him, not the police."

"Thank fuck. Has he called?"

"Whoa! Everyone stop right there. Who the fuck is Evan and why the hell do you think he can find my sister. What the fuck are you trying to pull? What aren't you telling us?"

"Evan is ex-military. They retired him with honors after his last mission. He is head of my security now. He's using his skills and contacts to find her. His means at finding information aren't exactly legal, but he will find her."

"This is all fucked up. You're fucked up! If it wouldn't have been for you and your crazy dysfunctional family, my sister wouldn't be missing right now." Robert is screaming at me. I take everything he has to throw at me. I am caught off guard, as he rushes at me, hitting me square in the jaw. I fly back into my chair, falling to the ground, but I don't get up. I allow him to continuously pound me into the ground. Phillip and Paul run to his sides, yelling at him to stop, but he doesn't and I don't try to stop him. They grab him by the shoulders, dragging him off me.

"Robert. That's enough. Beating a broken man isn't going to bring her back. Can't you see he's dying without her right now? You and I both know that we can't stop Eve from doing whatever she has set her mind to. You can't blame him for that."

I push myself to my feet, grabbing my jaw. Shit that hurts. "I know she's missing because of me. Don't you think that I know that? I hate myself. All we can do is wait. Either the detectives or Evan will let us know when they have something. Until then, all we can do is wait." I set my chair back up on its legs. Glancing at the table beside me, I notice *Alice's Adventures in Wonderland* laying on the table. My fingers brush its spine. Holding it up, I inspect it. As I turn the pages, I can smell the draw of the pages pulling me in. Now, I get why she smells the books. A soft smile plays on my lips, as I remember finding her in here, sniffing one of the books, as she sat in the chair. It fades quickly, leaving my heart feeling empty and hollow. I will die without her.

"That's her favorite." Linda sniffs and I look over at her. She wipes her nose again and nods to the book in my hands. "That's her favorite. She can recite most of it word for word."

I hand the book over to Eve's mom, as my phone rings. The whole room is silent. No one breathes as I answer it.

"Theron...Fucking Christ! When was the last visual on him? Okay, have them run everything on him...run her too...Fuck, Evan. She knew them...Find her. Call me when you fucking find her. Do you hear me? Fuck the God, damn police! I don't give a shit, you fucking call me first!" I am furious. Anger penetrates through my body. I drop my phone onto the table, and my eyes meet Kayla's. None of this makes any sense. Kayla walks to me and places her hand on my arm. I can't look away from her.

"Kayla...I don't...I'm sorry."

"It's okay. Just tell me."

"Did you work with a Benjamin Harper?"

"Yes. Tell me it isn't him. No, no, no. It can be him. Why would he do this?"

"My question for you Kayla, is why Anne would be with him?"

"What?" Kayla's legs fall out from underneath her and I catch her in my arms. Paul grabs her from me and carries her over to the sofa. Eve's family is staring at me, wanting answers and all I have for them is more questions.

"Evan was able to gain access to the security footage from one of the buildings across the street. There was a suspicious car stopping in front of the building letting out a man, and then it drove away. He ran the plates and they belong to a Benjamin Harper. His informants say that Ben used to work with Eve. There was also a female they were able to capture a visual of driving the car. They believe it to be Eve's friend, Anne. He is alerting the police of what he has found now. He is putting a price on Ben's head. It won't be long before he messes up. Someone will see him or recognize him."

"A price? Like the fucking mob? How can you do that?"

I turn, facing Robert. Ice flows through my voice as I whisper harshly into the air, "Money can buy anything, even people."

It has been an hour since I have heard from Evan. It is just past seven o'clock. The sun is starting to set. The fear of the night and darkness eat at me. Rebecca has brought us drinks and some snacks over the past couple of hours. The food has barely been touched, but we've run out of coffee twice. The room is quiet and the tension is palpable in the air. My phone rings, every feeling of hope that I am holding onto rushes to the surface. I swallow twice to find my voice, as I answer the phone.

"Theron...Thank fuck...Don't move unless you have to. You wait until I get there. Inform your men. Anyone who so much as touches her before I get there will be personally eliminated by me. I mean it, Evan. You wait for me, unless you don't have a choice. Do I make myself clear? Good."

I run my hands through my hair, taking a deep breath I turn to face her family. "Evan found her. Ben has her locked up in a house on the other side of town that he is renting under a fake name. They don't have any visuals on her yet, but they believe her to be either in the basement or attic. They have visuals on Anne and Ben, but nothing on Eve, yet. I am going there now. Phillip, Robert, you may join me if you like. Paul stay here with Kayla and Linda. I don't want to risk anymore lives, if I don't have to."

Robert grabs my arm, as I walk away. "What will you do when you find her?"

"I'll take her home with me, where she belongs."

"And when you find Ben?"

"For his sake, I hope the police beat me there. I plan on killing him."

CHAPTER 16

EVE

A warm breeze blows across my skin, I am back on the beach again, and I find myself sitting on a dock with my toes just barely in the water.

"Have you decided, yet?"

I turn my head, and my heart breaks, knowing this is only a dream. "I thought that you left me. Didn't we already say our goodbyes?"

"We did, but I think you need me now. Are you going to go to him?"

"Yes, I'm just not ready, yet. I'm so tired, Matt. I can't find the strength to open my eyes. I don't want this to be real. I want to wake up warm and safe in my bed. What if when I wake up, everything I had is gone? What if I don't get to see him again?"

"Ssh. Don't think like that. He'll be there for you, I promise."

"How do you know? What if I'm hurt too badly, what if they took my happiness from me?"

"I don't know. I just do. I can stay for a while if you want, but I'm going to need you to try and open your eyes soon. Staying here won't help you. If you stay too long, I'm afraid you won't be able to go back."

"Just stay with me a little while. I just need to rest a little longer."

We sit on the docks for a while longer. My head is resting on Matt's shoulder. I hear someone call my name, but I don't see anyone else around. I look up at Matt with questioning eyes. He smiles as he says, "Go. Open your eyes for me. Just try." His voice fades and I feel something wet on my skin.

A warm cloth brushes over my eyes, and I try to pull back my head. It doesn't matter, I know that I can't go anywhere.

"I'm sorry that it's gone this far, Eve, but I can't go back. I hate the way your face looks. Ben got a little carried away, but I calmed him down. Can you try and open your eyes for me?"

"No." My voice is barely a whisper. My head is throbbing. My body is in so much pain that I am having a hard time focusing.

"I need you to try. Ben is going to call Theron with a deal. If everything goes right, we'll leave you here and we will be out of the country before anyone finds us. Theron is just going to finance our little trip. Once we have the money, and we make our landing, I'll call from a prepaid phone and let him know where you are."

"I don't understand, why?"

"Eve, we have been over this already. Your boyfriend got involved and took something I wanted from me. Now I am taking something of his. The only difference is that I'm giving what I took back."

"No." I swallow trying to wet my throat. I feel nauseous as I try to open my eyes. My left one won't open at all, but my right eye opens just barely enough for me to be able to see around me. My vision swirls and sways. My thoughts won't process. I can't form the words that I need to say. I try to focus on Anne. She is sitting at the end of the bed that I am tied to. Trying to gather my bearings is wearing on me. My head lolls to the right. I notice that the windows are boarded up with what looks like some kind of cabinet doors. There is old gray and red carpet on the floors. It looks like the ceiling has some kind of carpet on it as well. My stomach knots, as I tr to focus on the room around me. I close my eye and take a deep breath through my nose. My mouth fills with spit and I swallow. I have nowhere to go if I get sick now.

"Damn, Eve. Any color you had left in your face just disappeared. How far down are your thoughts taking you?" Anne laughs, as if she has just told some kind of joke. Stretching with my fingers on my left hand, I can make out the edge of the bed, letting me know that I am closer to the edge of the bed on that side. Turning my head to the left, I feel a sharp pain sear through my cheek, as my face lays against the mattress. I have little room to move with my arms, but I can't move my legs at all. The knot in my stomach rolls and I know that I can't hold it back anymore. I push my shoulders to the left and vomit, trying my best to get it on the floor and not the bed. I don't want to lay in my own puke.

"What the fuck, Eve? Jesus Christ! That's just disgusting."

Loud footsteps enter the room. "What's disgusting?" It seems Ben is back.

"Eve just vomited all over the place. I didn't sign up for this shit. We were supposed to keep her until we got our money. In no part of the deal, did I agree to almost killing her, or cleaning up her puke. This is fucked up. Did you call him, Ben?"

"Yeah I called him. He has the account numbers. I am watching the bank. Once it is transferred, we are ready to go. Car is packed." His loud footsteps get closer to the bed. He grabs my face, gripping my cheeks in his hand and turns my head to the right. He holds my face still, as he smacks my left cheek. Pure white fire burns through my body. "Bet you could use some of that ginger ale now, couldn't you?"

I say nothing. Tears slide down my cheeks, as I try to catch a sob trying to escape my throat. With every breath I take, my chest pinches. I am fighting so hard to keep my focus. I moan out in pain, as someone tries to move my legs.

"What the hell would ginger ale do for her? She's puking because you've beat the shit out of her."

"Not where it would really count, I haven't. She better hope it doesn't come to that." His footsteps fade and I hear Anne call after him.

"What does that mean, Ben?"

"Oh, Eve, she doesn't know. Tsk-tsk. Look whose keeping secrets from her friends. Eve is pregnant, Anne. Surprise. Surprise!" He laughs as his voice trails off.

"Pregnant? Fuck. Eve, I didn't…I didn't know…I'm sorry."

There is a loud crash downstairs and Anne takes off. I hope someone else is here, someone who can help me. I swallow a couple of times, to wet my throat and take a couple of deep breaths to fill my lungs with air. I scream with every single breath that I have left. I scream for Theron, I scream for me, and I scream for what we were supposed to have.

There is another loud crash. I can hear a woman scream, followed by another loud crash. The voices are getting louder, but none of what they are saying is making any sense. Everything is muffled. There is an odd popping sound that I have never heard before, and then everything in the house goes still. There's another scream. Someone yells for no one to move. It is quiet and my vision starts to fade.

No. Damn it! I need to stay awake. Think of Theron, think of anything. Don't fall back to sleep. Scream or do something, anything. My mind is racing with ways to keep me alert, to keep me holding onto hope. Come on, Eve. Focus on what is around you. I stretch my fingers in my right hand, feeling soft linen between my fingers. My eye roams the room, noticing the carpet isn't just on the floor and ceiling, there's some on the walls as well. There's also doors nailed up sideways along the walls. Where am I? There is no closet or any furniture. It is just me, tied to a bed in a room with no lights. The sun is going down, and darkness starts to fill the room.

With the darkness coming for me, fear takes over my mind. I swear that I hear footsteps getting closer to the room. I don't want to look. I close my eyes and try counting to ten. I make it to five, before I fall deep down the rabbit hole once more. I feel like I am falling, spinning, around and around. My body sways and turns. I lose all control over my mind, and I let go into the black abyss waiting for me at the bottom of the hole.

Chapter 17

THERON

My phone rings before I even have a chance to leave. "Theron."

"Good evening Mr. Rowe. I have something of yours. If you want her back, you will need to do exactly as I say. I am going to give you ten different account numbers. I want you to wire four million dollars to each account directly. Once I have acquired the funds and make it safely out of the country, I will call you with the coordinates of her location. The police are not to be involved. I will know if they are. I am not to be followed by anyone, including your security team. If for any reason something goes wrong, or I even get the sense of you disregarding my rules, I will kill her."

Bile rises in my throat, as I realize who is calling me. It's Ben. I wave to Robert and Phillip to stop. Ben is rambling about money and accounts. I motion Robert over to me and I have him take out his phone, so I can record the account numbers. He wants four million dollars deposited into ten different accounts. I immediately agree, there is nothing that I wouldn't give to have her safe and back in my arms. What he doesn't realize is that I already know where she is. He also doesn't realize that there is a tactical team already in place, waiting to take him out.

Robert and Phillip slide into the car, as I shut my door. I race through town, once again, blatantly ignoring every traffic law in place. I pull up across the street from the address that Evan gave to me. It is an ordinary, gray Victorian style house with white trim. It looks like every other house on this street. The landscaping is well kept and there are even flowers planted along the sidewalk leading up to the front steps. Nothing looks out of place, until I focus on the windows. The upstairs and basement windows look like they have been boarded up from the inside. There is no sign of other cars parked near the house. Evan and his group have parked several blocks away, arriving on foot. I can see them in their black camo gear, flanked around the house. I doubt anyone in that house has a clue to what is going on out here.

"Stay here. I'm going to meet up with Evan, and go from there. I need you two to wait for the police. Let them know we are in the house with the suspects. I'm going to go get, Eve." Neither her brother nor dad make a sound. I give them a nod of my head and step out of the car. I walk down the road a bit and approach it from the other side of the street. Evan meets up with me, informing me of where his tactical team is located and hiding.

"Have you called the police, yet?"

"Just got off the phone with Detective Hallows. They are on their way, but he warned us not to do anything rash."

"Rash? They have my Eve in there. God only knows what they have done to her."

"Sir. With your permission, we would like to head inside. My alpha team has a read on her. She's reported to be upstairs. Two of my bravo team are already in place inside the basement. No words on any other movement at this time."

"Do it."

"Theron, I must warn you that what we may find might be horrific. I can't guarantee what we will see when we enter the house."

"You think I don't fucking know that, Evan? You think I don't know? There was blood at the store for fuck's sake. Her God damn fingernails were stuck in a floor board. You get in there, and you give me an all clear. I don't care what you have to do, but you do it now. I want in there, and then I want him!"

"Sir." Evan speaks into his left shoulder, and the men start moving by pairs into the house. The sun is starting to go down, giving the surrounding trees long shadows. I wait in their cover, until I see one of Evan's men wave to me from the doorway. I stay close to the frame of the house, as I approach. Carefully taking the steps up to the front door, I enter the house, walking into a very large room, which is basically empty with the exception of a small table and a lamp. There is a large doorway leading back to the kitchen through a long hallway. I can see a trail of blood leading from the back hallway to the stairs to my right. My Eve is up the stairs.

Evan motions to his men, closing his fist and pulling his arm down. Everyone drops to their knees, guns ready. Someone pulls me against the wall, my heart is beating so hard. It is eerily quiet. I can hear someone laughing above us. Then a door creaks open, followed by heavy footsteps. I can hear each step they take, the stairs creak and groan underneath their weight. My head grows dizzy waiting. I realize that I am holding my breath. It's Ben, I can see him clearly now. I want to rush at him, take his throat in my hands and squeeze every, last breath of his life out of him. I want to watch him die. I don't realize that I am starting to move towards him, until an arm reaches out, pulling me back against the wall.

Ben steps off the last step, turning towards the back of the house. He doesn't realize that danger is waiting for him right around the corner. He must see one of Evan's men because he takes off running the other way into the living room, where I am waiting with two other men against the wall. Ben bolts for the front door, but one of the men beat him to it. He blocks the door, knocking Ben back into the room. He falls into the table, as he tries to gain his footing. I stand, as Evan's men tackle him to the ground. Ben tries to fight them off, but his strength is nothing compared to theirs. They hold him to the floor, his arms bent behind his back. One of the men zip ties Ben's wrists together. Then they pull him up onto his knees, dragging him to the center of the room.

I see Evan motion out of the corner of my eye. Someone else is coming. They must have heard the noise. I slink back up against the wall. The footsteps are soft, slow, and cautious. They know something is wrong. Then I hear the rawest feral sound that I have ever heard in my life. My body jolts to life. Eve is screaming. It is loud, awful blood curdling screams. I charge towards the hallway, as Anne reaches the bottom of the stairs. I trip over my feet and crash into a wall. One of Evan's men reach to grab Anne as she screams, but she is too quick.

She spins around, grabbing something from the back of her pants. She is holding a pistol, aimed directly at me. Everything stops. I watch, as she slides the safety off on the gun. It is obvious that she has done this before. I close my eyes and take what I think is going to be my last breath.

"Don't move. Put your weapon on the ground!" My head snaps up and my eyes open to see Evan and his men with their guns drawn on her. She looks over her shoulder, towards the back door and then back at me. She lowers her arms, as she realizes that she is surrounded. Tears stream down her face in a silent cry. I wait for someone to move, and then I notice one of Evan's men coming closer. She sees him to. She looks at him and then back at me. I watch as her expression goes vacant, as she gives up all hope. I don't want to make any sudden movements, but I want to get to Eve. I take a small step forward. Anne catches me by surprise, as she spins her body while pulling the trigger, hitting Ben square in the chest. His body twists, as he falls to the floor. His eyes are open and vacant, as I watch his blood pool underneath his limp body.

Anne screams, as Evan's men grab her, knocking the gun out of her hand. The front door flies open and a swat team swarms the house. Their guns are pulled, directly aimed at the rest of us. I hear someone yelling at them to hold from the outside. One of them yells for us to drop our weapons. With Evan's signal, his men lay their guns at their feet and raise their hands in the air. Detective Hallows walks in, greeting me with a shake of his head.

"I said don't do anything rash. This looks rash."

"We had it under control."

"Is that so? How'd this happen?" He gestures with his head over in Ben's direction.

"Ah, that. Well, you can ask the lady in the hall. I believe she can recall every detail for you."

He gives me a nod of his head, and motions for his men to lower their weapons. After receiving permission from the detective, Evan and his men retreat outside. I am standing at the bottom of the stairs, staring straight up into a black abyss. My Evelyn is up those steps.

"Let my men go first, they will make sure that the house is all clear, and that no one is left hiding up there ready to surprise us. Good?"

"Fine, but I want up there. I don't want anyone touching her unless they have to." I wait for what feels like an eternity at the bottom of the stairs, watching the swat team carefully climb each step, making sure that everything is all clear for me to join them. I wait for what feels like minutes, but it is only seconds. The detective stands at the top of the stairs and flashes a light towards me.

"Come up, but I want to warn you that this is bad. We have a medic on standby outside. We are going to need them to be able to move her. She needs immediate medical attention."

I nod my head and swallow the bile in my throat. With every step that I take, my body comes alive. It is as if my soul recognizes her before my mind does. Nothing could have prepared me for what I found when I walked into the room. Everyone has their flashlights on, trying their best to illuminate the small dark attic. My eyes rest on the horror that is before me. My beautiful Eve is strapped to a bed. There are metal handcuffs on her ankles and cloth straps tying her to the bed frame. Her face is mauled, bloody, and swollen. I can barely recognize her. Her left leg is twisted and blue. Without a doubt, I know that it is broken. It's positioning is completely unnatural. Her hair is strewn around her head, some of it laying in vomit. Jesus Christ. My heart stops and starts a million times. They have broken her. She has been mutilated. If it wasn't for the police standing in the door way, I would find my way to Anne. I would make her pay for all of this.

I walk over to the bed and try to brush some of her hair off her forehead. I fall to my knees, as I see how destroyed she is. My strong beautiful girl is laying broken and shattered in a bed, all because of someone else's greed. Someone drags me away. A gut wrenching sob rips through my soul, as I watch medics move around her. They carefully untie her limbs and check her breathing. They start yelling things to each other, as I watch one grab a bag from the floor. Tears fall from my eyes, as I hear someone yell, "She isn't breathing!" and watch them check for her heart beat. One person, starts doing chests compressions, while someone else breaths into her mouth.

They cut her dress off and I hear the sound of the paddles before I see them. Someone yells, "Clear!" I can't watch anymore. I drop my head to the side and pray to God they can save her. If she goes, I will follow. I can't breathe without her.

"She's back. We've got her back. Get her ready and onto the stretcher." They rush around her, bracing her neck and leg before carefully lifting her onto the cot. I stand on my feet, moving into a corner, so that they can move her down the stairs. Someone grasps my shoulder and I turn to see Detective Hallows standing beside me.

"They will take her to the hospital in town, but I'm sure she's going to be airlifted from there to Chicago. Come on, I'll drive."

I follow him down the stairs and into the cool night air. Phillip is holding her brother, Robert back, as he screams for her. I have seen too many people break in my lifetime. I walk over to him, wrapping my arms around him. He clings to me, begging me to tell him that she is all right. I can't find the words. I can't lie to him. All I can say is, "She's breathing." It is all that I have to offer him. Phillip takes Robert with him to get the girls. I slide into the detective's car and we follow the ambulance. The bright red and blue lights flash across my face. Sirens blare into the night, and I am silent, as we follow the love of my life to the hospital.

Doctors meet the ambulance as it pulls up. They rush her inside. I am pacing in the waiting area. They won't let me back there with her. I am told that she crashed once on the ride over. They are going to stabilize her and then she will be airlifted to Northwestern Memorial Hospital in Chicago. I am also informed that I can't ride with her in the helicopter. Only patients and the medical team are allowed. I call Evan, telling him to pack a bag for Eve and me. I am not leaving her side. I'm going with her, even if I have to follow by car. Once she is stable, they load her into the helicopter. The medevac nurse gives me the floor and room number where she will be, once she is stable and has been evaluated. Grabbing a pen from a clipboard, I write the numbers on the back of my hand.

Someone asks if I'm related to her. I open my mouth to speak, but the detective speaks up for me. "This is her husband. He's to go where she goes." He winks at me, as he nods his head and shakes my hand before walking away. I couldn't be more grateful for his little white lie and for his help. I watch, as the medevac lifts from the roof of the hospital, taking my life with it. Evan is waiting for me outside the emergency room. This man is my savior. He has everything I have asked for. We slide into the car, driving into the darkness, headed towards Chicago.

I don't go to church. I am not a religious man. I don't know if God exists or not, but I pray anyways. I pray to anyone who will listen during the long drive. I pray they bring her back to me and pray for the life we created together. I offer my body up to take their place. I would offer my life for hers, but I can't. I am just an empty shell because my life is soaring in the clouds above us, fighting for hers.

CHAPTER 18

THERON

The room is full of cool and calming colors. It's as if they know, I might break soon. They tell me that she is stable now. I am pacing back and forth, waiting for an update on her. She was so badly beaten, I will never in my life forget how she looked tied to that bed, battered and broken. Eve's parents arrived shortly after I did. Linda is beside herself. She keeps crying, mumbling about her baby. Phillip is sitting by her side with his arms around her shoulders. She keeps asking him questions, but she is crying so hard that he can't understand her. It doesn't matter. Nothing he could say would give her any solace.

Robert is leaning against the wall next to the vending machine. He hasn't said a word. I can feel him staring at me, as his eyes bore a hole into me. I know he hates me, but it is nowhere near the hatred and contempt that I feel for myself. I can't look at him. I try not to look at any of them. My reflection catches me off guard, as I pace in front of the windows. The man I see before me is not someone I recognize. He is a hollow shell of who I used to be. There is nothing left in me without her. There is no hope, no light. There are only dark shadows twisting and consuming inside the hollow spot where my soul once was.

Kayla went downstairs for some coffee. This must be so hard for her, since Eve is the only real friend she has left. When Evan said Anne was involved, I had my doubts. He had to be wrong, but when I saw her there, holding that gun to my face, I knew she was never the person that Eve thought she was. Someone in a white jacket walks past and we all hold our breath. As they pass us by, we collectively exhale knowing there isn't any news, yet.

Fuck. Why is this taking so long? This pacing is making me feel sick. I want to vomit. Sliding into a chair, I drop my elbows to my knees, hanging my head. My face stings from wiping it so much. I know men can cry. My gram told me when my mom passed, that love and heartache will cause grown men cry. What she failed to tell me is how much I could love someone else. She didn't mention losing the love of my life either, but then again she didn't know. I rub my hands over my face and through my hair.

"God damn it! What the hell is taking them so long?" Robert kicks the garbage can beside him into the wall. If he wanted attention, he now has it. He starts pacing where I left off. I look up when a pair of black boots stop in front of me. Robert is standing over me, his fists clenched at his side. I know he wants to hit me. I am not sure what is holding him back this time. I want him to hit me. I want him to pummel me until there is nothing left of me. I want to writhe in that pain, knowing I might catch a glimpse of what my Eve is going through.

"I'm Doctor O'Connell." My body jumps to its feet, as we all turn around to face the man in the long white coat. "If I could speak to Mrs. Davidson's husband."

"I'm sorry?" Linda looks around confused. Robert catches on and starts to say something, but his dad kicks him in the leg.

"I believe he means, Theron." Phillip pushes me forward and I follow the doctor to the other side of the room.

"I'm sure you are aware of her multiple injuries. She's been through a lot of trauma and right now it doesn't seem her body wants to wake up."

My ears are humming and I can barely make out what he is saying. I swallow, trying to regain my nerves. "I don't follow. Can you be more specific?"

He flips through papers on the clipboard in his hand. This can't be good if he has to read them off. "There's quite a lot. She has an isolated skull fracture with a cerebral contusion. In layman terms, it is bruising of the brain, most likely caused by a blow to the head. She has some soft tissue abdominal bruising along her sides, as well as deep tissue bruising on her back. She has three fractured ribs and renal trauma. Her kidneys are most, likely bruised from a severe blow to her back, which would also explain two of the fractured ribs.

The other one is fractured on her chest. There is also more bruising along her ankles and wrists. Her shoulders will be sore from the state of the positioning she was kept. She also has a broken tibial plateau with a severe bicondylar fracture. She will have to have surgery and will most likely have screws put in place. Her knee is severely dislocated, as well as fractured. We were able to make her as comfortable as possible and she is stable. I want you to know that we have also run tests for traces of semen."

Shit. The ground sways under me. What the hell did that fat bastard do to her? If he wasn't already dead, I would kill him myself. "Was she…did he…tell me she wasn't raped."

"No, she wasn't. We had some concerns when we saw the bruising on the inside of her thighs, along with her fingernails missing, it leads us to believe that was defending herself. As I said, there were no traces or any injuries to that specific part of her body. We did run some blood work, x-rays and labs. Were you aware that your wife is pregnant?"

"What?" Robert yells from across the room. "Are you fucking kidding me? She is pregnant and you let this happen to her. I'll fucking kill you!" Leaping onto a chair, he knocks it over, as he jumps towards me. I don't move, I'm frozen in place. Kayla and Paul come back just in time for Paul to help hold Robert back. Paul and Phillip are holding onto Robert's arms. He is yelling, spit flying from his mouth. He looks like a deranged, rabid animal.

"Do I need to call security?" The doctor is looking at us, as if we have all gone insane.

"No, I'm sorry. As you can see we all love her very much, and we are deeply worried. You said, 'is pregnant.' Is the baby okay?"

"We did an ultrasound and everything seems to be okay. We will keep a close eye on her and monitor any changes while she is here. The orthopedic surgeon and anesthesiologist are with her now. Once she is out of surgery, and we make sure everything is as comfortable as possible for her, we will take her to her room. I was informed that you already have her room number."

"I do. I wrote it down before they took her in the helicopter."

"Good. You may wait here, until she is settled. Anyone wishing to visit her, must be signed in. No one may stay overnight, with the exception of you, since you are her husband. As I said earlier, her body has been through a lot of trauma and she doesn't seem to want to wake up right now. She is breathing on her own, which is a good sign. Sometimes the body puts itself into a coma. It is her own way of healing. I can't guarantee you when she will wake up, but I do know it will be on her own terms."

"What do I do now?"

"You wait. That is all any of you can do. Once she's in her room, I will send a nurse to collect you." He shakes my hand and gives a nod of his head to everyone else. I watch, as he walks out of the room and down the hallway, disappearing from my view. I turn around to face everyone, now staring at me. I am sure they heard most of what he said, but I feel the urge to explain a little.

"Eve's knee is pretty fucked up. They are taking her back to surgery now. She has some broken ribs, a skull fracture, and lots of bruising." All I see are eyes staring back at me, waiting for me to tell them some kind of a miracle, but I can't. I am praying for one as well. "The baby is fine, but Eve is in a coma. The doctor told me that it's her way of healing, and she will wake up when she's ready."

Linda starts to softly sob, as Phillip embraces her in his arms. Kayla falls into a chair, burying her face in her hands. She is not sobbing, but I know that she's crying. Paul sits beside her, rubbing her back. I look back over at Robert. He looks as if he has seen death himself. He walks past me, as if I'm not even there. I slide down the wall next to me, bending my knees up to my chest, I sit on the floor. Now we wait.

Time slowly creeps by. No one has left the waiting room, besides to use the bathroom. I have no idea how long I have been sitting on the floor, but my legs are stretched out in front of me, completely numb. A nurse in pink scrubs walks into the room. My legs wobble, as I clumsily try to stand. "Mr. Davidson, if you'd like to follow me, I can take you to her now."

"Wait just a moment, please." I walk over to Linda, placing my hand on her shoulder. "I'm going to go see her now. Will you come with me? I can't do this alone." Her head lifts up with confusion and her eyes search me for something. I have nothing to offer her, but my fear of what I will find waiting for me in that room. She takes my hand and kisses her husband and son on the cheek, before stopping to pat Kayla's back. We head down the bright hallways, following the nurse.

We get to her room, and I push open the door. There are two nurses in blue scrubs moving machines, and propping Eve's knee up on pillows. Despite her outer appearance, she looks peaceful as she sleeps. Her face is different hues of purples and blues; some are mixed together, creating new colors. Her leg is in a cast type brace that is almost the entire length of her leg. A hand squeezes mine, and I turn my head to see Linda with tears sliding down her cheeks.

"What did they do to my baby? Why Theron? Why would anyone ever hurt her? She is so sweet and gentle. She'd never hurt a soul." Another sob escapes her and she places her hand over her mouth, trying to catch it as she walks over to Eve's bed. The nurse brings Linda a chair, and I help her into it. Brushing Eve's hair out of her face, she turns to look at me. "I know this isn't your fault. I don't care how you are connected to it. It is not your fault. I see the way you look at her, you love her. She needs you now, even more so with the baby on the way. She's going to be broken and sore, not just physically either. It's your job to put her back together, give her whatever she needs to survive this. Don't forget to love her. This is going to be hard, but you will have to be the one who holds everything together. Can I count on you to do that?"

"Yes, ma'am. I wouldn't have it any other way. I have loved her since I was fourteen. I have never stopped loving her, and I always will."

"Good. Let me sit with her just a few minutes longer, and then I'll leave you two be. I will let everyone else know that they can come back in the morning. Do you need anything?"

"No. I'll let Evan know to bring my things up."

Linda gently places a kiss on Eve's hand, just above her bandages. "How is Evan?"

"He's doing as well as expected."

"Give him my condolences, please. I know this must be a hard time for him."

"You knew?"

"Your gram came by the house with him. She wanted my permission to contact Evelyn, so she could explain some things. I watched them together. I could tell something was there, you could see it in the way he looked at her." I watch, as Linda checks over Eve with one hand, gently touching her bruises and arms. She wipes away her tears, while still holding Eve's hand, never letting it go. "I believe that I'm exhausted. I think I'll head home now. Call me immediately if anything changes, good or bad. I want to be the first to know."

"Yes, ma'am." She stands and briefly kisses me on the cheek. Then she leaves me alone with my sleeping beauty. I send Evan a text, letting him know that I need our luggage brought up. Making myself comfortable in the chair, I take her hand in mine and watch her as she sleeps.

It is not long before Evan comes into the room with the bags that I asked for. He doesn't say a word. He doesn't need to. Nothing he could say could make this any better, so he just stands beside me. After a few minutes, he squeezes my shoulder and then leaves me alone with Eve. I should never have left her alone. I wish I would have gotten to her sooner. I also wish that Anne hadn't shot Ben. I wanted to be the one to pull the trigger. A nurse comes into the room and records some stuff onto Eve's chart. I suddenly feel exhausted. I excuse myself into the bathroom and change my clothes. When I come out, the nurse is gone. She laid out a blanket and a pillow for me on the blue couch by the window. It takes me a couple of seconds before I figure out how to pull it out into a bed. It's not very big. In fact, I am too long for it. I try to make myself as comfortable as possible. Turning onto my side to face Eve, I lay quietly just listening to the beeps of the machine and her breathing. I don't know how long I lay there waiting for sleep to claim me, but eventually it does.

Nurses came in and out all throughout the night. Sleep seems pointless. Even without the constant stirring of people, I wouldn't be able to sleep. Worry and the feeling of helplessness is eating away at me. I give up around five in the morning, and get dressed. I have just finished brushing my teeth, when I hear a knock on the door. I step out of the bathroom, as a young doctor walks in.

"How is our patient this morning?"

"Asleep. She looks like hell, and she's still asleep." I don't mean to come off as an asshole, but it happens. I don't care how I'm perceived or about anything else around me, except for my girl.

"I know how frustrating this can be. She's healing and the rest is exactly what her body needs right now. I'm going to check the sutures on her leg. The swelling in her face has gone down immensely, which is a great improvement."

Anger seeps through me, as I watch him check her vitals and inspect her injuries. If I could get my hands on Anne…I would burn her alive. I would light the match and take joy in watching her body burn to ashes. I want to hear her scream, knowing that I am the cause of her pain. She deserves every second of torture at the mercy of my hands. I am pulled from my inhumane thoughts, when I see the doctor standing in front of me again. He looks like he is waiting for something.

"I'm sorry. I'm lost in my thoughts. Did you say something?"

"It's quite alright. Letting her rest and taking care of yourself in the meantime is exactly what she needs. The nurses will be back in for their rounds in a little while. Do you need anything or have any questions right now?"

"No."

The doctor leaves and once again, I am alone with Eve. I would give anything for her to wake up and just tell me that everything is okay. It seems as though I will just have to wait. I fix the sofa I was laying on, folding up the blanket and placing it in one of the drawers across from her bed. Pulling a chair next to her, I carefully take one of her hands in mine, and watch the clock at the seconds tick away.

For four days, I watch as the seconds, minutes, and hours inch by. Her family comes and goes. Kayla and Evan keep checking on me. I refuse to leave. I don't want her to wake up and be alone. Her mom stays with her a few times, while I shower or grab something to eat, but I always rush right back. She is laying so peacefully. Closing my eyes, I rest my head on her bed and pray for her to wake up. I am afraid of what I might do if she doesn't wake soon.

CHAPTER 19

THERON

There is a tap on the door and I jerk my head up. I must have dozed off again. It is just after ten. Evan walks in and hands me a coffee. I take a drink and shudder at the bitter taste. Eve would hate this coffee. She would have to drown it in creamer and sugar before she drank this crap. I haven't slept and all I have to rely on for caffeine is this horrible tasting sludge in my cup.

"I know. It's shit, but it is all they have on the floor. I figure I can get you something better later. I wanted to get here, so I can give you a heads up. Detectives Hallows and Markz called me. They wanted to approach me first, so I could get a read on you."

"What happened, Evan? I don't have any patience for bullshit or games." He leans against the counter across from me with his legs crossed and stretched out in front of him. His face isn't giving anything away.

"From what I understand, Anne had quite a lot to say the night they took her in. They want to make sure that you're stable before they come up here. They need to ask you some questions, and Hallows was insistent on it being today."

"Fucking cops. I get that they have a job to do, but shouldn't I get some kind of time to process all of this. Fuck, Evan. Look at her. They fucking broke her!" Running my hands through my hair, I stand and start pacing back and forth. Why does it have to be today? I look over at Eve. Anne needs to pay for what she has done.

"Whoa. You alright?"

I stop dead in my tracks and glare at Evan. "What?"

"What are you doing in your head, Theron? Your face twisted, you look dark. A dark man does dangerous things. I don't know what you are thinking or planning, but stop. She needs you right now. If you're behind bars, it won't do her any good."

"Set up a meeting with the detectives for later today. Linda and Phillip will be here after lunch. Try to set it up so that Eve is never alone."

"Will do." Evan turns to walk out, but I grab his arm.

"I mean it, Evan. She is never to be alone." He nods his head, as he walks out the door.

The rest of the morning slowly creeps by. The only sound is of her machines and her breathing. I watch her for a while. She is laying so perfectly still. This is all so surreal. At noon, one of the nurses brings me a can of pop. I didn't ask for anything, but I can tell that the nurses feel awful. Every time one of them comes to check on my Eve, their faces are full of pity. I stare back out at the lake through the window, watching the boats pass by. I bet Eve would like to sail. She always loved when the wind blew through her hair at the beach. Closing my eyes, I picture my beautiful angel the first time that I met her. I am pulled from my thoughts by voices outside of the door, and I stand from the window ledge that I am sitting on. Linda and Phillip walk in, whispers ceasing when they see her.

"Jesus Christ." This isn't the first time that Eve's dad has seen her since everything happened, but every time he comes here, his reaction is the same. All of the color drains from his face, as he walks around her bed. Linda doesn't say a word. She adjusts some lines and Eve's blankets, but never looks at Eve's face. I don't think that she can handle it.

"Theron, how was she during the night?"

I shrug my shoulders and drop my head. My voice is so tight it cracks, as the words leave my lips. "Nothing has changed."

"She's just resting. You'll see. My brave girl is stubborn and she is a fighter. We'll make it through this."

I swallow hard and nod my head, as Linda takes a seat in the chair beside the bed. Looking over to Phillip, my expression matches his. Lost, anger, heartache, desperation, hatred, and fear all play their parts on our faces. With her parents here, I decide that I could use a few minutes out of the room, even if it's just to gather my nerves.

"I'm going to step out for a minute. I won't be far. I'm just going to the family lounge to get some coffee."

"That's fine. We have her."

For some reason, Linda's words offer me so much comfort. They have her. I know she will be okay if I step away. As I walk down the white hallway to the family lounge, my phone buzzes in my pocket. "Theron."

"It's Evan. The detectives would like to see you. They swear that it's urgent. It's not my place, but I feel that they are withholding information."

"I'm not sure what they could withhold. Her parents are here now, so I'm getting a fresh cup of coffee. How long before they get here?"

"I'd give an ETA of about twenty minutes. Maybe less."

"That's fine. I'll be waiting." This is hell. I have been in hell for almost five days now. It feels like it has been so much longer than that. The family lounge is small. There is a microwave, mini refrigerator, chairs, coffee pot with paper cups, and a bathroom. I make myself a cup of coffee, as my brain tries to make sense of everything that has happened. I don't understand Ben's obsession with her. Was he like this before, or was it knowing how much I was worth that spurred his actions? My phone buzzes in my pocket and I almost spill my coffee trying to answer. "Theron."

"We're here."

"We?"

"Yeah, listen I have a really bad feeling. Something's off. I wasn't going to sit by and let you meet with them alone. I met them in the lobby. Where are you?"

"In the lounge on her floor. There's a visitor limit. How can you come up with them?"

"Cops don't count as visitors when there's an investigation going on."

"Right. Okay." I end the call and shove the phone back in my pocket. My stomach sinks, as I accept that fact that this isn't over, yet. Sitting in one of the chairs, I start bouncing my knees, as I stare at the door. I have to keep moving. I need to do something or I am going to lose my mind. Evan walks in, followed by both detectives. Standing, I shake their hands. "Detective Hallows. Detective Markz. Have a seat. That black shit behind you in the pot is supposed to be coffee, if you want a cup."

"Now with a sales pitch like that, I'd say that I'll have to pass. Though, I don't think we have anything better at the station. It all tastes like shit to me. I'm not really the sitting type, but I think Markz will have a seat." Hallows nods with his head towards a chair, and Markz finds himself a seat. All three of us stare at Evan, waiting to see if he is going to sit or stand. He slowly sits down in the chair to my right. Markz clears his throat and our heads turn in synchronization towards him.

"I know how bad this looks. I know how bad this is, but I want you to know that this case is our priority. Obviously, her coworker, Ben was a huge player in this, but we believe that he was just simply a piece in a game of chess. Anne had a lot to say the other night, but she got real quiet when her lawyer showed up."

"I bet. Any lawyer would advise their client not to talk." Evan says exactly what I am thinking.

Hallows turns around, making himself a cup of coffee. "I think what should interest you is who her lawyer was." I stare at his back, waiting for him to tell me. He turns back around and I stare him dead in the eye.

"Who?"

"Ronald Guzman."

"Mother fucker." Once again, Evan says exactly what I am thinking. Out of all the lawyers around, my dad's personal attorney shows up.

"God damn it!" I stand from my chair and kick the door as hard as I can. It slams shut. It only offers me a second of reprieve from the anger boiling inside of me. Hallows grabs my shoulder, but I shake him off. "I should have fucking known. At first I knew it was him, but at the board meeting he honestly looked surprised when I mentioned the notes."

"We couldn't figure that one out, either. It seems that Anne didn't even know about the notes." Hallows takes a sip of his coffee, looking over at Detective Markz before he continues. "She also didn't know about the hundred grand Thomas had transferred over to Ben that morning. It seems our man Ben was keeping secrets from everyone."

"Theron, I don't think this is over, yet. What does your dad have against you?"

A sharp laugh escapes me, as I look at Markz. "My life. He has hated me since the day I was born. He blames me for my mom's death, and would love to see me shatter. He wants nothing left of me, but a shell. I'll tell you something, he's already fucking done that. My life, my reason to breathe, and the reason my heart still beats in my chest is lying in a hospital bed, mangled by people she thought were her friends. They turned her over for money, as if she was nothing to them, just a paycheck. Well, fuck them! Fuck, Thomas! Fuck anyone who stands in my way! Unless you have him in cuffs or his feet are buried in buckets of cement sinking to the bottom of the lake, stay the fuck away from me."

"I get you're hurting right now. We all do. Don't do anything rash. Detective Hallows and I can only protect you legally from so much."

"Rash? Rash would be me waiting outside his house in the middle of the night. Then just as he falls asleep, I slip in through his window, startling him awake. I'd make him watch, as I carved his body with a sharp blade before I slit his throat. That detective would be rash. I'm not doing anything rash. No, I'm getting vengeance." Hallows grabs my shoulder again. I stare straight into his eyes, so that he can see exactly how capable I am of holding true to my words. He pulls in a breath and drops his hand. I don't turn around, as I turn the handle of the door. "Evan." It is all I have to say, he knows to follow me.

"Theron. Calm yourself down, man. If you go back to her like that, what kind of vibe will you give off? Eve needs you. I'll handle the detectives."

My stride never falters, as I continue to walk back to her room. Without stopping or looking back, I give Evan his direct orders. "I want to know every move Thomas makes. I want to know when he's sleeping, where he goes, and when he eats. I want to know if he sneezes or blinks an eye. Do I make myself clear?"

"Sir."

"Get on it." My hand touches the handle to her door, and instantly the current in my body changes from one of pure hatred to one of heartache. Walking into the room, I find Linda reading to Eve from one of the hospital magazines. Phillip is sitting in a chair with his hands in his face. They both look to me and I offer them a weak smile. There is no reason for me to mention the detectives or Thomas. They need to focus on her. I will handle the rest.

"She hasn't moved. Her heart rate has sped up a couple times. The nurses said she might be dreaming." Linda's voice is just a whisper, but it is so quiet in here that I can hear it clearly.

I gently place my hand on her shoulder, as I walk over to the window taking a seat on the ledge. "I know she needs her rest, but I want her to wake up. I'll settle for just one eye to open. Anything. I know you don't know me from Adam, but I love her. I can't breathe without her." I turn my head to look out the window, as a tear slides down my cheek. I need to be stronger than this, but I am breaking apart.

"Robert called. He will be here later and Kayla's coming with him." Linda's voice is soft and quiet. Her words are slow, as if to fill the emptiness in the air. I close my eyes, absorbing the warmth of the sun shining on the windowpane.

"I can't do this. I can't just sit here and wait for her to wake up. Linda, I need some air." Phillip stands, holding his hand out for his wife. She looks to me, worry written all over her face.

"Go with him. I won't leave her." She nods her head and walks out of the room holding her husband's hand. Once the door closes, I make myself as comfortable as possible in the chair beside her. I gently take her hand in mine, softly brushing her knuckles with my thumb. God, I love her. Holding her hand isn't enough. I need to be in her, I need to feel her and I can't. It is absolutely killing me. Turning my chair, I scoot it closer to her bed. I stretch out my legs under her bed, and lay my head by her waist on the mattress. Tears fall from my eyes, as I place soft kisses on her arm. I take her hand in mine again, and I cling to her hospital gown with my other hand.

"Fuck. Wake up, beautiful. Come back to me. I can't…I can't do this without you. I can't breathe. My lungs are suffocating. They are burning, baby. My heart is barely beating, I'm nothing without you. Beautiful, please wake up." Begging through the sobs that tear from my chest, I bury my face in the sheets, crying until my tears are replaced with hate. It calms me. It's an eerie feeling. Finally closing my eyes, I drift to sleep. Maybe she'll be in my dreams.

"So, we're just going to pretend that this isn't what it looks like?"

"Robert, shut up. That man hasn't slept. The nurses said when he does sleep; he calls out her name. She doesn't need your attitude and neither does he. If you can't behave yourself, you can go."

"Seriously, mom? He's clinging to her. You can't tell me he's not hurting her. Why is his arm under the sheet? I don't trust him…Oh."

"Now, don't you feel stupid, son. He's clinging onto both of them. That's how you're supposed to love someone. Now quit your bitching."

"Whatever, dad."

Someone is arguing and my arm suddenly feels a lot cooler. My vision is hazy. I let go of Eve's gown to wipe my eyes, it is hard to see with them being so dry and raw.

"Way to go, Robert. You woke him. Sorry, Theron. Robert is being an ass." I look over to the voice that is speaking to me, recognizing the curly blonde hair instantly.

"Kayla."

"Yeah. I'm sorry he woke you."

As I push myself up a little off the mattress, I realize where my other hand is laying. I softly move my fingers, rubbing her stomach. I remember needing to feel her before I fell asleep, but I guess I needed both of them. I make sure that her hair isn't in her face, smoothing it behind her ears. It's not. She hasn't moved besides the nurses changing her clothes and the sheets, but I do it anyways. I don't care who watches me look at her. She is mine. I would do anything for her. Someone clears their throat. I guess I am making them uncomfortable.

I sit back in the chair, looking up at Kayla.

"Time." My voice cracks, my throat is so dry.

"Just after six." She tosses me a bottle of water. I can see why she and Eve are so close. Kayla seems to be great at reading people. There is no need to fill the air with words. Subtle gestures seem to be her language. I take a sip of water. It is just what I needed.

"How long?"

"Oh, I don't know exactly. Mom and dad said you were sleeping when they came back in, so they went and got an early dinner. Robert and I just got here about twenty minutes ago. You were out cold."

Running my hands over my face, I glance at everyone around the room. "Sorry. I needed her."

Linda smiles and shakes her head at me. "In this family, we don't apologize for loving each other."

"Noted. Has Evan called or stopped by?"

"If you mean the angry sasquatch standing outside the door like a God damn guard, then yeah. He's here."

A nurse walks in to check on Eve, raising her eyebrow; she looks pointedly at all of us. "There's a limit of visitors on this floor."

"It's alright, Miss. It's their shift. It seems that I had fallen asleep. They were just drawing straws to see who would wake me."

"Who won?"

"Eve's brother."

"That was nice of him."

"I'm sure he was ecstatic. If you'll all excuse me, I need to meet with the Sasquatch in the hall." I give Kayla a wink.

"Go ahead, Theron. I got her."

With a nod of my head, I leave my Eve with her family. Evan is leaning against the wall next to the door. "Update."

Hearing my voice, Evan jumps. "He hasn't left his house. All of his vehicles are parked or stored. I did get confirmation of his exact location. He's been on the phone with someone in his study. It's not his regular phone. I'm sure it's either a loaner or a burner. Thomas looks as though he's waiting for something. I'm not sure what."

"If anyone comes or goes from that house, I want to be the first to know. Are the police aware that you have a visual on his location?"

"No. I'm here. My phones, computers, and tablets are all searching at home hospital care and sailboats, per your request."

"Good. Evan, I want you to be aware of the situation I'm putting you in."

"I am, Theron. I'm aware, on board, and I'd love to take over driving, but this is your call. You have more to lose than I do."

"I know." Fuck. I want to watch Thomas suffer before he dies. I need to find out what he is protecting, what he is holding onto, and I need to destroy it before he destroys what I have left.

Linda and Phillip leave a little after eight. They both look exhausted. I don't think Phillip has said more than a couple of sentences the whole time that he has been here. Robert follows them out. It is just Kayla and I now. She waits for the door to close, before she pulls a chair up, sitting down directly across from me. Leaning back in her chair, she raises her eyebrows at me, while twisting one of her curls.

"It's cool, Theron. I got time."

"Time?" What the fuck is she playing at?

"Don't be coy. I know you're hiding something. Evan wouldn't be here, if you didn't need him. I've been watching you two. He's not watching you, he's watching someone else, but he's reporting to you. Isn't he?"

Shit. Kayla is really, good at reading people. I let out a sigh, running my hands through my hair. "He's watching, Thomas."

"Okay. Why?"

"The police have evidence that suggests he paid Ben off. I'm not entirely surprised. It's just that the notes are making sense. Thomas is a lot of things, but he's a horrible actor. When I questioned him about the notes, the shock on his face was real. He didn't know about them. So, either he didn't know Ben was leaving notes, or he didn't know the extent of which Ben was taking things. None of it fucking matters, though. He can't hurt me anymore. I'm going to fucking destroy him."

"Shit. That's twisted, Theron. Eve told me that your dad hated you, but this isn't hate. I don't know what it is, but it isn't natural. This is worse than hate."

"I know."

"So, what's the plan?"

"There is no plan, at least not, yet. I've got eyes on him. He's up to something. He thinks he's going to be able to get to me, to make me come to him, but I can't figure out how. My mom is dead. My gram is dead. My poor beautiful girl is lying in a hospital bed because of him. I don't have anything left."

"Maybe it's not what you think."

"Maybe." No sooner do those words leave my lips, my phone rings with Evan's name lighting up the screen. "Theron."

"He's got a visitor."

"Who is it?"

"Ronald Guzman."

"Fuck. It's almost nine. Why would someone invite their attorney over so late?"

"Whatever it is, I don't see it being any good. They are both in the study now."

"Keep a visual on him. Let me know if either of them leave." Ending the call, I look over at Eve. She is sleeping so peacefully. I carefully bring her hand to my lips, softly kissing it, before I lay it back down on the mattress. She takes a deep breath and my heart skips in my chest. "That happened, right?"

Kayla rushes over to the other side of the bed and meets my stare. "It happened. I saw her. I heard her. That wasn't regular breathing that was a really deep breath." We watch her closely for a few minutes, but nothing happens. The nurse walks in and stares at us, as if we have both lost our minds. I am sure that we look really, crazy leaning over her bed, staring at her.

"She took a deep breath."

The nurse gives me a sympathetic smile, and continues to go about her job, as if I have said nothing of importance. Kayla and I just stare at each other. I know my beautiful girl, and I know that was something. Kayla sits with me for another twenty minutes or so, before she leaves. Maybe we did imagine it. I fix the couch into a bed again and lay down for the night, but not before making sure to charge my phone. I don't want to miss any updates on Thomas. My eyes close and I dream of vengeance. I dream of my hands closing around Thomas' throat, his body thrashing, while his fingers dig at my tight grip. I dream with a sweetly sick smile on my face.

Chapter 20

EVE

There is so much pain. White searing lights flash behind my closed eyes, burning and blinding me, even in my dreams. I try to raise my hands to block it, but I can't move. My head is throbbing, and my legs feel numb, except for the stabbing pain surrounding my knee. Voices float around me. I strain, as I try to grasp onto them. Am I still in the house? I faintly remember a loud sound, followed by Anne's scream. Someone else was yelling, there was a popping sound, and then it sounded like someone was coming up the stairs, followed by darkness and silence.

I could feel my body swaying. It felt like someone was pulling at me, but then my body went still. I can't move anything. My mind isn't cooperating. I want to feel something, anything. I try to move my fingers again, and pain soars through my veins. Hot, intense pain spreads over me. The light fades and it is dark again.

There is something about the lake that calms me. It is not just one particular thing. The sounds of seagulls, the cool breeze on my skin, the waves lapping at the sand, and the feel of the water rushing over my toes, sends me into a blissful state. I am sitting in the sand with my knees bent and pulled to my chest. My white skirt billows in the air. Trying to trap it, I wrap my arms around my knees. The cool water rushes over my toes. I feel at peace.

I am not sure how long I sit here, before my heart grows lonely. I miss him so much, but my body is stuck on this beach. A million thoughts bounce around in my head, but nothing makes sense. I need him. I need to hear his voice, and feel his breath on my skin. I am getting anxious. I worry what will happen if I don't leave this place soon. My desperation overcomes me, and I swear that I hear his voice.

His scent wraps around me, his voice rings in my thoughts. He is so close and I can't reach him. I am not sure if he even sees me. God, I just want to open my eyes. I need to know that he is okay. My heart is breaking at the thought of knowing that I could have lost everything. The pain is so intense, I think of dying, but I can't. I can't let go of him. My heart is pounding, as the darkness pulls me under once again.

The sun is warm on my skin. I revel in it, but then I remember him. Why can't I stay with him? Why can't I just focus? Everything is so cloudy and confusing. I imagine the feel of his lips on my skin; it feels so real. My skin is buzzing just from the thought of him. Taking a deep breath, I try to breathe him in. The current under my skin fades, and his scent drifts away. A sob wrecks my body, when I finally accept the fact that I can't reach him. At first, I thought this might be heaven, but it has to be hell. Anywhere without him is.

Turning my head, I notice someone walking towards me. Matt smiles, his teeth are so perfectly white. "Hey."

"Why can't I go back?"

"Do you want to?"

"Yes, I want to go back. I need him."

"Are you sure? It's going to be painful. You will hurt, Eve." Matt sits beside me and I lay my head on his shoulder.

"Thank you for coming to get me."

"Anytime. I love you."

"I know. I love you, too."

Oh. My. God. Someone needs to turn off that awful sound screeching in my ears. My eyelids flutter as I try to open them, but it seems pointless. Is that someone's alarm? I try to turn my head to follow it, but it hurts so bad to move. It stops. Thank fuck. Something clicks. A door, maybe?

"I'm sorry to wake you, but the doctors should be here shortly."

"It's fine. I set my alarm, so I was just getting up anyways."

"How was last night?"

"She's still asleep."

"I can see that. She will wake up when she's ready. Her body needs the rest."

"I know. I just need her."

Theron? He is here. Oh God, he is here. Someone else is here too, but I don't recognize the voice. My eyelids are so heavy. I try to open them. I want him to see me. Fuck this. I need to do something else. I stretch my fingers in my left hand. Shit, they hurt! I hear some more movement, but no one speaks. There is another click and I can only assume that I am alone again. My heart slams in my chest. I suddenly feel overwhelmed and very warm. They are leaving me. I can't be alone. Please, oh God, please don't leave me alone. I stretch the fingers in my right hand, and I feel material bunch under my fingers. It is soft and cool. I need to get their attention, obviously moving my body isn't going to work. Swallowing some of my spit, I try to wet my throat. I use my tongue to wet my lips, as I spread them apart. Taking a deep breath in, I mutter the first word that comes to mind.

"Theron." I wait. There is nothing, not one sound. Oh God, they did leave me. Something brushes against my hand, and I jerk away from it. Please don't let it be Ben, please don't let it be him. Bile rises in my throat, as I Imagine his face above me with his hands brushing over my skin. "No!" The scream rips from my throat, as I frantically try to move my body. Someone grasps my shoulders, holding me still. I am going to die, and Theron will never know how sorry I am. He will never know how much I love him. Tears slide down my face and I am able to open my eyes a little. White light seeps into my vision, as the dark clouds looming over me turn into shapes. I can make out the shape of a body leaning over me. Hearing a click, I release a bloodcurdling scream. I try to dig at the hands holding me down with my right arm, but it takes so much for me to move. I am easily pinned down.

"Jesus Christ! Help her. Fucking help her! What did you do? What did you give her?" It is Theron again. He is back. I turn to the shadow coming closer to me. Please, be Theron. Please, be Theron.

"Mr. Davidson, I didn't give her anything. I called for the other nurses. I have her, let her go. Calm yourself, you won't be any good to her if you are frantic like that."

Mr. Davidson? My dad is here? I could have sworn that I heard Theron.

"The doctor is coming. I promise he will be right here."

The pressure on my shoulders releases. I relax and drop my hand back down by my side. A doctor is coming and someone is talking to my dad. Where did Theron go? I know that he is here. "Theron." A shadow comes closer. I blink trying to focus my eyes. He runs his hands through his hair, but the one lock is stubborn and falls to his forehead. I love that lock of hair. I drink in the features of his face; his beard is rough around the edges. My man needs a trim. My eyes trace the shape of his lips and then his nose. Looking into his eyes, I find myself lost in a sea of colors. Each color pulling me a different direction. A tear runs down my cheek, as I blink again. Theron is right above me. His thumb catches my tear and he brings it to his lips, licking it away.

"Beautiful, I thought you would never wake up." He stares at me and I stare right back. I have never seen something so perfect in my life.

"You're here."

"Yeah, I'm here. I haven't left your side. I'm not going anywhere."

If Theron is here, where is Anne? Where is Ben? My heart races, tears pour down my face. I find his forearm with my hand, and I grab onto him. I cling to him. I need to know. "Ben?" My voice cracks, my broken pieces showing through, as I say his name.

"Gone, beautiful. I found you. I never stopped looking for you. He can't hurt you anymore. I promise."

"Anne?" More tears slide down my cheeks, as I recall my so-called friend, sitting beside me in that dirty bed, defending Ben.

"The police have her. You're safe. I have you." He gently wipes my tears away. I hear a click and I turn my head to locate the sound. That is when I notice that I'm in a hospital. There are wires on my chest and an IV in my left arm, with bandages on my fingers. Looking down, I notice that my leg is in a huge blue and black brace. No wonder I can't move.

"Evelyn. It's so great to see that you're awake. Your husband told me you have incredibly beautiful blue eyes. I can see that he wasn't lying. You've been through a lot in the past four days. You have some bruising on your face, back, and sides. You've suffered a broken and dislocated knee, three broken ribs, and an isolated skull fracture. Does anything hurt that I haven't mentioned?"

"Everything."

"I'm sure it does. I'm going to have the nurse come in and up your dosage of morphine. We are going to try to help you get better, so you can go home. Your husband has been by your side the entire time. That's quite a guy you have."

I furrow my brow, looking over at Theron. Since when do I have a husband? He winks at me when the doctor turns to write something down. So, now we are playing husband and wife? Excitement runs through me, as I picture myself dancing in a white dress with him. I wouldn't mind being his wife. I watch Theron's hand softly brush my stomach, and my heart sinks. I open my mouth to ask what my heart fears, and the only sounds is a broken breath.

"Eve? What's the matter, baby?"

Theron looks at me. He looks so worn and broken, it hurts knowing that I am the reason for it. I take another deep breath, puffing my cheeks out, as I release it. Looking down where his hand lays, and then back to his eyes, a tear slides down my cheek.

"Everything is fine. The baby is fine. I promise." The tension in my body eases at his words. Thank God. I am so happy that I didn't have to ask. He knew exactly what I was thinking. Theron softly kisses my forehead and looks back up to the doctor. "When can she come home with me?"

"We need to check her vision and some other things first. As long as everything is okay, I don't see why she shouldn't be able to go home tomorrow. She's not doing anything here, that she won't be able to do at home. She's going to need lots of rest, and will have to stay off of her leg for quite a while."

Theron beams at me. His smile is huge. I so badly want to be in his arms. The doctor walks out, leaving me to be with my 'husband'. I nervously bite my cheeks, as Theron grabs my hand, bringing it to his lips. "I've missed you."

"I needed you. I swear I could feel you, but I couldn't get to you. I needed you so badly." My voice cracks, as I start to cry.

"Beautiful, don't cry. I've got you now." He cups my face with his hand, and I turn into it, letting him catch my tears. My lips press against the soft skin of his palm. The comfort I get from knowing that he is here with me is immeasurable. My body soars from his touch and I know everything is going to be okay.

Time has moved so slowly the past couple of days, and it seems to rush around me, as it tries to catch up. Theron called my family and Kayla, as soon as the doctor left the room. I could hear my mom crying over the phone. I couldn't make out what my dad or Robert had said, but when Theron called Kayla I could hear her scream with excitement. By lunch, I had seen everyone, but Evan. My room was full of beautiful flowers. I kept asking Theron who they were from and he just shrugged. I know most of them must be from him.

It is a little after two and my mom is sitting in a chair beside my bed. Her, my dad and Robert are recalling stories from when I was little. They must be funny because Theron keeps booming with laughter. I smile, as I watch all three of them go back and forth, completely mortifying me with embarrassing stories. My eyes grow heavy. I look over at Theron and he catches my stare. He gives me a wink, and I smile back. I close my eyes, as my family surrounds me with love.

I'm not sure how long I have slept, but it must have been at least a few hours. I clear my throat and reach for the remote attached to my bed. I hit the button, and my bed moves, helping me to sit up.

"Hey, look who's up." Theron kisses my forehead and I turn my head to find Kayla and Robert sitting where my parents were.

"Mom?"

"They went to get something to eat. Kayla and Robert are here now. They will only allow you so many visitors."

"Oh." Why the limit on visitors? I am sure they have their reasons, but I want everyone to be here. My stomach rumbles. Theron must hear it because he smiles and pours me a glass of water. The sound of the water rushing into the glass suddenly makes me want to pee very badly. "Bathroom."

"I'll call the nurse. You could probably just let it go, though. You still have a catheter in."

Fuck my life. That needs to go. "Can you call her, please? I want to use the toilet."

"Sure, babe."

It is not long before the nurse comes in and removes it. It pinches, as she carefully pulls it out, but at the same time, I feel relief in knowing that I no longer need it. The nurse and Theron carefully help me into a wheelchair and then roll me into the bathroom. Theron keeps asking me if I am okay or if anything hurts. I keep shaking my head 'no' because I'm afraid that my words will betray me. By the time, they have me sitting on the toilet as comfortable as they can possibly manage, my body is covered in sweat. Relief floods through me, as I am able to use the bathroom. Who knew peeing could feel this good?

They help me back into the chair and then into the bed. My body is shaking and I hiss through my teeth, as they move me back onto the bed. Theron bumps my fingers, as he tries to gently lay my leg back down on the pillow they have propped under me. "Fuck!"

"I'm sorry. I'm so, so sorry."

I can't manage any words, as the pain spreads its way through my body, setting my nerves on fire, so I just nod my head. I know he didn't mean to, but my body fucking hurts. The nurse gives me another dose of morphine through my IV. The pain calms and I drift to sleep again.

I open my eyes and find the room lit dimly. The lights are glowing softly. Grasping the remote in my hands, I push the button, raising my bed so that I can sit up.

"Ssh." Following the voice, I see Evan sitting on a couch by the window. "Theron's asleep." I look beside me and see Theron reclined in a chair beside me. He looks so peaceful. "How are you feeling?"

"I hurt."

"Yeah. That's going to happen. He hasn't left your side." Evan nods to Theron and a soft smile plays on my lips.

"So, I've been told. Evan, how did they find me?"

"Who? The police?"

"Yeah. How did they know where I was?"

"They didn't. Theron made it my job to find you and I did."

"You found me?"

"I was just doing my job. He loves you, Eve. He'd walk through the hottest fires in hell to get to you. I've never seen fear like that before, and I have held soldiers in my arms, while they took their last breath. He needs you; he doesn't exist without you. I thought he was going to kill them when we found you, but he didn't get the chance."

"What happened?"

"It's not my place to tell you. You'll have to ask him." I look to Theron and he is still sound asleep. Evan doesn't say anything else. The nurses come to check on me, and someone brings me a warm bowl of soup. I finish with my dinner and look over at Evan. Theron is still fast asleep.

"Evan."

"Yeah."

"I'm sorry." I take a deep breath, causing my sides to pinch, as I try to hold back my sobs. "Everything, all of this, is my fault. If I would have just told someone sooner, if I wouldn't had hidden things. I'm so fucking sorry."

"Eve, no, this isn't your fault. You couldn't have known what they were doing."

"Does he hate me? Is he mad at me?"

"Do you really think he would be here if he did? That man loves you. Don't question it because of some wrongly placed guilt you feel."

"I just—"

"Stop." I glance at Theron and his face is twisted with anger. "Stop, right now. None of this is your fault. None of it. I have a list of people to blame and you are nowhere close to being on it."

"Can one of you please tell me what happened? How did you find me?" Neither one of them will look at me. "Evan?" He looks to the ground, avoiding my gaze. "Theron?" He doesn't answer. Silence fills the room; you could hear a pin drop. "Damn it. Somebody tell me!" Theron jumps at the sound of my voice.

"No. Not right now. That's my final word on the matter."

"Final word? What the hell, Theron? I deserve to know." Theron stands and starts pacing beside my bed. Raking his hands through his hair, he lets out a sigh.

"You do. I won't deny that, but I don't trust myself to tell you right now. I don't know if I can tell you and control my actions at the same time. Right now, I want to crush those people beneath my shoe. I want to skin them and hang their bodies out to dry in the hot sun. I want to take everything that they've ever had from them and destroy it. I want to torture them by breaking their minds, before I break their bodies. I don't know if I can hold back my anger. I just got you back. I'm not going to risk losing you because of my hastiness. Let me pull my thoughts together. When we get home, it's just us and you're wrapped in my arms in our huge soft bed, I'll tell you anything you want to know. Just not now. Please don't make me do it now."

"Okay."

"Okay?"

"Yeah. Okay." I lean my head back against the pillows, trying my best to keep tears from falling. Reclining in my bed, I close my eyes.

CHAPTER 21

EVE

Ouch! I stretch my arms out above me, trying to loosen my muscles. If he would just let me out of bed, besides to shower or use the bathroom, I would be able to stretch my muscles a little bit better. I have been laying in the bed for six days. I need to move. My sides are still a little sore, but it doesn't hurt to breath anymore. My leg still hurts, and I know that it is only going to be worse when I start putting weight on it. I have a follow up appointment with the orthopedic surgeon. Getting out of the house is going to be interesting. I can still remember Theron and me arguing, as he carried me up the stairs when they released me from the hospital.

He was so insistent on me sleeping in our bedroom. I thought it would have been easier downstairs in a spare bedroom, but he refused. For one thing, there wouldn't have been so many stairs involved, not that I was walking up them anytime soon, but he had to carry me up the stairs. Although, being cradled in his arms with my head laying on his chest, breathing in his intoxicating scent wasn't really a bad experience. Just thinking of his strong arms around me, has me closing my eyes and wishing that I could clench my legs together. That is another knot that I need worked out, and I am afraid that he is not going to touch me anytime soon. I know that he doesn't want to hurt me, but if he doesn't touch me soon, I may die.

I push myself up onto my elbows and wiggle my hips, scooting backwards until my back is flat against the headboard. Leaning over, I try to reach for the brush that is sitting on the table beside me, but my sides are still too sore. I hiss through my teeth, as Theron walks through the door. He rushes over to me, daggers shoot from his eyes right towards me. I can't avoid them either.

"Why do you insist on making me crazy?"

"I don't insist on anything. You do this to yourself. I can brush my hair, Theron."

He sits beside me and reaches for the brush. We sit in silence, as he brushes my hair. I can't take much more of his hovering. If it's not Theron jumping at my every movement, it is my nurse, Kelly. It's not like Kelly does much, Theron won't leave me alone. The poor girl just waits around. She has only brought me pain pills once or twice. Other than running me a bath, she just hangs around the house. I am tempted to tell Theron that I don't need her, but he is so on edge with everything. He is constantly jumping when other people walk into the room. I know that he is holding back on me, and I really wish that he would just tell me what is really going on. My frustration turns into anger, as I sit there with the brush sliding through my hair. I am not a weak person. I may have dealt with some crazy shit, but I am not weak. Is it because he doesn't want to burden me? Tears sting my eyes, as my emotions consume me. A few slide down my cheeks, and I hear him sigh. I quickly wipe them away because it is obvious that I am bothering him.

"Stop."

"Stop what?"

"This, Eve." Theron points to my head, as I cast my eyes downwards, looking at my hands fidgeting in my lap. I start chewing on my cheek to help with whatever this is. Anxiety? Nerves? Fear? I don't know what it is, but it's eating me. He lifts my chin with his fingers. I revel in his touch, as I look into his colorful eyes. "Whatever you have going on in here, just stop. Talk to me, don't keep it locked away."

"You're one to talk."

"What's that supposed to mean?"

"I've noticed how jumpy you are. I can see the weight of your thoughts on your shoulder. You're keeping things from me, yet you want me to talk to you. You talk first. Then I'll talk."

"I don't think we are ready for this conversation."

"Ready? Jesus Christ, Theron! I was fucking dragged out of my work, beat, tied to a bed, and left to lay in my own urine and vomit while I'm told, by someone who I thought was my friend, that I'm being held for ransom. Ready? Fuck you. All I want is for you to be honest with me. I died without you, Theron. My heart felt like it was ripped from my chest." Tears pour from my eyes, as I try to talk through my sobs. "I just wanted you and you weren't there. They were going to take me from you and I couldn't...I couldn't make them stop. I wanted to die, but I couldn't. I couldn't let go of you, and I couldn't let go of what we created together."

"Beautiful, I came for you."

Wiping my eyes, I look over at Theron. "You came for me?"

"Yeah. I knew something was off. When I opened the door to the store, I felt like I had died a thousand deaths. There were books and shelves everywhere. Then, when I saw the blood, I knew. I knew someone had taken you from me. I didn't wait for the police. I mean, I had Evan notify them, but I wasn't going to wait around for them. Evan was in the military for years. His specialty was finding and recovering objects, as well as people. I gave him orders and he followed them directly. He knew where you were before the police did."

"You came for me?"

"Baby, I'm trying to tell you. You wanted to know. So, this is me telling you what I know." He swallows and I just stare into a sea of colors. I knew he was close because I could feel it. It is like our souls recognize each other. He takes a deep breath and looks up at the ceiling. "Evan notified the police of your location. They warned me not to do anything rash, but I couldn't sit around waiting on them. So, your dad, Robert and I drove to where they were keeping you. It wasn't anything fancy or rundown. To be honest, the house looked normal. Nothing stood out, until I noticed the windows seemed to be covered or boarded up from the inside. Evan had his men surrounding the house. They went in for you and I followed. Ben came down the stairs first. He tried to run, but he didn't make it out of the house before he was restrained. Then Anne came downstairs. I just couldn't believe that she was there. Evan had told me, but it still fucking shocked me. She pulled a gun out and just when I thought she was going to shoot me, she shot Ben instead. I watched his body slump over on the floor, and jealousy ran through me. I knew I would never be able to hurt him like he hurt you. The police brought the paramedics with them."

"You don't have to keep going. Thank you for coming for me." I lay my hand on his leg to stop him. Tears are sliding down his cheeks. I don't want to be the reason for his pain.

"You need to know that Thomas was behind this."

"No, it was Ben and Anne."

"I know you saw them there, but Thomas paid them. The detectives followed his money trail and it led right to Ben's bank account. Then Thomas' personal attorney showed up for Anne. He's not done, yet. I don't know what his plans are, but I know that he's not done, yet."

Fear slices through me. Now I know why Theron is so jumpy. He is afraid that Thomas is watching us. I wouldn't doubt it if he was, but I have faith in Evan. Surely, he would know if Thomas was close. Theron grasps my chin once more in his hand and ever so softly, he kisses my forehead. I take a moment and breathe in his scent. The heat from his lips scorches my flesh. Goosebumps spread across my body, and I shiver.

"Cold?"

"No. I just need you."

"You have me."

"No, I need to feel you. This is the only time that you've actually touched me without having to help me out of bed or change my clothes. I need your touch, Theron. It's highly addicting. If you don't touch me soon, I'm going to crawl out of my skin."

"You need me that bad?"

"Always. I always need you." Light explodes in his eyes. His lips curve into a delicious smile.

"Beautiful, you have me. I'm keeping you. Do you think this is wise?"

"Theron, I don't care. I need you. For fuck's sake just touch me." My heart is pounding in my chest and my skin is burning for him. How does he not get what he is doing to me?

"I'll make you feel good, but you have to help me. I want you to scream my name, while I watch your skin glow from my touch. Can you do that, baby? Can you scream my name for me, while you come undone from my touch?"

"Yes. Fuck yes."

"Alright. Let me help you lay back. I got this." Theron gently lifts my body into his arms and lays me in the center of our bed. It has to be difficult to move me so carefully without hurting me, but he moves me, as if I am just a feather. I lay my head back on the mattress, my wild brown locks fanning out in every direction. He props my broken leg up with a pillow and gives me a wink. What is going on in his head? I watch, as he stands at the foot of our bed and slowly pulls his t-shirt over his head. His body is perfection. He slowly undoes the buttons on his jeans, slides them down and then kicks them to the side. My breath catches in my throat. He pauses, as he hooks his thumbs in the waistband of his boxer briefs. I can already see his hard cock through the straining fabric. He gives me another wink and then shakes his head.

"Theron. Please." I am not beneath begging. I know what he is capable of making my body feel. I am dying to get on that ride.

"Ssh. Let me take care of you." His hands drop from his sides, leaving his boxers in place. Disappointment fills me, but I am easily distracted, as he very carefully slides my panties down my legs. "Tell me if I hurt you. This will only work if you're honest with me. I don't want to push you too far."

"You won't." His lips softly kiss the tips of my toes and work their way up the inside of my right leg. My skin prickles and I can feel my body dripping for him. His fingers caress and dig into my thighs. My nerves are on fire. His nose skims my pubic bone, before planting soft kisses on my stomach. He is teasing me, taunting me. I am going to shatter. He grasps the hem of my t-shirt and rolls it up my chest, just below my neck.

"Don't move." I don't need to be told. It is not like I can just get up and walk away. My eyes are focused on his perfectly round ass, as he rummages through the closet. He turns around with a white rectangle shaped box in his hands. "I was going to give this to you before everything, but I couldn't keep my hands off of you long enough to actually grab it. There are seven speeds, but according to reviews, it goes from 'this is nice' to 'oh my fucking, God! Don't stop!' to 'unidentifiable sounds erupting from my body in heavenly tunes'. Which one should I start with?

My mouth goes dry. I can't answer, so I try swallowing a couple of times, but it doesn't help. He walks around the bed and sits beside me, with my new vibrator clasped tightly in his grip. My tongue tries to sweep across my lips to bring some kind of moisture to my mouth, instead my mouth forms an O shape, as Theron's hands find my nipples. He pulls and twists my nipples into hard peaks. My breaths are short and fast, as I watch his hands manipulate my body to his liking.

"Bend your right leg for me." I do exactly as I am ordered, and he scoots down towards the end of our bed and positions his body between my legs. "I'm too afraid to hurt you, but you say you need me. I can't say no to you, beautiful. You own me." My heart soars at his words. If he only knew that it was him that owned me. I hear the buzz of the vibrator before I feel it. Little fireworks explode, as he slowly slides my new toy in and out of my wet pussy. A soft moan leaves my throat and floats around the room. "This must be the 'this is nice' setting. That won't work for me, baby. I want you begging me to stop."

The vibrations increase and so does his speed. He's tilting it up, and my body shakes from the feeling. If I could close my legs, I would. I grab his wrist, trying to slow his movements, but all I earn is a smack to my clit. "Oh, my God!"

"I'm not God, baby, but I'll be your God if you let me." He is such a smartass and I love him for it. "You're so slick. Jesus, baby. I'm going to come just from watching you." He twists the vibrator, while thrusting it in and out of me, as his fingers massage my clit. Moans escape me, as that familiar feeling crawls up my body. I feel his mouth on me, sucking and lapping at my juices, while never stopping his hands. My body explodes and my eyes roll back and close. I feel like I am soaring. "Ohmigoddon'tstop!Fuck!Theron!" My words jumble together, as I scream out in ecstasy.

"Yeah, baby. Fucking let go. Let it all go. God damn, you're so fucking hot. Open your eyes, Eve."

My eyes pop open and another moan escapes me, as I take in the sight before me. Theron's hand is gripping his cock, pumping himself up and down. Fuck this is so incredibly hot. The muscles strain in his neck, the veins in his arm bulge, as he closes his eyes. "Open your eyes, Theron." His eyes open, dark with desire. "On me, baby. Let it all go on me." I turn his words back around at him, and the look in his eyes consumes me.

He kneels between my legs and I watch, as he clenches his jaw trying to hold himself back. "Fuck, Eve!" My name roars from his lips, as his release shoots across my stomach, marking me. I have never witnessed anything so incredibly hot in my life. If it wasn't for my leg, I would be straddling him right now.

Leaning back on his legs, he drops his head forward with his chin resting on his chest. "Fuck. You undo me, beautiful. Everything about you undoes me. Every wall I have ever built around myself, you have knocked down. Every barrier I have fought to put up, you have managed to cross it. You make me feel loved, but it's not just that. You make me feel deserving of your love. I'm such a better person when you're with me. I am keeping you and never letting you go. I can't, Eve." Theron raises his head. Tears fall from his eyes, and my heart explodes with love for him. "I can't breathe without you. I'll die if you ever leave me."

Words fail me, as tears slip from the corner of my eyes. "Babe—"

"Wait. Let me clean you up first." He carefully slides off the bed, heading towards the bathroom. He brings back a warm washcloth washing between my legs, before he wipes off my stomach. Climbing into bed, he lays back on the pillows and props up on his arm, as he gently lays his leg over the right side of my body. "Is this, okay?" I nod my head. Just the feel of his arms around me makes me feel safe. Everything was taken from me so easily and I don't want to ever experience anything like that again. The thought of him being left without me or me taking everything from him, crushes me. My tears turn into gut wrenching sobs, as I recall every detail I can remember of that day. He doesn't say anything. He just holds me, as I let go of all the pain that I have endured and held onto. I bury my face into him, as I break. This isn't the first time that I have broken in front of him and I doubt it will be the last. He is the only person that can rebuild me. He knows exactly where every piece fits. I lay there, draped in his arms, as I drift off to sleep. I am not worried about where my dreams will take me because I know that he has me.

I wake to the sounds of birds singing a sweet sound outside the balcony. As I stretch, I take notice of how loose my muscles are now. My shoulders feel lighter and I am not as tense. I guess my body needed Theron as much as my heart did. The curtains blow in the breeze, looking out the French doors, I see him sitting at the small table. His long legs are crossed, his feet propped up on the railing. I clear my throat and he turns to look at me.

"Good afternoon, beautiful. How was your nap?"

"Perfect." His smile is infectious. I feel myself grinning like an idiot, as I admire him from our bed. I don't know what he sees in me. Beautiful is far from how I would describe myself, but when he says it, I feel beautiful. I own it as if it is my name, and I wear it just for him.

"What shall we do today?"

"Am I allowed out, yet? My sides are just a tiny bit sore. My headaches are gone, and I can see perfectly."

"What about your leg?"

"People get broken legs all the time, Theron. I need out. I don't care where out is. In fact, just out of this room would be a great relief."

"Evan went to pick you up a chair. I thought today would be a nice day for a cookout. Are you up for company?"

"It's the middle of the week, don't people have plans?"

Pushing his chair back, he stands and walks towards me. I drag my bottom lip through my teeth, as I take in the sight of him. He gives me a gorgeous smile and kisses the top of my head. "Their plans are to come and see you. I have already set it all up. It's gorgeous outside and you could use some fresh air." I am lost in my own mind, as my eyes roam his body. He must have showered recently because he smells of soap and the cologne he always wears. "Eve?"

"Hmm?" Is he still going on about the cookout?

"If you keep looking at me like that, I'll have to take you again and as tempting as that may sound, I'm not sure you're ready for me just yet. I don't want to risk hurting you. When I do take you again, it will be hard and rough, and it will last all night. So, keep that lip out of your teeth and stop fucking me with your eyes, or I won't be responsible for my actions."

I swallow so hard it echoes in my ears. Fuck. He has such a way with words. My body shivers from the thoughts of what he could do to me. This man owns me. Theron walks away from me, my heart drops, thinking that I have done something wrong, but I shake away the feeling. I know that he loves me. He walks into our closet and comes back with a beautiful lilac colored dress in his arms. He lays it on the bed and steps back into the closet. The dress is lovely. It is a soft silk dress with thin braided spaghetti straps that crisscross in the back. There are silver flowers that start at the bottom and climb about half way up the dress before they stop. A silver ribbon wraps around the entire waist, meeting in the center with a tiny bow. It is beautiful. I am sliding the material through my fingers, when Theron comes out holding one silver sandal in his hand.

"This does belong to a pair, but since you can only wear one, I've left the other in the closet. I had these ordered just for you. Do you like them?"

"The dress or the sandals?"

"Both."

A smile spreads across my face, as I look at my man standing nervously in front of me. There is no chance of me not liking it. I would love anything that he gave me. "They're beautiful. What's the occasion?"

"Beautiful things for a beautiful girl." Gently laying the sandal next to the dress, he stands beside me. His eyes darken, as he runs his hands through my hair. Holding my face in his hands, he brushes my bottom lip with his thumbs. My eyes never leave his as he leans in, branding my lips with a kiss. He holds me still, as I open my mouth to him, letting him claim me. My hands fist in his hair, I hope that this fire between us never dwindles. He pulls back, leaving me breathless. "The occasion is that the love of my life was in a horrible accident, so I kept her locked away in an ivory tower for almost a week, and her family is going crazy because I'm not sharing her with the world. So today, I'm releasing my beautiful dove from her golden cage, so she can soar through the garden. Will that do?"

I blush at his words. "Yes, that will do."

"Good. I have some other things that I need to tend to. Kelly will be up here in a few minutes. She will help you shower and get ready. I'll see you soon." He kisses the top of my head and just like that, he is gone. I wonder if I would have fallen so quickly for him if none of this craziness ensued. Would I still have loved him if Matt was here? I dismiss the thought immediately, of course I would love him. I was born to love him. Kelly knocks on the door, pulling me from my thoughts and helping me into the shower. I can't wait to get out of this room.

Chapter 22

EVE

I am sitting in front of the vanity, softly running my fingers through the curls that I just finished putting in my hair. Sliding a silver bobby pin with three white pearls on it into my hair, I pin back the left side, just behind my ear. I spray a little bit more hair spray and gently move my head back and forth, making sure that the curls pinned back are secure. With a touch of lip gloss, I am ready. After I adjust the straps on my dress, I call for Kelly. She helps me stand with my crutches and walk back into the bedroom.

Theron is standing by our bed waiting for me. He looks so incredibly handsome in his dark gray suit. The purple tie not only matches my dress, but also makes his eyes pop. I am not sure what kind of cookout we are having, but I doubt that there will be hotdogs or burgers on the grill. Taking in the sight of him, I catch my breath.

He reaches out for me and I gladly take hold of him, as he wraps his arms around my waist. I lean into him and he carefully picks me up in his arms. He refuses to let me walk anywhere. Not that I am complaining, just stating a fact. I like being wrapped up in his arms. It is where I feel the safest.

"Are you alright?"

"Yeah. I just wasn't expecting to see you like this."

"I wanted to surprise you. Are you ready?"

"Yes." I hoped that my answer sounded convincing.

"Stop chewing on your cheek. You'll like this. I promise." I must really be nervous. I didn't even realize that I was doing it. He promises that I will like my surprise and I don't doubt him. Laying my head against his chest, I take a deep breath, letting his scent wrap around me, as he carries me out of the bedroom. I truly love this man. As we reach the bottom of the stairs, the faint sound of music fills my ears. It is a beautiful melody. I think I have heard it before, but since there are no words, I can't be sure.

Kelly and Evan are waiting for us with a wheelchair. I hate using my crutches, so the chair comes as a relief. Theron gently sets me down in the chair and pushes me through the house and out into the garden. I can hear Kayla's laugh before I see her. I am pushed along the stone pathways and finally we come to a clearing. Kayla and Paul are sitting at a beautiful stone patio table. My brother and dad are standing by a small fountain, talking amongst themselves. I look for my mom, but I don't see her. Then I hear a violin. I knew that I knew that song. My mom used to play it for us on her violin when we were little. It is soft and sweet. Kayla waves to me, as Theron pushes me past everyone to the front of a cedar gazebo. Ivy winds its way up the pillars and around the lattice roof. I feel as if I have been transported into *The Secret Garden.* My mom stands in the center of the gazebo, playing her violin next to a metal chair. Theron lifts me from my wheelchair and carefully sets me in the chair. Tears brim my eyes and he hasn't even said a word. My heart hammers in my chest with love for him.

He stands in front of me and nervously wipes his hands on his pants, before he kneels down on one knee in front of me. "Beautiful, I have loved you since the first time that I saw you on the beach. You looked like an angel and I knew right then that you would be the one to save me. I built a wall of stone around my heart. I built it strong, so nothing could ever break it down, but I wasn't expecting you. No wall or force would ever be strong enough to keep me from loving you. You're the reason that I breathe, the reason that my heart beats in my chest. I'd rather die than live without you. You have my heart and my love. It will never be enough because you deserve so much more, but I want to spend the rest of my life proving my love for you always. I want to wake up with you beside me every morning for the rest of my life." Tears fall down my cheeks, as I smile at this beautiful man in front of me. "Evelyn Davidson, can I keep you?"

Theron pulls a small box from his pocket. As he opens it, my eyes fall on the most beautiful ring that I have ever seen. Its silver band twists with diamonds, it almost looks as if it is braided. In the center of the band is a beautiful round diamond. He holds it up for me and the sun hits it. Little lights flicker and bounce around the gazeebo. I am in awe of this magical moment. I swallow, trying to calm my nerves.

Finding my voice, I look deep into his colorful eyes. "You're wrong. I don't deserve more than your love, it's you who deserves more than what I can offer." A look of worry flashes across Theron's face. I take a breath and finish my thoughts before he can worry any further. "But, I promise to prove my love to you every single moment for the rest of my life. Yes, you can keep me. I love you." I have never seen a happier person in my life than Theron at this very moment. A huge grin is plastered to his face, and I don't believe that it is ever going to fade. His eyes glisten with tears, as he slides the ring onto my left hand. He lifts me, cradling me against his chest, as he leans down and softly kisses my lips. The salt from our tears mingle with our tongues, bringing a new sense of our love for each other to our kiss.

Applause and laughter brings me back down from the cloud that I am floating on. I was not expecting this when I woke up this morning. It was the best surprise that I have ever had.

"Hey you two, get a room!" I look to see Kayla smiling back at me. She is laughing, while jumping up and down, her blonde curls bouncing all over the place. "I can't believe we are both getting married! This is going to be so much fun planning our weddings together." I roll my eyes and look up at Theron. Chuckling he sets me back down in my wheelchair.

"Are you ready for your lunch now, beautiful?"

"God, yes. I'm starving."

He pushes me back towards the patio table where Paul is still sitting. My dad gives me a wink, as he turns the steaks on the grill. Everyone gathers at the table and my mom pours us all a glass of lemonade. My perm-a-grin isn't fading and I don't think it will for a long time. The afternoon flies by with my family telling more stories of my childhood, most of them at my expense. I laugh along at the jokes Paul tells and my eyes keep glancing back towards, Theron. His smile is just as big as mine, if not bigger. The only one who seems put off by this situation is Robert. Hopefully, he gets over whatever it is that is bothering him soon, otherwise things are going to get awkward.

As the afternoon turns to evening, our guests slowly leave. Eventually it is just me, Theron, and Robert sitting outside. I yawn and Theron jumps to his feet.

"Are you falling asleep on us, beautiful? Would you like to go upstairs and take a nap?"

"That sounds lovely. Could you go upstairs and fix my bed for me?"

"I'll just ask Kelly."

I would really like some alone time with Robert before he leaves, so I bend the truth just a little. "You could, but you do it so much better. She never gets my pillows right."

"That won't do at all. I guess that I should go fluff the queen's pillows. It was nice seeing you again, Robert."

Robert nods his head at Theron. I wait a few minutes before I say anything. I want to make sure that Theron can't hear us. "Okay, spill it."

"What?"

"Don't what me, Robert. I know you and I know something is bothering you. So spill."

"I just don't see how any of this is you. You've always been so down to earth and calculated. Here you are pregnant and engaged to some guy that you've barely known for a couple of months. Don't you think that it is too soon? I know that he was engaged before. What makes you think that you are any different?"

"For starters, he loves me and I don't doubt him for a second. I feel alive when I'm with him. If I have learned anything in the past couple of months, it's how quickly you can lose someone you love. I'm not going to risk losing him because of something as frivolous as the amount of time I've known him. Maybe you can't understand it, but you don't need to. You need to accept it and I need you to support me. I love him, Robert. There is nothing that will ever change that. We could be poor and homeless living on the streets and I would still stay by his side. He calms me. He keeps me from over thinking things and staying in my head. My lungs don't burn from trying to breathe when he's with me. I need him like flowers need water and sunlight. I need him like you need air to breathe. He is my life now. Learn to accept it, or you are going to end up putting a rift between us. I don't want that." My voice quivers and a few tears escape from my eyes.

"Shit, Eve. Don't cry. I didn't mean to make you cry, kid. If you love the bastard, then fine. I will love him too, just stop with the crying."

"Really?"

"Yeah, really. Come on, let's get you inside. I hate all this mushy bullshit."

Once again, a huge grin appears on my face, but this time it is because my brother has gone soft on me.

"Get rid of that stupid ass smile, too. You'll never hear me admit I like him again, got it? You leave this mushy conversation between us. I don't want anyone else to know that I'm a softy."

"I love you."

"See? That's what I mean. Now you are just going to expect me to admit my feelings all the time. It's not happening, Eve. Do you hear me? It's not happening."

I laugh, as Robert pushes me back into the house.

"Something funny?" Theron steps down off the last stair in the foyer and lifts me into his arms once again.

"Nothing you'd understand."

"I'm okay with whatever it is. I'm just glad that you're laughing again."

"If it makes you feel any better, trust me when I tell you that she's laughing at my expense. I have to go, kid. I'll see you later."

I wave at Robert and yell, "I love you!" as he walks out the door. I am rewarded with his middle finger, but I know what he means.

"Do I want to know?"

"Nope."

"Didn't think so. Let's get you into bed."

Theron lays me on our soft bed, positioning a pillow under my leg before sitting beside me.

"I meant everything that I said."

"I know." I lean back against the pillows and my hands naturally rest on my stomach. He places his hands on mine and leans down to gently place a kiss above our hands.

"Your mommy said I can keep her. I'm keeping you, too. I'll love you both until I breathe my last breath."

Theron looks up at me, his eyes are filled with love, but I see that hint of mischief. "What are you planning?"

"Who says that I'm planning on doing anything?"

"I do. I know that look in your eyes."

"Oh?" He moves, placing his body between my legs, bending my right knee with his hand. My body clenches from the possibilities that await me. "Maybe I plan on making my beautiful girl scream. Do you want to scream, baby?"

Fuck. Electricity snaps in the air, goosebumps spread across my skin at just the sound of his words. "Yes."

"Hmm. I don't think I believe you." He gently pulls my panties down my legs, being extra careful with my left one. Picking up my right foot, he begins placing kisses, as he crawls back up my leg. A moan escapes me, as he slides his fingers into my pussy. He doesn't need to check because I know I'm more than ready for him. I watch, as he sucks his fingers into his mouth, licking off my wetness. Fuck, that is hot. My eyes are hooded, as he spreads me open with his fingers. His tongue licks me back to front, as if I am a lollipop. Sucking my clit into his mouth, I feel his teeth graze me.

"Ahh."

"Now, that I believe. I'm going to make you scream until you come all over my face."

"Fuck!" His words hit me, and my skin ignites. I am desperate for him. He thrusts two fingers into my pussy, my walls clench around his fingers. A scream leaves my throat, as he curls his fingers up, hitting my wall. "Oh my, fucking God!"

I come apart, as his fingers relentlessly stroke me to orgasmic bliss. I am floating on my high, when I slowly start to recognize him saying my name. "There she is."

"Hmmm?"

He shakes his head with a laugh and that lock of hair falls to his forehead. He looks so incredibly sexy. I rake my bottom lip through my teeth, as I undress him with my eyes. He has on way too many clothes.

"Theron. Take off your clothes. I want to see you." A devilish grin slides across his face. He stands, kicking his shoes off to the side, and then drops his pants to the floor. Sliding his jacket off his shoulders, he starts unbuttoning his shirt. My breath hitches when his shirt falls open. I take in every detail of his body. His hair falling around his eyes, his perfectly trimmed beard, his strong shoulders, his perfectly taught abs, and then I let my eyes linger over the design of his tattoo before I finally lock eyes with him again. He is so incredibly handsome, and he's all mine.

"Now what?"

"Come here, so I can taste you. I want you to straddle me and place your cock at my lips. I want to hear you scream my name."

"Holy shit."

He carefully climbs over me and straddles my waist resting his weight on his knees. Leaning down he presses his forehead to mine. "You fucking amaze me."

"I try." I softly press my lips to his. His tongue sweeps across, asking for permission. I open to him and tongues crash in a fire of pure sex. I fist my hands into his hair, my fingernails scraping his scalp. He moans into my mouth and I know that I have him right where I want him. He pulls back, his eyes already hooded. "Scoot closer, babe."

He scoots up with his knees next to my breasts just under my arms. His hard cock is staring me straight in the face. I lick my lips in anticipation, before taking him into my mouth. His hands twist in my hair and he lets out a soft moan. I swirl my tongue around him, as he pumps in and out of my mouth. He tastes so incredibly good. Moaning, I pull my lips back just a bit letting my teeth barely scrape him.

"Fuck, Eve." His fingers tighten in my hair, pulling my head back, and opening my throat to him. He slams into the back of my throat. My eyes water, but I love what I am doing to him. He is losing control. I grip onto his thighs and my nails dig into his skin, as I take him into my mouth. I hollow my cheeks, and continue to swirl my tongue, making sure to pay special attention to the tip every chance that I get. I can feel his legs tighten in my grip. "Fuck, baby. Shit. Just like that." I swallow, preparing myself for his release. His cock hits the back of my throat, as he screams. "Fuck. Eve!" His salty warm release shoots down my throat, I gag a little and he pulls back enough, so that I can swallow. He is breathing heavy and his fingers go loose in my hair. I love the immense power I feel, knowing that I am the one who does this to him. He leans back onto his legs, rolls off me, and lays next to me, resting his head on my right shoulder.

"Amazing. Absolutely, fucking amazing."

"Thank you."

"I love you, Eve."

"I know." Grasping my face in his hands, he gently places a kiss on my forehead and then one on the tip of my nose. I stare into his bright eyes, butterflies flutter in my stomach. "I love you, too."

"Can I still keep you?"

"Forever." Theron gives me a sweet smile, before laying his head back down on my shoulder. My fingers play in his hair and soon we are both drifting off to sleep.

CHAPTER 23

EVE

The rest of the week flies by and we spend most of the weekend in bed, wrapped in each other's arms. Sunday comes and I can't shake this nervous feeling that I have. I told Theron about it, but he said that it is just my nerves, since my appointment is tomorrow. I am hoping that they give me a walking cast, so that I can start moving around more. Although, I doubt that will happen. Theron really seems to enjoy carrying me everywhere. I have mainly been wearing dresses and skirts, since wearing pants is completely out of the question. I am digging through the rest of the clothes that my mom has collected for me and brought over. I find a beautiful long white skirt with small green flowers on it. It is definitely one of my favorite skirts. I have had it for years. I tend to wear it to the beach a lot or whenever I want to pull off a hippie look.

I pull on a white tank top with lacing along the hem. I plan on lounging, so why not be comfortable? Kelly helps me slip into my skirt. Standing, I hold onto my crutches, as Kelly zips up the side of my skirt. The material pulls and I can tell that it is tight before she even gets close to finishing with the zipper. Fuck my life.

"Kelly, can you just get Theron for me?"

"What about the skirt, sweetie?"

"Just forget it. I'm going to hibernate in my bed all day and gorge on chocolates."

"Alright." She helps me back out of the skirt and back onto the bed. She leaves to get Theron, and I lay back against my pillows.

"What's with the sad face?"

"I'm fat."

"What? Where is this coming from?"

"I tried to wear my favorite skirt and Kelly couldn't get it to zip up. I can't go anywhere or do anything. I sit around all the time or you carry me. Now I'm fat."

"Beautiful, you are not fat. You're pregnant."

"Who the hell starts showing this early?"

"It's not really that early. You're probably around twelve weeks now. When's your next appointment?"

Shit. When is my next appointment? I grab my phone from the table beside me and open my calendar. "Friday at ten."

"Didn't she say come back in four weeks? So, it really isn't that early. Besides, I can hardly tell."

"That's because it's not from the baby. It's fat."

"Pregnant?"

"Fine. Pregnant and fat."

"No. Pregnant and absolutely beautiful."

"Whatever. I'm not leaving this bed." Theron raises his eyebrows and I try my best to ignore his smugness.

"What if I promised you a day in the library, with a picnic lunch in the garden?"

"The library?"

"And now, I have your attention. Baby, pick a dress and I'll help you into it. Then we can spend the day in the library."

"Fine."

"Fine." He stands from our bed and walks over to the closet. He slips inside and comes back holding a plain light blue cotton summer dress in his hands. It is simple and looks incredibly comfortable, perfect for lounging around in. Sitting up, I raise my arms, as Theron slips the dress over my head. Handing me my crutches, he helps me to stand. I put most of my weight on my right foot and relax my shoulders. Standing is a lot easier than walking. The dress falls down my waist and ends mid-thigh. It is tight around my chest, but still loose around my middle. Theron runs his hands down the sides of my waist, and then places them just below my belly button. I can feel his hands rub my stomach, and I look down, noticing just the slightest bump to my stomach. Great. It starts.

"I like the way you look."

"Will you like the way I look when I'm huge and you can't put your arms around me anymore?"

"I will always like the way you look. You're beautiful. I don't call you that just for fun, I mean it every time that I say it. Come to the library with me, and relax a little. Tomorrow, we'll see the doctor and find out if you can get a different cast. Let me carry you around one last day."

"Like you still won't try to carry me."

"You're right, I probably will. So, what's stopping you today?" A smile plays on my lips, as I process his words. Who am I kidding? I would never say no to a day in the library.

"Okay."

"Yeah?" I nod my head, and just like that, I am cradled in his arms once again. He tries to carry me into the library, but I argue with him, so when we reach the bottom of the stairs he sets me in my wheelchair. "You are incredibly stubborn."

"You should remember that." He shakes his head at me, before grabbing the handle to my chair and pushing me into my favorite room of the house. To be honest, it is my favorite room ever.

I am sitting in one of the leather chairs by the windows and my foot is propped up on a small ottoman that Theron has pushed over for me. This is literary heaven. The way the books feel in my hands, the power of the thin pages, and the smell of the words pouring through the room is absolutely, sinful. I have had a hard time picking just one book, we are only in here for a short while, but I have already had Theron create me a pile of books. He comes across a few books that I know Olivia would love, so I have him make a pile for her as well. We can drop them off after my appointment tomorrow.

My thoughts stray to the bookstore. I imagine Olivia is in the back stocking shelves, as the front of the store somehow manages to operate on its own. Smiling, I think of the first time that I entered that bookstore. Poor Harold was trying to talk Olivia down a ladder. She had climbed higher than she realized and was frozen, refusing to come down. When I walked in, he asked me to call the fire department. I couldn't figure out why anyone would need help getting down off of a ladder. I asked him if he had any more ladders. He ran from the room, leaving me with a strange woman, clinging to the shelves above me for dear life. Harold placed the ladder in front of me and I climbed up until I was face to face with Olivia. She had tears in her eyes, but I told her not to cry because the books would have to suffer water damage. She laughed and we climbed back down the ladders together. Olivia never took her eyes off me until we got back down to the floor. I fell in love with the store and its owners that day.

I picture the store in my mind, seeing everything in detail. I close my eyes, reminiscing in my time spent there, when suddenly I notice something on the hard wood floors. Bending down to take a closer look, I notice that it is someone's fingernails sticking out of a crack. My heart slams in my chest and I am frozen to the spot. My arms and legs feel heavy and my head lolls around on my shoulders, as someone screams above me. Their words cut through me like swords made of ice, chilling me to the core. I try to move my legs, but something is forcing me to stay in place. Hot searing pain scorches my skin, I scream as Benjamin walks into the room, laughing at my plight. Someone else screams my name, but I refuse to open my eyes. I can't. I can't do this again. I won't make it. I know that this time I will die.

Something cold and wet drips down my face. I blink, as the water runs over my eyes. Looking up, I realize that I am still in the library. Theron is kneeling in front of me, gripping the arms of my chair and his face is pale, as if he has seen a ghost.

"I…I wasn't here. Ben…Benjamin." My voice falters, as sobs escape me in a guttural plea for help.

"Ssh. It's okay. You're with me now. He can't ever get to you again, baby." Theron places his palms on the sides of my face, wiping my tears away with his thumb. Confusion consumes my mind. I don't understand. It seemed so real.

"Was I dreaming? Did I fall asleep?"

"No. You were reading, but you just seemed to space out on me. I kept calling your name and waving my hands in front of you, but you couldn't see me. You looked right through me then you started screaming. I didn't know what to do. I yelled for help, I didn't know what to do." His voice shakes, as the fog lifts from my mind. Oh my God, I completely freaked out on him. Holy shit. Taking deep breaths, I try to calm my nerves, but the tremors in my hands won't stop. Before I realize it, I am shaking all over. My skin feels hot and clammy. I am going to be sick, my stomach wretches, as I quickly cover my mouth with my hand. Theron rushes across the room and comes back with a small trash bin.

I am not going to be sick. I am not going to be sick. I am not going to be sick. I desperately try to breathe in through my nose and out my mouth, while repeating that mantra in my head, but it fails me. My sweet man is holding my hair back, as I sit in a chair throwing up all the contents of my stomach into a small bin. I gain my composure. I wipe my forehead and realize that it is wet. I look down at my hand, noticing the water droplets on my fingertips.

"I didn't know what to do. I threw my glass of water on you, and it worked." He shrugs his shoulders, as if there is no better reason for what is taking place right now. Voiceless, I nod my head. Bed. I just want to go to bed, curl up in the softness of my covers and pretend my little melt down never happened. Jesus Christ. I am a complete mess. I am broken. My eyes cast downward from embarrassment, how could he even want to be with someone as fucked up as me? "I think we need to give the books a rest for a bit. Bed or garden?" As hopeful as his voice sounds when he says garden, I know that I won't be going out there today.

My eyes never look up. I keep my head down with my eyes cast to the side. "Bed, please."

"Beautiful, talk to me. What happened?"

"Don't. Just take me to bed, please."

Theron lifts me into his arms, I try to take comfort in his touch, but something is still off. It is as if I know something is wrong. I lay my head on his chest, he tries to set me in my chair, but I shake my head 'no' at him. If he lets go, any sense of reality I have is going to come crashing down around me.

"Oh, beautiful." His words are soft like silk wrapping around me, saving me from myself. His heartbeat thrums in my ear, as he carries me up the stairs to our bedroom. He doesn't speak, but he places several kisses on the top of my head, before he sets me on our bed. He pulls the duvet over me and I twist my hips as best as I can, so I can comfortably lay with the side of my face resting on my pillows. I don't know how long he sits at the end of the bed before I fall asleep, but I know that it's quite a while. Every time that my eyes start to close, I jerk myself awake from fear of what I might find in my dreams.

Warm enticing smells pull me from my slumber. The sunlight peaking in through the balcony window is soft and subtle. I search for him with my eyes, my heart sinks when I realize that I am alone. Next to me, I find a bowl of chicken soup and a piece of freshly baked bread. I prop myself up onto my pillows, then eagerly reach for the piece of bread, bringing its deliciousness to my lips. I smell it before I take more than an ample size bite.

"So, she smells bread as well. It's not just books."

A shy smile graces my lips, but quickly fades. Looking up at him through my lashes, I give him the best apology I can offer. "I'm sorry. I don't know what happened. One minute, I was thinking about the bookstore, and the next minute I was back in that room with Ben. It was so real."

"Don't apologize for that. Ever. If I had it my way, I would have tortured him for years before letting him finally die, but only after he begged for relief. Don't. Ever. Apologize for what that fucking lunatic did. We clear?"

He doesn't want me to apologize, but I definitely feel like I am in trouble now. How am I going to move past this without hurting Theron or dragging him along with me? He has had enough pain in his life. I don't need to add more.

"Stop. I know that you're in that head of yours. Whatever you're thinking, whatever excuse you are trying to concoct to make yourself believe you're responsible...it stops now. I told you that I'm keeping you. That means all of you. Every beautiful inch of light and every fucked up shadow that follows you. You can't hide from me, Eve. I've lived with guilt and blamed myself for years for situations that were way beyond my control. The weight almost drowned me, until you came along. You reached out into my dark abyss and pulled me out. All I could see was a beautiful angel coming to save me and I followed you out. I'm not going to let you drown. My shadows still loom around me, but when you're near, they dissipate from the pure light of your touch. It's my turn to pull you from the shadows. Don't hide from me. Don't apologize for things that you can't control. Just let me love you. Let me take care of you. Let me carry you when you're too weak to go on by yourself. I love you." He leans down, taking my face in his hands and kisses away my tears. The dam around my heart bursts open, as my pain from the last couple of months explodes around me. He doesn't ask any questions instead he just holds me. I cling to him, as if he is my life raft in a sea of turbulent waves crashing down around us. There aren't any words to describe the way that I feel, as he saves me from the dark abyss. His word, his touch, his love, wraps me in a cocoon of security. I know anything we face together we will be able to conquer.

He sits with me the rest of the night, as we talk about random things. The conversation is light over dinner, neither one of us bringing up the shadows hiding in the corners. Instead, we relish in each other's company. As he crawled into bed with me that night, everything finally felt safe. I embraced his hold around my body, his fingers circling my belly, even after he drifted to sleep. My heart soars with love for this man. I close my eyes and eagerly greet my dreams because tonight I know the sooner I get to sleep the sooner I will wake up in his arms again.

Chapter 24

EVE

"Are you sure?"

"I'm telling you, we have him located and he hasn't moved. Something's not right."

"Fuck. I have to take her to the doctor's today. I want you to follow, even if you need to locate another vehicle. I don't want him to recognize you."

"I understand, Sir."

I close my eyes, as I hear our bedroom door push open. I can hear Theron's footsteps. An uneasy feeling comes over me, as I recall their conversation. I am sure they both thought that I was asleep, but I am restless. "Who is Evan watching?"

"What?" Theron stops, his back turned to me. His shoulders tense and it is at that moment that I am sure of who it is.

"It's Thomas, isn't it? We haven't heard anything else from him. The detectives are still searching through his accounts, right? So, if he knows the cops are watching him, why would he try something else?"

"Thomas is relentless. He isn't deterred easily. In fact, it becomes more of a game to him. We have now become a game in his eyes. He will do anything to make sure that he comes out the winner."

"But he's a smart man, surely—"

"I never said he was a smart man, I said he was dangerous. He's deadly, Eve. I don't want you anywhere near him. So, today while we are out, Evan will be close behind."

I don't say anything else, even if I did, I'm not sure it would make any difference. After everything that has happened, I'd prefer Evan to be close by. I actually find it kind of comforting. Kelly and Theron help me with my shower and get me ready for my appointment. I still can't shake the awful feeling that I had yesterday, I chalk it up to nerves.

Everything went well at my appointment. The doctor is actually surprised at how well I am healing. I am fitted with a different cast. I can put weight on my foot now, just not a lot. I will still need crutches, but at least now, I will be able to make it to the bathroom without having to call for help. Gray clouds now cover the blue sky and rain begins to fall around us, as Theron helps me back into Badass. It is still the best name that I have ever given anything and this car fully lives up to its name.

I watch the windshield wipers flick away the rain, as we drive home. Evan isn't too far behind us. We end up losing him at an intersection, but Theron doesn't slow to wait for him. The rain has turned into a deluge now, and visibility on the road is almost gone. I suggest pulling over to wait for it to let up, but it seems that just my words alone have caused a break in the clouds. The rain eases up, as we pull into the drive.

That awful feeling is back, accompanied with my arm and neck hair standing on end. I place my hand on Theron's thigh, as we enter the gates. Something is off, normally the gates make a grinding sound when they first open, but they were oddly quiet. In fact, I am not sure they were entirely closed. I look over at Theron, but he doesn't seem to notice. We pull up in front of the house. Theron parks as close as he can to curb of the walkway, so that I won't have far to go in the rain.

Everything happens as if it is in slow motion. Theron steps out of the car, and I watch him walk around to my side to open my door. His hand pulls on the handle. He stops still, when a figure comes out from behind one of the trees. My heart is slamming in my chest, my lungs burn. It is then that I realize that I am holding my breath. I try to push open my door to open it, but Theron won't move. He stands in front of it, holding it closed with his body leaning up against the car. The figure slowly walks around to the front of the car. The rain comes to a stop, as my vision clears to see the man standing in front of us. Thomas.

"No, no, no. It can't be him. Theron! Theron!" I slam my palms against the window, but Theron still won't move. Thomas is holding something in his hands. It is black and fits comfortably in his hand. It's a gun. "Fuck! Theron! No! No!" I am screaming, as if my voice is going to save the two of us from the deranged man in front of us.

Thomas is screaming at Theron, but I can't understand all of it. It is too muffled from inside the car. Theron isn't buying whatever it is that Thomas is throwing at him. I can hear him perfectly outside my window.

"Just go. What the fuck do you think you're going to accomplish here today? Waving around that fucking shit in your hand doesn't make you a man. I'm more of a man than you'll ever be. You are nothing, but a piece of fucking shit. I've taken your business. Your name has been run through the mud, nothing is left of you, but the trash that you are. Get the fuck away from us!"

"Theron! God damn it!" I desperately need out of here. I take my shoulder and ram it into the door, while pulling on the handle. It barely budges. Theron's fist pounds into the side of the door. I am not giving up. Thomas' right arm raises into the air at the same exact time that I hear tires screech outside my window. It is enough of a distraction for Thomas to lower his arm, turning away from us. Theron yanks open my door, quickly pulling me from the car. He sets me on the ground behind the car.

"Beautiful, stay down. Fuck. Whatever you do, please stay down. Jesus."

"I'm not done with you, boy!" Thomas' feet crunch on the gravel beneath his shoes. Theron stands, turning away from me. He leaves me alone behind the car. I can see Thomas' feet get closer, so I try my best to scoot myself around to the driver side of the car. That is when I see, Evan. It was his tires, I heard screech. His arms are raised, as he makes his way around his car. His eyes never leave Thomas, his fingers rest on the trigger of the pistol in his hand.

"Put down the gun!" Evan yells, towards Thomas. Most people would probably cower from a gun pointed directly at them, especially when it is common knowledge that the man holding the gun is a trained marksman. My skin crawls when Thomas releases an eerie laugh.

"Do it. Pull the trigger, and I'll pull mine. Who should I shoot first? The bastard child who ruined my life, killing my reason for existence, or the whore cowering behind a car, as if it's going to save her or the bastard child she's carrying?"

"Put down the gun. I will not say it again. This is your last chance to comply." Evan's feet spread to the width of his shoulders, his back straightens, but his aim never changes.

"Comply? Comply? I will never fucking agree to anything you have to offer me. He ruined my fucking life. He's a murderer! He killed his own mother, and here you are protecting him."

"I. Did. Not. Kill. My. Mother."

"Sure you did, son. The moment your waste of a body came out of her, she started dying. You took her strength, leaving behind a weak woman to take care of child who wanted nothing more than to destroy our lives since its very first breath."

"Fuck you!" I am unable to sit there any longer, listening to this man blame Theron for all of his hate. "Fuck you. You are nothing, but a worthless piece of shit. You are nothing. You have nothing, but that's too much for you, isn't it? Your dick is even smaller than your intelligence, both are almost nonexistent, and now you're angry with the world. You're trying to overcompensate for what you will never have."

"And what's that? What could you possibly know? You're nothing but a gold digging whore."

"I know what it's like to love, and you will never know the joy of having someone to experience that with. She was afraid of you, she never loved you." Gravel crunches, and I know that he is coming for me.

"Drop the fucking gun!" Evan screams at Thomas, as he comes around the front of the car. His feet must twist because he trips, either that, or karma is truly a bitch because his body twists, as he holds me in his aim. Thomas turns his head to Evan. Someone screams my name, and I hear the sound of two simultaneous clicks.

I am told that if someone experiences something so horrific, they can block it out. It is as if your brain is trying to protect you, keep you from living in the hellish reality surrounding you. Everything blurs around me. I feel hands pulling me from the ground. A voice looms around me, trying to pull me back to reality, but I can't get rid of the loud ringing in my ears. Then it hits me.

Two clicks. I frantically pull at the hands trying to carry me away. I am desperate to see what has happened. Where is Evan? Why can't I see Evan? Someone is screaming, crying. I can't hear over the noise. It is so loud that I can feel it rumble in my chest. Fuck. It is me and I am the one frantically screaming. Why isn't anyone listening to me? I can't lose anyone else. I can't do this again.

"Evelyn!"

My name registers somewhere in my consciousness, turning I find the face that belongs to the voice. Theron is kneeling beside me on the steps, trying his best to calm me. Our eyes meet, my heart thumps in my chest, and I know. I know someone is dead.

"Beautiful, stop. It is over. It is all over. The police and an ambulance are on their way over." He pulls me into his lap, rocking me back and forth. "It's over. It's all over." He clings to me. I am not sure if his words are for me, or more for him. No words escape me. I can't even begin to put together everything that has unleashed here today. I am not sure if God exists, but I know with everything in my being that the devil does and he was here tonight.

Red and blue lights flash among the trees, accompanied by loud whirring sirens. Theron doesn't let me go. The scene becomes a chaotic mess of people, as both police and paramedics rush onto the scene. Words are spoken, but in low hushed tones. All I hear is, "he didn't make it." My heart drops, tears sting my already hot cheeks, and anger boils beneath my skin. I watch as the paramedics push someone into the back of the ambulance, but I can't quite make out as to who. Theron won't let go of me. I honestly believe that he is panicking. We are still rocking back and forth when someone walks over, asking if we are all right. He briefly lets go of me, so that they can look me over to make sure that I am alright. He pulls me back into his arms when he is satisfied with their assumption of my wellbeing. I wrap my arms around him, and he buries his head in my neck. I am not prepared for his words. They catch me off guard, stabbing me through my heart in one swift motion. "He's dead."

My eyes scan the chaos of lights, and people moving around us. I still can't find Evan. The ambulance pulls away and that is when I notice the black shoes laying so still on the ground. This can't be real. Someone covers the figure with a blanket. I close my eyes and bury myself into the man holding so desperately onto me. My awful feeling has come to fruition, and I can't help but wonder if I am not to blame. If I hadn't spoke up, what would have been the outcome? Theron stands and carries me back to the car. Where are we going?

Maybe he just needs to get away, and perhaps this has finally all been too much for him. I don't ask him what his intentions are, I just accept them. It doesn't matter where we are going, as long as I am with him, nothing else matters. Tears blur my vision, as I watch the trees pass by outside the window. Nothing has really ever happened to me. I have never had any huge surprises, catastrophes, or excitement of any kind until these past couple of months. It is odd how quickly things can change.

CHAPTER 25

EVE

I am sitting in a hard vinyl chair. My right knee is pulled up to my chest with my arms wrapped tightly around my waist. Theron keeps trying to get me to eat, but I can't. Hot and clammy sweats keep taking over my body. Panic is hiding just below the surface, and it is boiling just under my skin, waiting to claim me. I watch him pacing back and forth before sitting in the chair across from me, then standing to do it all again. I wonder who is more broken. Is it me, Theron, or the man lying beside me in a hospital bed? All of us are shattered into to so many pieces that I wonder if someone could even possess enough glue to make one whole person out of us.

Theron hasn't slept in two days. He is insistent on staying at the hospital. I can't blame him, if it was Kayla, I would never leave her side. The doctors were able to remove the bullet with minimal damage. It turns out that Evan has great aim, but Thomas didn't. He moved at the last second and aimed his gun at Evan. The bullet hit its victim, but it was the left shoulder that took the bullet. Evan had a clear shot. His bullet didn't miss its target, and it slipped through Thomas just above the bridge of his nose, killing him instantly. We are hoping that Evan will be released tomorrow if he wakes up, otherwise it may be a few more days, yet.

Bridgette has shown up twice at the hospital now, demanding to see Theron. I had her removed by security. I will deal with that crazy psycho once we are back at home. One panic attack at a time seems to be easier to handle. My mom is here with me. She keeps bringing me hot tea to sip. She has tried to mother Theron as well. He is so unfamiliar with being taken care of that he just gives her looks of confusion when she tries to comfort him. My heart breaks knowing his confusion is all because his father, the man that was supposed to love him and raise him, but instead held Theron accountable for the death of his mother and the destruction of the world Thomas was so clearly accustomed to. I can't fathom how someone could hate their own child. I don't think that my mind will ever be able to wrap around it. Perhaps, it is because all I have known in my life is the love of my family and friends. Never before, have I ever been so grateful for everyone in my life, especially Theron. Even if he doesn't see it all the time, he is my everything.

"Hey girl, are you planning on staying here all day again?"

I turn to see Kayla peeking in through the door. Her tight blonde curls are piled on the top of her head in a crazy mass. For some reason, I find this to be absolutely, hilarious. I am not sure if it is from the lack of sleep, or if I have gone mad. It is probably both. A giggle escapes me, catching both Kayla and Theron off guard. Their expressions of shock, only add to the hilarity I am finding in this situation. Doing my best to stifle my laughter, I bury my face against my knee. What ensues after is a not a sound most humans make. I am laughing silently, my face growing hotter from the breath that I am holding. I breathe in at the same time that a laugh like sound escapes me. I sound like a braying donkey.

"What the hell was that?" I look to Theron, but he shakes his head letting me know that it wasn't him asking.

"Jesus Christ, you sound like a fucking mule being murdered." Kayla is now laughing with me. I try to catch my breath, but I am failing epically. The sound escapes me again, this time followed by a snort. White little spots appear outside the corner of my eyes. If I don't calm down, I am going to faint from not breathing.

"What the hell was that? Did you just fucking snort?" The voice is groggy, cracking as it questions the horrible sounds coming from my mouth.

"She did, Evan. She fucking brayed like a damn donkey and now the crazy cow is snorting. Jesus, Theron get your woman under control. We are in a hospital of all places." At the sound of Kayla's words, I pull my shirt just over my head and breathe deeply. I am now hiding like a turtle inside its shell.

"I can't control that, I've tried and it only gets worse. Last time she fell out of the chair she was sitting in. I am not risking it. Just let her calm down. As for you, how are you feeling?"

"Like shit. God, damn my shoulder is on fire. What happened?" Evan's voice is rough, but it brings me back from the psychotic break that I was starting to edge over.

"Thomas shot you. Evan, you saved us." It is my voice that answers him. It is soft and muffled from inside my shirt, but I know that he hears me because of his sharp intake of breath. I peek out from my hiding place, not making eye contact with anyone. Laughing now would be completely rude to the gravity of the situation we now find ourselves.

"Have you regained your sanity now?"

"Yes, mother." I scrunch my nose up at Kayla. She is so bossy sometimes.

"Ladies, although your concern for me is more than I could have asked for, could you let me talk to my man for just a minute?"

I am a little put off by Evan's request, but I comply. He is Theron's right hand man. I am sure there are things they need to discuss. I follow Kayla out of the room and down the hall. She stops in front of the Family Waiting Room. My eyes focus on the door. I have encountered so much loss in that room. Seeing my hesitation, she follows me, as I continue to walk through the ending hallways, making my way to a bench outside the main doors.

It is almost two o'clock, the sun is shining brightly, high in the sky. Yesterday was unbearably hot and humid, while today has a slight chill to the air. Mother Nature is such a tease. Once you get comfortable accepting the idea of one season, she changes her mind, just to mix things up a bit. Kayla sits beside me, neither of us say a word. It is not that we need to, there is just no reason to fill the silence. I take comfort in the little warmth the sun is offering, the birds singing in the trees, and the knowledge that no matter what is in store for all of us in the future, we will face it together.

A yawn escapes me, as I lay my head on Kayla's shoulder. "I'm suddenly very tired and very hungry."

"That's probably because you've finally let go of the stress that you've been carrying around for way too long. Why don't you let me take you home? I can help you get everything ready for everyone to finally come home. We can order pizza, rock out to some Pandora, and just let everything go. A stress free night."

"Is that a good idea? I mean, what will they think of me just leaving them here? I should be with them."

"You were. Now you need a break. You need to take care of yourself, too."

"I know."

"Then it's settled. Stay here, you don't need to gimp around so much. I'll get Theron." She kisses the top of my head and heads back inside with a little bounce in her step. As I sit outside waiting for them, I can't help but take notice of the elderly couple walking out of the building and into the parking lot. He is using his cane to help support both of them. She has both of her arms wrapped around his free arm, and their steps are short but balanced. You can see the concentration on his face, as he makes sure that his wife is safely following him. A soft sweet smile is on her face. She has complete faith in him. I wonder what it will be like when Theron and I are older. Will we still love each other so desperately and passionately as we do now? I believe that we will, and I hope that it is so much more.

"I hear my beautiful girl wishes to go home and put her leg up." Looking at Theron, tears well up in my eyes. Grasping my face with his palm, he wipes away the stray tear that has escaped and is now rolling down my cheek. "Hey, what's this for?"

"I love you."

"I love you too, but why the tears?"

"It's just because I love you so much."

He leans in and ever so softly places a kiss gently on my lips. It is just a feather of a kiss, but it resonates throughout my entire body, electricity courses through my veins, searing the fireworks from his touch to memory. "Go get some rest, beautiful. I've got this." I nod my head, turning my lips to place a kiss against his palm. He helps me to stand, as Kayla pulls her car around.

Opening my door, he helps me slide into the car. He shuts my door once he is satisfied with my seatbelt. I place a kiss on the tip of my fingers and place them on the window as we drive away. My shoulders feel incredibly light. Closing my eyes, I rest my head against the window and drift to sleep during the short drive home.

Kayla helps me into the house. I am so tired that I head straight to bed. I promise Kayla that it will only be a short nap, but I know that is a lie. She wakes me around six, when the pizza arrives. We eat our meal in silence on the balcony, mainly because my mouth is so full of food, talking would basically lead to choking at this point. I gulp down my lemonade, the glass clinks, as I set it back on the table.

"Feel better?"

"Much."

"I would hope so. Jesus, Eve. I've never seen someone scarf a pizza down so quickly in my life and I have brothers!" I shrug my shoulders. What did she expect? I said I was hungry. The evening fades into the night, as we sit on the balcony talking and laughing at just about anything we can think of. It feels so good to be able to relax like this. No worries, no drama, it is just us. It is just like it used to be when all three of us lived together. My thoughts stray to Matt, but I don't encounter sadness this time around. Instead, my thoughts of him bring a smile to my lips.

"Kayla, do you remember when we convinced Matt that there was a monster in the lake?"

"Oh my God, that was great. He wouldn't go near the water for the rest of the summer."

"I know. I can't believe that he fell for it. It took us forever to get him back in the water and that guy was snorkeling, and he popped up in the water right in front of him. That was hilarious. He was scared shitless."

"Right? Who snorkels in Lake Michigan anyway? The odds of that happening was slim to none, but it worked out for us!" We continue telling stories, laughing through the night until my eyes can barely stay open any longer.

"Kayla, I think it's time to call it a night. I'm exhausted and my bed is taunting me with its amazingly soft pillows."

"Okay. Let me help you up, and get you to bed."

"The help up I'll take, but I'm just going to throw on one of Theron's t-shirts, so I'll be fine. Could you stay here tonight? It's a big house, and with everything that's happened, I'd rather not be alone."

"No problem, sweets. I'll raid your clothes for something to sleep in. Where am I bunking?"

"You may pick any room you want on the other side of the parlor. Rebecca keeps them clean, and ready to use, just in case."

Kayla nudges my shoulder with hers, as we walk back into the bedroom. "You know, I'm jealous of you. You have someone to cook and clean for you, your fiancé is loaded, you have a beautiful house...You have a lot, Eve." I am not sure what to say to any of that, so I just watch her, as she digs through my stuff. She grabs some clothes and places her hand on my forearm. "But you've been through so much. You deserve every bit of this sweetie. This house isn't too big for you." She gives me a wink then heads out the door to find herself a room. She knew exactly what I meant when I said the house was too big. I don't feel like I belong here or deserve any of this, but Kayla is right. Taking comfort in that thought, I make myself comfortable in my huge bed and drift off to sleep. I am hoping that tomorrow goes pleasantly and that there won't be any drama.

CHAPTER 26

EVE

The sudden jolt to my core brings me from my slumber, my body stirs from the sensation between my legs. My eyes open to the sight of a naked Theron slowly kissing his way up my body. I am now wide awake and completely alert to his every move. If I could, I would choose to wake up every day like this. His grin is contagious, as he crawls up towards my face, causing my smile to match his.

"Good morning, beautiful."

"Good morning. What is this? Not that I'm complaining, but why aren't you at the hospital?"

"Evan's sister is there. She suggested that I take a break, plus I know I've neglected you."

"Oh." My voice is a breathy whisper. "Wait. Kayla will hear us." I would never hear the end of it if she heard us.

"I sent her home." Theron places a soft kiss on my lips and I close my eyes, enjoying the sweetness of it. "No more neglecting." His lips skate along my jaw to my neck, his tongue sweeping across my skin, as he nips just below my ear. I shiver from the electricity of his touch. His hands slide under my shirt, cupping my breasts, his rough fingers teasing my nipples. I arch my back pushing my breasts into his hands. I could come just from this alone. My nerves are knotted and explosive to the touch. Pulling my shirt over my head, his mouth finds my breasts. My nipples are teased and pulled into hard peaks, as his mouth assaults my body.

"Oh, God!" Moans escape me as his hands drift between my legs, slipping between my wet folds. My hands grip his shoulders, my nails digging at his skin. I am desperate for him, for his touch. "Theron, please. I need to feel you."

"You are so wet. Do you know how much you turn me on like this? Just knowing that I'm the reason your body comes alive, is enough." I need more, not just his hands. I need his hard cock slamming me into oblivion.

"Please. Fuck me, Theron. Please!" He coaxes my words from me, along with moans, as my body heats into a roaring inferno of lust. No amount of finger play is going to take me where I need to go. "Theron, now!"

"I don't want to hurt you."

"You won't. I need you, baby, please." His fingers slip from me, his hands moving to my hips. He lifts my right leg over his shoulder, spreads my pussy open for him.

"I love your slick cunt. Who am I to deny you of what you need? You ready for this?"

"Yes!" He positions the steel head of his cock before slowly pushing into me. My body stretches to accommodate his size, a burning sensation takes over me and I revel in it. His pace is slow and steady. I clench my walls around him, as he drives me towards my orgasm. I am just on the brink, but I can't get there. I need it rough. Using the heel of my foot, I push onto his ass forcing him to pound into me.

"Baby, no. I won't be able to hold back."

"Fuck holding back." His eyes darken, and I know that I am going to be rewarded for my smart mouth. His fingers dig into my hip, his other hand wraps around my thigh, as he thrusts into my pussy pushing me farther into the mattress. "Theron! Like that. Don't stop."

"Fuck. I'm not going to last." My body jolts from the force in which he is slamming into me. Hard. Rough. My mind spirals out of control, everything clears, and I am flying high, as my body loses control.

"Theron!" His name leaves my lips in a moan of pure ecstasy, as my walls clench around his hard cock, pulling him deeper into my pussy. My hands fist in the sheets, as my body arches towards the heavens.

"Fuck!" His grip tightens, his body stills and his release pours into me, filling me. "Holy shit."

"Mmhmm." My breathing is ragged and sweat clings to me. Slowly pulling himself from me, he drops to his side. Theron lays his head on my chest, his arms wrapping around me and his fingers make soft circles on my skin in a random pattern. I feel completely sated. That was unbelievably good.

"Are you broken?"

"Mmhmm." He tilts his head back, letting out a deep laugh. My mouth curves into a huge smile. I am so incredibly in love with him.

"Get some rest." I lay awake with him wrapped around me. His breathing slows, letting me know that he is asleep. My fingers lazily stroke up and down on the skin of his back. I lose track of how long I lay there with him. I am too lost in the high that I get when I am near him.

The sound of his phone brings me back down from the clouds. I nudge his shoulders, but he only responds with grunts. "Hey, caveman. I know that I wore you out, but what if that's Evan?"

"Ugh." Pouting, he rolls over and grabs his phone off the nightstand. "Theron." Why can't he ever say hello like a normal person? "What the fuck do you want?" He sits up, his body speaking a thousand words to me without ever making a sound. His posture is rigid and frustration is coming off of him in waves. Who is he talking to? I am not sure what is being said. Not only do they have his attention, but they have now pissed him off. "I'm not in the mood for games. Eve and I have been through enough bad shit to last us a lifetime. You have an hour. Do you hear me? You have an hour to get here and explain whatever it is you feel that I need to know." Theron ends the call and tosses his phone across the room. It slams against the wall.

"Who–"

"Don't. Do not question me right now. This needs to be dealt with and I'm doing this my way. Come on, I'll help you get dressed. Bridgette is on her way over."

"Are you fucking kidding me? I told her to leave us alone."

"Aren't you the one who told me she's pregnant and carrying Thomas' baby?"

"Yes, but that was before any of this."

"Before what? Her lies or you hiding shit from me?" I gasp. His words sting, as they scratch against my surface. "Well, which one is it?"

"Fuck you."

"Too late. You already did." What the hell did she say to him, and why is he taking it out on me? I thought we were past all of this.

"Get out. I don't need you to babysit me. I can dress on my own. I'll meet you downstairs. I know you're pissed right now, and I'm sure that it's because of the cunt that was on the phone. I'm not her. I will never be her. You need to pull your head out of your ass, now. I've been through too much to let you walk all over me when something doesn't go your way. You are not Thomas. Do not act like him."

Theron spins on his heels. The angry glare in his eyes fades into sorrow. "Beautiful, I–"

I put my hand up to stop him. "Don't. I'll meet you downstairs."

He rakes his hands through his hair. He knows that he has hurt me. The pain and regret of his actions written all over his face. "I didn't mean it. I'm sorry."

Hot tears spill over onto my cheeks, turning my head away from him I whisper, "Just go." The door shuts quietly behind him. More tears pour down my face and it takes me a minute to catch my breath. I am angry with Theron for his response to her, but my hatred is solely focused on Bridgette. She is like a roach that just won't die. Well this time I am arming myself with my best high heels. I am going to step on her, enjoying the sound of her body crunching underneath my shoe. Two can play at this game.

By the time, I get ready and make it downstairs, Theron is already in the kitchen with Bridgette. She is sitting at the table smugly drinking, what I assume is either tea or coffee. Who am I kidding? She is the devil. It is probably full of souls that she has collected over the years. It would explain why she always looks so picture perfect, her beauty must survive on their essence. Her hair is pinned back in a French twist with two chopsticks sticking out of it. I so badly want to rip them out of her hair and stab them into her neck, watching her blood pour out, as she gurgles her last breath. I shake my head, releasing the thoughts, though a slight grin still plays on my face. The sound of my shoe and boot hobbling across the hard floor, alerts her of my presence.

"I didn't realize that Eve would be here." Only her words acknowledge me, her eyes never leave Theron.

"That was a pretty fucked up assumption, wouldn't you think? She goes wherever I go. Eve and I are inseparable. I need her like you need Botox to survive. She is not going anywhere. What is it that you had to tell me in person?"

The look of shock on her face is priceless. I walk around the table, stopping next to Theron. I start to pull out a chair, but he pulls me onto his lap instead. I make a mental note, not to acknowledge her until I have to. "Is everything okay, babe?" Placing my right palm on the side of his face, I search his eyes trying to find the light we just had. The light Bridgette's phone call stole from us.

"It will be." His words are soft and steady. His brows furrow, his eyes brim with tears. Sorrow written all over his face. I lean in, never breaking eye contact, and softly place a kiss on his lips. *I forgive you.* I don't tell him with my words, but with my body. I only hope that he understands. He closes his eyes, before taking a deep breath. He opens his eyes, as a different man. I know this man. This is the man that I saw take his father's business out from under him. He is determined and unwavering. Whatever it is that she thinks she is going to get from this, won't happen. He has already made up his mind. Check mate. The game is already over before her first move.

Bridgette clears her throat, as if to remind us that she is still here. Oh, I know that you are here, sweetie. I am just taking my time before I make it perfectly clear that you are never allowed near us again. "I'm pregnant."

"I already know this. Weren't you the one who tracked down my fiancé in a doctor's office, coming up with some elaborate lie, claiming it to be Thomas' child?"

"It's not a lie. It's his."

A deranged laugh escapes from Theron. What does he know that I don't? Raking his hands through his hair, his eyes steel and his face hardens. "It's his, is it? I'll tell you a little secret, Bridgette. Something only my mother and I know. Since she is no longer with us, I guess the secret was left only with me. Thomas couldn't have any more children. He despised me so much as a child that he had a vasectomy to prevent any more 'mistakes', as he would call it. I know this because he made damn sure to remind me daily of his hatred for me. I ruined his life, and there was no way that he was going to waste his time raising another useless parasite, sucking him dry and sending everyone around them to an early grave. His words, not mine."

My mouth falls open. It is not his, it has never been his. My lips curl up into an evil grin. Her lie has snapped back in her face like a rubber band, stinging her face and leaving her red with embarrassment.

"That's not true. It can't be." She backpedals. I may be enjoying this a little too much.

"It is. Which brings me to my next question. Who were you sleeping with besides my father? If you were supposedly so loyal to him, how is it that you're pregnant? That might be a baby you are carrying, although it's debatable since you are the devil's incarnate, but that baby is of no relation to me. It has nothing to do with any of us. So, I suggest that you go through the list of men you were screwing on the side and start issuing out paternity tests."

"I...I...this can't be right. Why wouldn't he tell me? He knew that I was pregnant, he knew that I thought it was his."

She can't be this naïve. "Maybe that's why he tried to pay you off. Maybe he was willing to pay to get rid of the whore he kept around, for obviously way, too long. You couldn't even keep your legs closed. To think that I came down here to destroy you, to prove to Theron that you aren't worth the waste of our breath. Instead, I find out that you're nothing, but a two-timing whore and that you have no clue who the father is. I don't need to put you in your place, you've already found it. It's with the trash in the dumpster. Now, I want you to leave. Get the fuck out of our house."

She places her hand to her chest, her mouth opening and closing like a fish. It seems the girl who knows everything is at a loss for words. Revenge is sweet, but karma is beautiful. Standing, she pushes her chair back so hard that it clatters to the ground. She bends down to pick it up, but I can't let her leave without being a bitch just one more time. "Just leave the chair. We are going to have to burn it anyways. Who knows what kind of diseases you've brought into our house." Her eyes turn into daggers, but they have no effect on me. She turns to leave and I send Rebecca to follow her out. I want to make sure that she actually leaves the property. I don't trust her.

"You are very ugly when you are catty."

I look up at Theron, and I feel just as ugly as my words. "I'm sorry. She brings out the worst in me."

"It's alright, beautiful. She brings out the worst in everyone." I lay my head against his chest. "At least she is gone now. There is nothing else that can come between us." His hand wraps around my side, sliding upwards, cupping my breast. His breath is hot against my neck. He knows my body so well. "I don't like fighting with you. We should makeup properly. Let's go upstairs, where I can show you how sorry I really am." My mind races with the possibilities of the next couple of hours, but my stomach has bad timing, as it rumbles loudly from hunger. "Perhaps we should feed you first and then we can go upstairs."

"Can't we just take the food upstairs with us?"

"God, I love you Eve. You always have the best ideas."

Theron slides me off his lap, and moves about the kitchen with such ease. Once he is satisfied that he has everything we need, he motions for me to follow him. I start to follow him, but then I have a great idea. I quickly limp over to the refrigerator. Finding what I need, I grab it and make my way over to Theron.

"What is that?"

"Oh you know, just something a little cliché." I hold up the butterscotch syrup. I squeal, as Theron drops everything and sweeps me up into his arms, carrying me upstairs.

"Let's just order in. I can't wait to get you into bed, naughty girl."

A giggle escapes me, as he lays me on the soft mattress.

"What's so funny?"

"Nothing. Everything is absolutely perfect."

"I'll show you just how perfect things can be. I'm going to make love to you until your body soars into the clouds." Theron holds true to his words. As we lay in our bed, his body wrapped around mine. I lightly stroke my fingers up and down his back. He is sound asleep with his hand spread out over my belly, his fingers still softly making circles on my skin. The sun peeks in through the curtains by the balcony, it glistens on the glass, sending little miniature rainbows scattering across the walls and ceiling. I rejoice in this moment. Our light has burst through the shadows, erasing them with its glow. Heaven is just under my fingertips, and I press my lips to the top of his head. My knight in shining armor, destroyer of shadows, and bringer of light. It might sound cliché and some may roll their eyes at it, but sometimes cliché is good. Our cliché had just a little more flavor than everyone else's. Butterscotch has never tasted so good.

Epilogue

THERON

Several Years Later

She is leaning against the doorframe of the nursery, her hand resting on the roundness of her belly, long brown locks flow over her shoulder. She is exhausted, but you can't see it on her. She refuses to stay home. I should never have bought her the Book Emporium, but when Harold and Olivia approached us about wanting to retire after all of the chaos that took place at the store that night, it was my natural reaction. We had thrown them a retirement party and were cleaning up after everyone left. Eve was quiet most of the night, I knew she was sad having to give up something that she loved doing. I walked up to her, put my hands over her eyes, and told her to keep them shut. The absolute joy on her face after I showed her the deed of sale, was priceless. I would have bought her a million bookstores just to see her smile like that.

I was lucky enough to witness the same exact smile after each of our children were born. My eyes roam her body, as she wears motherhood so well. She is still so incredibly sexy. God, if I don't want her right now. I lock her gaze with mine and give her a quick wink. She rolls her eyes at me. I chuckle and look down at the project at my feet. I have just finished putting together the new basinet that she had to have. I don't see how this one is any different than the other two that we have had, but I would do anything for her. Whether it is a new bassinet or the world, I would give it to her.

"They are waiting for you."

I pull her into my arms, my lips press against hers, sweeping my tongue into her delicious mouth. I slide my hands up her sides, cupping her breasts, teasing her nipples through her clothes. "They can wait. I need to feel you." I lean in, nipping that spot just below her ear, knowing that she won't be able to say no much longer. A soft moan leaves her lips, causing my cock to harden. Fuck, I want her.

"Theron. Stop. You can have me after they're in bed." She pulls out of my reach, holding her hand out for me. "Come on, God, time to say goodnight."

"Am I your God, beautiful?"

"Always." She leads me from the nursery and down the hall to a bedroom full of giggles. I push open the door, catching both of them off guard. It always takes me a minute to catch my breath when

I see them. If it makes me a push over then that is fine, but I have never felt more of man than when I am with my family.

Matthew Thomas is the oldest. I am still not a fan of his middle name, but Eve wouldn't budge. Something about how good things can still come from darkness, I still don't understand it. He is quick to jump into bed, as if I didn't just catch him wrestling with his brother. They both have Eve's beautiful brown locks. Matthew has her eyes and her stubbornness, too. Andrew is the spitting image of me. He even has my eyes, one brown and one green. Eve tells him that they are magical. It is a load of shit, but all of them believe it. Andrew is our youngest, for now. The boys and I are going to be in a world of trouble when Isabella arrives in the next few months. There is already little bits of pink being spread about. Hell, the nursery looks as if a fairy princess already lives in there. It is going to be amazing.

I get both of the boys tucked in and Matthew asks for a story. I know that it is just a ploy, he would do anything to get out of going to sleep, but I play along.

"Once upon a time, there was a lonely prince."

"Eww, dad. Not this story. They always kiss at the end." Matthew scrunches up his face in disgust.

"There's nothing wrong with kissing."

"Yeah. My friend Justin, at school, he says all the girls have germs. That's just disgusting." I shake my head in laughter. I swear the things these kids say are just too damn funny sometimes.

"You may think kissing is gross right now, but you'll like it when you're older."

"Nope. I'm never going to do it. Me and Andrew promised that we are never, ever doing that. Didn't we, Andrew?"

"Yeah, that's icky."

"Alright fine, but you're missing out on a great story. A princess comes along and saves the prince. He loved her so much, he made her queen of all the kingdom, and they lived happily ever after." I look over at Eve. She always blushes when I tell them that story.

"Whatever. Night, dad."

"Night boys. I love you."

"Love you, too!" They both yell out, as I walk out of the room, taking their mom with me. I pull her with me into our bedroom, gently laying her down on our bed.

"It's true, you know."

"What is?"

"The story that I always tell the boys."

"Tell it to me."

I lay on my pillow, pulling her close to me. "Once upon a time, there was a prince named, Theron. He was lost and all alone. One day he met a beautiful princess named, Eve. Her beauty was so magnificent, even the angels were jealous. She loved Theron so much and he was never lost or alone again. So, in return for her love, he loved her more than anything in the world and made her Queen of all the kingdom. They had three beautiful children and lived happily ever after in a castle at the top of the hill."

"I like that story, but you left some parts out."

"I know. It was the short version, the longer one takes too long and right now I just want to bury myself inside of you." I softly place a kiss just under her ear, in that spot that I know she can't say no to. She sighs, and melts into me. This is amazing. Nothing can be better than this. I look down at my wife lying beside me. Never in a million years could I have imagined how great life can be.

Other Books by Amber Lacie

SHADOWS
BOOK ONE OF THE SHADOWS SERIES
Available at: Amazon

Eve was content getting lost in her books, while living with her best friends. She's a beautiful girl surrounded by her friends and family. In her twenty-six years of life, nothing exciting has ever happened to her. Everything is going perfectly for her. Little does she know, one summer at the beach could change her life forever…

Theron is the son of a cutthroat multi-billionaire business tycoon. He thought he left behind the world his father created, but things change. Now, he's devoted himself to his eccentric grandma. His only hope at overcoming his past, is finding the one person he lost so very long ago…

When Eve bumps into Theron, their worlds collide. Nothing can prepare them for the instant fireworks and roller coaster ride waiting for them.

But…One has a secret. Can their love overcome tragedy, lies, and secrets?

About Amber Lacie

Website: www.amberlacieauthor.wix.com/author-blog
Twitter: @amber_lacie
Facebook: http://www.facebook.com/amberlacieauthor

You can contact Amber Lacie at amberlacieauthor@gmail.com

Amber Lacie grew up in Chicagoland and now lives in a quaint little town in Northwest Indiana. She has two beautiful children and a husband who worships the ground she walks on (or at least he should). She is an avid reader and coffee drinker. The love of being able to be transported into another world and experience adventures through someone else's imagination has always captured her attention. Now, she is expanding that love into writing and is looking forward to producing many books.

Made in the USA
Middletown, DE
09 February 2016